The Erotic Cryptids Collection

THE *Erotic* CRYPTIDS COLLECTION

HONEY CUMMINGS
URBAN LEGEND EROTICA COLLECTION

4 Horsemen
Publications, Inc.

Published By: 4 Horsemen Publications, Inc.

4 Horsemen Publications, Inc.
PO Box 417
Sylva, NC 28779
4horsemenpublications.com
info@4horsemenpublications.com

Cover & Typesetting by Valerie Willis

Library of Congress Control Number: 2022949658

Paperback ISBN-13: 978-1-64450-709-4
Audiobook ISBN-13: 978-1-64450-711-7
Ebook ISBN-13: 978-1-64450-710-0

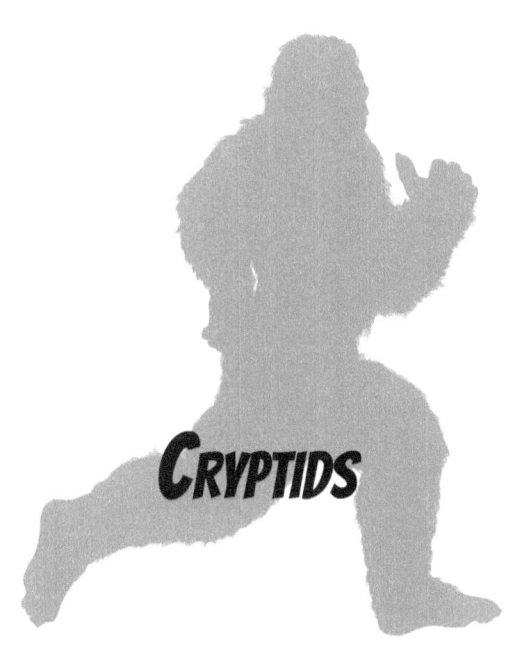

CRYPTIDS

Sleeping WITH SASQUATCH

HONEY CUMMINGS

URBAN LEGEND EROTICA COLLECTION

TABLE OF CONTENTS

DEDICATION

To Erika

Thank you for talking me into this insane idea!

XOXO

Honey Cummings

Night with the Boys

Bif's hair stood on end, signifying the time to shift drawing near. *Fucking new moon.* He gulped down his beer, glaring at the other men and women gathered around the campfire. Unlike his fellow shifters, he had a mop of golden locks and piercing blue eyes. Most of it hid under his ball cap, which only made his chiseled jaw and muscular neck and shoulders stand out. He shifted in the camp chair, and it creaked under the weight. Unlike the cozy office jobs his companions preferred, he'd spent the summer working odd jobs and hay bailing. His skin had turned a rich tawny color, as if the warmth of the sun had soaked into his flesh and stayed.

It wouldn't be long now before the change came over them all. Every new moon, they gathered here in the National Forest to walk the night as the notorious urban legends of the woods. They'd set camp and checked that no human had camped within a twenty-mile radius. Even the trail cams from hunters and researchers had been turned off, and any signs of tree stands checked and checked again. Being caught on camera caused a huge uproar in their secret community of shifters, whether a Sasquatch or a Chupacabra, it didn't bode well.

Twisting off another beer cap, Bif hated what came next. Everyone's cell phone alarms went off in unison and the ritual started. He watched with bitter disdain as the men and women around him started to shed their clothes. Bare skin glowed orange in the firelight and he was the only one celebrating alone. Again, Bif found the bottom of his beer and snorted. Seeing the smiles, the way hands glided to the more intimate parts freely and without obstruction only added to the misery he endured.

Last time he'd brought someone, one of his own kind, but she had broken up with him shortly before tonight. He thought it had gone well. They had screwed all night, and when the sun came up, they had one more round for good measure. He should have noticed after that the relationship was a bust. She hadn't been calling or texting. When they did talk, she was busy, but at last it came to a head three days ago when he caught her after work.

He could still hear her words stinging in his chest. *'I found someone else to spend the new moon with. Sorry, Bif. It's not you; it's me.'*

She had spun on her heel, giving him one more gulp of her perfume before sliding into a car. Not hers, but her new man's Dodge Charger, and it had roared away. In his mind, it had sounded more like laughter, and he wondered if she had used him for the last new moon.

"Bif, come on! Time to strip buddy! We can't have Big Foot running around in a wife beater and cargo shorts," Satch snorted, pulling his girlfriend closer to him.

His friend may have been just as tall but lacked the bulk of muscles Bif carried. He was just as attractive in his own way with his pompadour haircut and the deep brown eyes matching the bony structure of his thin face. Out of the group of friends, Satch was the playboy, the one who always got whatever girl he set his mind and dick on. Granted, he wasn't afraid to use dirty methods to get that done, and Bif hated that part of Satch the Sasquatch.

"Oh leave him be. It was a bad break up," Abe chimed in as Bif shed his clothes and grabbed yet another beer. "Leave the poor guy alone."

Then there was Abe the Skunk Ape. His family had moved up north from Florida after most of their new moon go-to spots had been flattened for progressive projects like theme parks and apartments. Unlike a Big Foot or Sasquatch, his kind never got big. He wondered if it had to do with the swampy regions they originated from, needing to be agile to avoid the panthers and gators, but Abe always shrugged when Bif asked.

"Ya, leave this poor guy alone," Bif winked at Abe. "Plus, ya'll got some ladies to wait on. Don't waste any more time on the third..." He paused, counting the others. "Make that fifth wheel."

"Ya-ya." Kissing his girl, Satch started to stumble into the woods, tugging her along. "I told you that Bethany chick was bad news."

Heat rose in Bif's face, the site of the lovey-dovey couples combined with Satch's remark adding to his frustration. *If I had someone else, I wouldn't be alone. And it's not like there's plenty of shifters like us to choose from asshole.*

Bif cracked open another beer and shouted after him, "Does Yeti Spaghetti know you're banging his sister?"

"No, and don't ruin it, Bif!" the girl hissed, her petite body pale as snow in comparison to her dark black hair. "And I have a name!"

"Yea, I know it, Yvonne. Ghetti bitches about you every chance he gets." Bif raised an eyebrow but as he turned to his other comrades, they had all fled into the forest.

"Fine. More beer for me." He flopped back into the camp chair as midnight crested.

Ghetti the Yeti couldn't come out with them this time around. He was some place in Vancouver for a job, but that cooler weather during a new moon probably felt amazing. They called him 'Yeti

Spaghetti' because he was more fur than man. Shifted, he looked larger than Bif, but the moment he went back to normal, he looked like a wet noodle. Bif chuckled to himself thinking back to the first time they met, and he had seen him shift. Shame he wasn't here to keep him company.

As the new moon crested, hair erupted across his body, and he groaned. Another beer, and he became more numb to the night and to the fact he was alone. Unlike some of his fellow shifters, he didn't grow bigger, just more hair or fur or whatever you wanted to call the fluff that came with the change. In human form, he was just a tall and overall huge man. He'd been labelled a body builder, Samoan, hell, even called a steroid junkie a few times.

Bif sat there, nothing more than a really drunk, miserable Big Foot. He'd spent plenty of new moons running the woods as an urban legend solo, but tonight, it hurt. Some part of him just hated getting a taste of something special, intimate even.

If only I had a girl to spend these nights with... a girl who would let me make her happy...

2
Start Your Engines

"Come on, Frankie," Ted lugged the tent into the back of his old Ford Bronco, right beside the fifty-gallon tub of motion sensor cameras and recording equipment. Tall and built like a wrestler, there was no mistaking he was one of the good-ole-boys that made a girl wet just watching him work. Military haircut teamed with a long, brown beard ironically matched with a farmer's tan and hazel eyes. He could make any girl ache to spend a night with him. If that didn't tickle your fancy, the man had big arms and a sex drive that never ended. "We need to get out there and set up before dark."

"I thought you said we were going camping as a couple's retreat this weekend?" Frankie crossed her arms, bottom lip puffing out as she gave him a heated glare from under her locks of bleached-blonde hair. She had worn some homemade daisy dukes, complete with her bikini top and a shirt tied up so she could flash as much skin as she could for her man—for easy access too. Even with her thick thighs, wide hips, and big breasts, she still felt dwarfed next to Ted and his heap of muscles. Despite it, nothing could tame the brilliant blue in those eyes when she had a goal in mind. "Why are you packed like we're going out there to film a full production movie?"

"If we're going out there, I'm going to do some Sas-hunting." And there was Ted's biggest flaw. Whether it was the redneck in him or the nerd, he had a section of his garage looking like a conspiracy theorist's assassination chart, complete with maps, photos, and newspaper clippings all centered around the local forest legend, Sasquatch. "Frankie, baby... please, you know how much this means to me. I swear I'll make it up to you, Sweet Pea."

Twisting her lips further, she hated when he cooed her name like that. "Stop it. You look like a sad, lost puppy." Deep down her heart sank. Last time they were out together and someone mentioned Sasquatch, it had caught his attention hard. So hard that he lost interest in her completely. They had gone home early from the bar, and she fell asleep while he spent the entire night reviewing his Sasquatch notes because some new information had been shared. "This better not end up like the night we came home from the Nice'nSleazy."

"Frankie, Honey Bee." He came closer, his hand gliding across her abdomen, riding over her hip and grabbing her ass. It was aggressive and he pulled her against him. Oh, how she loved it rough, dirty, and the more domineering the man, the more she came. "You know I'm really going out there to have fun with you, Baby."

"Stop it with the sugary pet names." Her resolve waned as his beard tickled at her neck and he began kissing her, lips hot as they suckled with the threat of leaving a hickey. "Ted, don't. Last time I had to wear a scarf around my neck for over a week, dammit."

"Oh?" He nibbled her, his teeth grazing her skin and she crushed her neck close. He moved on to new grounds, suckling at her ear, sending chills across her skin. The heat of his hands crawled all over her, making her ache for more. *Who cares if we get carried away in the front yard? Let him bend me over and teach me a lesson for daring to give him a hard time with his nice hard...* "Don't worry. I have other places I can leave those."

She grinned, his free hand slipping under her shirt, snaking under the bikini. Fingers gripped her breast, squeezing until she moaned. "Ted, the neighbors might see us."

He laughed, twisting her nipple and his voice breathy in her ear. "Let's give them a show—right here, right now." Another twist made her squeal and she wiggled against him, his monstrous arm wrapping around her waist, keeping her from escaping him.

Frankie arched her back and Ted began kissing down her neck and across her collarbone. Oh how she loved the way his beard tickled her skin. Her fingers gripped his shirt into balls, and he slipped his knee between her thighs. She moaned and it only egged him on. Hot lips wrapped around her nipple and a silken tongue flicked it, each time sending a throb of want through her. Frankie closed her eyes tight, enjoying the overwhelming foreplay and secretly hoped the neighbor would be watching from between the blinds.

Hope the crazy old bat has her binoculars!

Catching her breath, she wanted to save this for when they were alone in the woods, but maybe that could be the encore. Nothing intrigued her more than the idea of losing herself to sexual pleasure in the wild, like the animal she craved to be from time to time.

No, I want to tease him, make sure he'll forget all about Sasquatch by the time we get there.

Pushing Ted off her, she spun out of reach playfully. "First, you give me that camping trip you promised, then maybe we can see about your little front yard fantasy." Her fingers caressed his groin before skipping off around the Bronco.

Ted licked his lips watching Frankie climb into his lifted Bronco, his shorts a little tighter at the thought of bending her over for all to see. Shaking loose from her tantalizing view, he finished tossing everything in the back. Leaning on the tail gate, his eyes scanned everything he had; there in those tubs were five wildlife trail motion detecting cameras, two remote feed video cameras, the camouflaged tent, cans of deer musk and scent cover, the laptop and pack of battery backups, folding table, camp chairs, and some MREs.

Smiling, Ted's thoughts said it all; *Good weekend to catch Sasquatch and a good fucking on camera.*

"We have everything?" Frankie leaned out the window and lifted an eyebrow. "Or are ya taking a piss back there?"

Snorting, he winked at her, closing the back up. Hopping in front of the wheel, Ted brought the Bronco to life with a roar.

3

HANGOVER

The sunlight dappled down onto Bif's face, his pounding head making him groan. Before going for a run in the woods, he had downed three more beers and gotten bored. The whole night had become a blur before spinning and going black. He rolled over, but it didn't feel right. He felt stiff and bulky, as if he was still not back to his normal body. Blinking awake, he sat up, looking at his hands. They were still the hands of a turned Big Foot. Dread came crashing down on him. Scrambling to his feet, he inspected the rest of his body.

"Holy shit! This can't be happening!" The sun was up, but the shifted form never left.

Rushing through the woods, it took him a few miles to find the camp again. At least the sense of smell and natural navigation skills were something they all had in or out of the shift. Stumbling into the clearing, he froze. Knots twisted in his stomach to see only his tent remained.

Did those assholes leave me here because I hadn't shifted back?

After several minutes lost in thought, Bif shook his head trying to think what to do next.

"Didn't Satch go through this?" Breaking out of his drunken stupor, he dug through his pack and pulled out his cell phone. "I thought it was a load of bullshit, but here I am ... stuck in a shift."

Pacing around the low burning fire, he took inventory of what they had left behind. At least his friends left him the essentials, all his things and a few other items. They were planning to come back eventually, but when? Scrolling through, he dialed Satch.

"Hey Drunk Ass!" Bif cringed, his hangover still haunting him. "Couldn't find you so we left."

"Fuck you for leaving me," he barked, anger seeping forward. "We both know you didn't even try hunting down my scent. But I've got bigger problems."

"You didn't step in a bear trap like Yeti?" Satch sounded a little concerned, his laughter ceasing. "Did you get it off? How'd you get to your phone at the camp?"

"I might've been shitfaced, but we cleared the traps before we started." Fighting the foggy sensation of his thoughts, Bif refocused. "I'm stuck in... well... I didn't change back. I take back ever making fun of that story and calling bullshit."

"No fucking way!" Satch started informing the other shifters in the car and everyone seemed to find it funny or scary. "I told you! That shit happened to me! It's no joke!"

"I KNOW!" He could hear his voice echo. *Great he has me on speaker phone.* "What in the hell did you do to shift back?"

"I had to go fuck someone ... a few times."

"No, really, what did you do?" Bif rolled his eyes, looking for the clothes he had taken off last night. "This is rather awkward, Satch. I'd like to go home and do so as the normal me."

"Dude, I was stuck out in Yellowstone for a fucking month. I'm not joking. You'll need to find a hook-up. One round isn't enough so prepare yourself."

Picking his shorts off the ground, he shook them off. "You can't be serious. Hook up with someone looking like Big Foot. I'm royally screwed, Satch. Who camps out here in this shithole of a National Forest? There's nothing. Not even a good bird viewing trail! How in the hell did you change back?"

"Look, some hipster chicks high as a kite came and camped nearby. It was some naked spiritual thing in the woods. Far as I could tell, they were on one helluva acid trip and then some. Anyhow, there was a chick there... She didn't care who was banging her by the time a group of guys showed up, nor do I think she could care less about where she was. She just wanted a good time." Yvonne started shrieking, and Bif pulled the phone from his head for a moment. "I was desperate, Yvonne! You don't get it..."

"Shut the hell up, Yvonne!" Bif's voice roared through the car. "What happened after that?"

"Anyhow, I banged her and turned back. A few hours later, the shift reversed, and I had to circle back and hope they were still there." The car had fallen silent, the situation serious as the story unfolded. "It took about three tries, so... find a camper and give her the ride of her life. We all know you're the king of fucks. You got this, buddy!"

"You've got to be fucking kidding." Bif tugged on his shorts, frustrated at the whole idea. He didn't mind hooking up, but this far outclassed the level of two people intentionally looking for a one-night stand at the bar. "I'm in the middle of a forest. How about you all come back and help me or bring me back with you? Sure, I treat the ladies well, but c'mon, Satch! I'm a big hairy ape in this state! If a girl does magically appear in the woods, what are the chances she'll even let me near her?"

"Oh no. We can't take you home. It's a little hard to hide Big Foot in the car." Satch started to laugh. "Look, let me take everyone home, and I'll come back with someone willing to help out. Maybe post a Craigslist ad."

"How long will you take?" Looking around, the cooler had been left behind. "At least you left me with food and water. Beer would have been nice."

"I'll bring more and keep you supplied 'til you change back. Hang in there, Bif."

"Satch, I don't think I can pull this off..." The phone beeped.

Bif sat on the cooler, looking at the smoldering fire. His life might as well be ending. Worse, his only lifeline believed that sex solves all, and he couldn't be sure how accurate that solution would be.

Is this what happens to a heartbroken Big Foot? Didn't this happen to crazy Uncle Lenny before he got shot by a hunter out here? Shit! That's right! Sasquatch Hunters tend to come out here ever since they caught Abe on camera. I'm royally fucked unless someone willing happens to show up. What are the chances of that? That Craigslist ad better work, Satch, or we may have to see if Ghetti's other sister is willing to put out.

4

Off Road

The truck made a hum on the asphalt as they travelled. Off-road tires had a way of doing that and the country music didn't drown it out, but Frankie thought it seemed as if she couldn't have one without the other. She had slid to the center of the bench seat once they hit the two-lane road with the sign saying *Welcome to the National Forest.* It was nothing but nature and them for miles. No streetlights, barely a sign besides the numbered markers for the various clay-road offshoots which led to more trees and reclusiveness.

Frankie kept creeping closer until her head rested on Ted's shoulder. He was wearing her favorite cologne, *Chrome,* and she couldn't help but still feel the heat of his hands on her. As her mind hungered for the lustful want, she began squirming in her seat. It wasn't the age-old twang of the *Nitty Gritty Band's Fishing in the Dark* that had added to the fire of desire. Even Ted shifted a lot, tugging at his pants to make room for the boys. Instead, when the low baritone notes from *Josh Turner's Your Man* began at the very moment the Bronco bounced down the last stretch of clay road, Frankie was feeling frisky. Her fingers slid over his thigh and squeezed. He tensed, grunting as he pulled her hand away.

"Baby, I've told you. You can't do that to me." He eyed her and she licked her lips before biting on them; she looked hungry, and he was on the menu. "Honey Bee, we can't. We'll crash."

"Stop the Bronco, then." She squeezed his thigh again and she could see his shorts tighten a little more. He couldn't say the idea didn't excite him, that he didn't want what she was offering him. "Come on, Teddy Bear. Let's have a little fun. You got my motor running and now I'm wanting more. Can't I play with you just a little?"

Her fingers snaked across his tightening shorts, both aching for more foreplay. He could feel her fingers through his cargo shorts, caressing his cock and balls and gripping them tight. Moans escaped his lips. She squeezed harder, stroking his dick through the fabric just enough to make him grow a little harder. Swallowing, Ted looked in his mirrors. No signs of anyone behind them, and no one had been seen in front for almost a solid hour. He let off the throttle, veering to the shoulder and without further ado, putting the Bronco into park.

Frankie licked her lips again in anticipation as Ted unbuttoned, unzipped, and flipped out his hardened length. Ted couldn't handle it anymore; he wanted what she was offering, and he wanted it now. He shifted in his seat and stretched his arms across the bench seat. It was all hers. The heat of Frankie's breath washed over his dick, and he moaned. Chills ran across his arms and his stomach tensed, aching to be in the wetness of her mouth. Silky and hot, Frankie's tongue glided from the base to the tip of his cock and circled there. He hummed, the sensation invigorating, and his hands fisted, fighting the urge to shove himself through her lips. The last thing he wanted was to skip this part. The way she played with him; the build that made the finish that much more satisfying.

Her lips were back at the base, suckling and kissing the underbelly as her fingers caressed his scrotum. The tip of her tongue tickled the flesh between the cushions of her lips as if she were French kissing his dick. Slow and in timed intervals, she worked her way up. Her breasts rubbed against his thigh, and he could feel her hard nipples. Each suckle closer to the top of his dick, only made him grow harder and Frankie smiled. She loved how Ted moaned, the humming of his pleasure in vocal form only made her wet with excitement. If he hadn't worn those work boots today, she could see his toes curl. It was pure torture for Ted when she started, and she wondered how long he would hold out before grabbing a fist full of her hair, aiming to finish.

I've got him right where I want him...

It had become a game, one where she knew she had the most control and it excited her. As she reached the top, she sucked the very tip, teasing him whether she would take him all the way in, her lips never passing the edge of the tip, but progressively daring to go farther. He moaned, his hips shifting, daring to cheat the game.

Nope, not yet. I want you to know what kind of weekend I aim to give you, Ted.

Pulling away, he grunted and frowned. She looked up to see his head tilted back, eyes closed tight. Snorting, she decided to change her method of attack. She began suckling and teasing the topside of his shaft as her thumb rubbed and caressed the underbelly. Again, a groan escaped Ted and the muscles in his thighs tightened. If she kept teasing, kept him wavering on the edge, he'd start to play with her as a means to encourage her to dive deeper and suck harder until her teeth nicked him.

If you want more, you know what you need to do.

Frankie wiggled a little closer, her pussy aching with want and her panties wet from the very idea she had Ted in a corner. His hand broke loose from the seat, riding the divot of her spine, slipping under her daisy dukes enough to force them off her ass. He squeezed her ass cheek, and she hummed against his dick. Ted grew harder, knowing full well if he wanted her to go further, deeper down on him, he would have to appease her needs. Another squeeze and another hum confirmed it. She would keep him teetering on the edge until he gave her a reason to go further.

That's a good boy. Give me what I want.

She scooted on the bench seat, positioning herself so Ted had full access to wherever he intended to play. Fingers caressed the folds of her pussy and she wiggled, enticing him to keep going. His fingers dove a little closer to just outside her vaginal opening, his fingers slick with her own anticipation. His cock pushed against her lips, he had gotten excited over the sensation, and she rewarded him for venturing that far. Her lips slid just past the cap and his fingers pushed inside her. They both moaned, wanting more. At once they dove deep together, lips wrapped tight around the base of his cock while his knuckles kept him from pushing any further inside her.

Yes, yes, yes!

There was something magical about the way he stroked her with his fingers in sync with the way she sucked and pulled on his cock. He was fucking her on both ends, feeling how wet she grew with his dick in her mouth and gushing as his fingers had their way with her. The tip of his cock hit the back of her throat and he moaned, losing his rhythm where he played. She sucked hard and pulled up and off with a pop. Ted moaned. Her tongue circled the tip and she wiggled her hips, hinting he would get nothing more until he continued pleasuring her.

Don't stop now! She suckled on the tip. *I'm not giving you any more until you play with me some more.*

Ted's agony peaked. His fingers dipped into her, hard and she returned the gesture with another round of deep throating. He wanted to finish, he was riding on the edge of coming and he wanted nothing more than to have Frankie swallow. She was dripping wet, but she hadn't been moaning like he wanted. Fingers slid out and she pulled up and off his dick; the mirrored motion agonizing for them both. He grinned, his other hand grabbing a fist full of her hair.

Oh, he's taking control. What will my punishment be?

Looking down at her, both their faces red-cheeked from the heat of their toying. His finger moved up, circling her asshole, making it slick from where they had been.

I've been bad enough to receive the full punishment for misbehaving, I see.

Frankie grew excited, breaking her stare with Ted and began sucking on the tip in order to beg for what he hinted, what his fingers promised to do to her. She rocked against his finger, daring him to enter that forbidden place she yearned to be played with. His other fist tightened on her hair, and all at once, he dove his fingers into her; *two in the pink, one in the...* She moaned with a mouth full of cock, grinding against his hand. He was so stiff, every muscle in his body tight with the build of his oncoming orgasm.

Please, a little longer...

He lost it. Coming, he pushed her down, his cock riding deeper than before. Her tongue shifted and she began swallowing, and he released hard. He loved the way the back of her tongue and throat tightened over him, swallowing down everything he had to offer her. His finger rode deep inside her only pushing her further onto him and she gushed, thighs wet with her own arousal.

Don't stop! I'm so close!

Finished, he pulled her away, panting. Grabbing a work rag, he wiped his hand clean and shifted in the seat. Satisfied and winding down, he tucked himself away, and Frankie puffed out her lip. She had hoped he would keep going, to fuck her there in the Bronco and make it rock to and fro.

I wanted to rock this bucket of rust until the Game Warden came to knock to see what wild animal he had locked inside until he saw my tits against the window.

Her body hummed with the weight of her want. He had met his peak, but she was still teetering on the edge, just shy of the promised orgasm throbbing at her loins.

Shit, I want to just ride this out a little longer… Fucking Ted.

"Dammit woman, can you suck a cock!" He gave her a glance, seeing the disappointment on her face, nipples hard and thighs glistening. "Oh, Baby Doll, don't look at me like that."

"But I wasn't quite done, Teddy Bear." Breasts heaving, she wiped her mouth and frowned.

"You wore me out, woman." He put the Bronco back in drive and started down the road. "I'll make it up to you after we set up camp. You'll be walking funny before we head home, promise."

"Promise?" Frankie's shorts and bikini bottoms were sliding down her shins as she spread her thighs open. "Because I'm going to have to play with myself on the rest of the ride. Make you watch and hear me satisfy myself since you couldn't." The playful jab made him snort and rev the engine.

"You do that, Sweet Pea." He reached over and gripped her left breast and pinched her nipple. "And I'll lend a hand to get you there faster, Baby Doll."

Frankie moaned, her hands diving between her legs to finish what he had started. Her fingers were slick and the way they glided over her hard clit was intoxicating. She enjoyed playing with herself, whether he fucked her or not, she was never fully finished without the cherry on top. Masturbating right after a session with Ted always felt different, elated compared to those moments where she was trying to satisfy herself without the foreplay.

He twisted her nipple the other way, and she hummed again. "Let me hear you sing… That feel good? You like it when I twist 'em?" Back the other way and she moaned. "Don't make me get rough. You better come for me."

Still, wanted your cock… but this… this might… this might do…

She wiggled and shifted, legs jittering. Her face reddened with frustration. She was so close to an orgasm, and it was driving her crazy. Shuffling off her bottoms all the way, a bare foot propped up on the dash so she could dive deeper into herself. He squeezed her breast, massaging and flicking her nipple and she started to arch her back. He saw her bite her bottom lip and like clockwork, gave her nipple another hard twist.

Yes! YES! Harder!

It broke the levee. She lurched forward, a loud coo and groaning filling the air like a wave of relief and satisfaction exhaling from her. Frankie only made that sound when she peaked, and he loved watching her make herself come.

Catching her breath, Ted handed her the work rag. "It's clean, I swear. You're a hot, wet mess over there, Sugar Doll."

Huffing, she took it and wiped up her thighs and the seat. She hadn't expected to come so hard, but oh did it feel so good with his hand on her breast while she finished. Cleaned up, she shuffled her bottoms back on and slid back to the window on her side of the Bronco, watching the endless trees passing by was hypnotic as her eyelids grew heavy.

NEIGHBORS

A Bronco had roared dangerously close to Bif's camp, interrupting his plucking on the guitar. He snuck through the trees and underbrush, curious who his new neighbors might be. Peering into the clearing, he watched as a good-ole-boy stepped out. Bif cursed under his breath.

Why couldn't it be a couple of Sorority girls on retreat?

Opening up the back of the old Bronco, the man propped it open with a stick and began rifling through the back. Bif caught the extensive amount of trail cams and equipment. The man lugged out the military pack and there Bif saw it. The local Sasquatch hunter's patch. They weren't the brightest hunters, but in his current state of being a daytime Big Foot, this could be dangerous.

Of course a hunter would come out and join me in my crisis. If I get desperate, he can knock me out of my misery or just capture it on camera. Good Lord, did he pack for a full production film or something? There's gotta be more trail cams in that pack than balls in a Walmart toy bin.

A growl rolled out of Bif's chest and he couldn't stop it. Part of him was angry and the other part felt cornered. In this form, he was half animal and there were things he couldn't keep from happening. The idea of his rational thinking being overridden by instincts rattled him. Squatting down, he continued his glower at the man. Bif watched as he set up a table and laptop near a tent. Lifting an eyebrow, Bif couldn't deny the man knew how to setup camp and fast. He was curious why so many blankets for one person, until *she* came out of the Bronco.

He brought his girl with him, but seeing how she's dressed, she ain't here for hunting. The scent of her wafted on the air and he shuddered. *Peaches. My-my, she's horny and ready to go. She came all the way out here for some fucking, and I don't think he told her why he came out here.*

He could feel himself harden as he took in her perfumed fragrance. It was like ripe fruit, sweet and sugary. It made him hungry in a way he hadn't felt in some time since he spent the summer as a farmhand and hung out with a Chupacabra scouting for cowgirls. Bif cursed under his breath. She might be ready, but her sights were on her man and not the awkward hairy apelike creature hiding behind the trees like a creeper.

How in the hell am I going to take advantage of this? I'm not like Satch, but...

Bif scanned the camp and sniffed the air. There were no signs of drugs or drinking. In fact, strangely he didn't really smell food or any other necessities. Looking it over, he had set up for a weekend and packed for a day out. He glared at the Big Foot Hunter and what now looked like a disgruntled girlfriend, and he grinned. Unlike Satch, he'd rather have a girl clearheaded, and if things went south between these two, he could get on board with that.

What fun is she if you can't tease her until she begs you for your cock? Poor thing probably thought he was going to be paying her all the attention the entire weekend. He's about to take this from pre-sumed fuckfest into fuckup if he doesn't take it easy on the Sasquatch Hunter routine.

"Ted, I thought this was about *us* this weekend." She frowned and Bif's eyebrows lifted high.

Called it.

"It is, it is!" Ted closed the back of the Bronco and Bif snorted. "Since you aren't gonna cover your scent, Frankie, just wait here, Honey Bee. Don't want your scent to scare 'em off."

YOU'VE GOT TO BE FUCKING KIDDING ME! Did that moron just ask his half naked, ready-to-go-at-it girlfriend to cover her scent! That's fucked up. Hilarious, but not right. Poor thing, she really wanted to have fun with him, and she got...

Bif's spying was short lived as Ted started to spray scent cover. It was pungent and Bif's eyes and nose stung. If that idiot thought it would hide him from one of his kind, he was sadly mistaken; though the scent of wanting from his girlfriend could draw him in far faster than doe in heat to a buck. It took every part of him not to walk out and give her what her body was demanding. Then again, Frankie's arousal had started to wane, and the smell of Ted's scent cover had brought both her and Bif to their knees.

I'll have to come back when it gets dark and Captain Deer Piss leaves. He's ruined the moment for me and... Frankie.

Unable to stand the scent, Bif marched back to his own camp. He had liked the feel of her name in his thoughts and wondered how a girl like her had ended up with a moron like that. Nothing in the Bronco or camp said he had packed to meet her needs. Well, besides the blankets, unless he was the type who didn't care to feel the ground under him. Back in camp, and far away from the stench, Bif grabbed his phone.

"Hey Bif! Don't tell me you're out of food already?" Satch prodded.

"Look, unlike you when this happened, I have a damn phone." Bif found the lack of urgency in his friend annoying. "And I'm in deep shit. It just got worse."

"Oh, c'mon now." Satch grunted over the receiver. "I'm posting the ad now, I swear! I think you can live for a while with a broken guitar string."

"Not that! There's a hunter camping next to me, Satch!"

There was silence.

"Is she hot?"

"Yes, I mean, he's not…" Bif covered his face, her scent still lingering in his nose despite the invasion of scent cover. "It's a hunter and his girlfriend."

"PERFECT!" Satch seemed too excited at the news. "I can delete the ad! You've got a solution to your problems. Good luck, Buddy!"

"Don't delete the ad," hissed Bif before a growl took over. "This is serious. There's not a drop of alcohol or drugs. This isn't like your little cult of naked hippie chicks. He's part of the local hunter's regime, but he's packing a crap load of cameras."

He could hear Satch typing on his keyboard. "I bet a hundred dollars he only sets up trail cams on one side of his camp. They're like a one-winged moth circling on a table. Couldn't find their way through the forest even if we put a yellow brick road down."

"That's not the point."

"Well, she's hot. And he's busy hunting." A squeak from a chair told Bif that Satch had no plans of bailing him out as he propped his feet on a desk. "Go over and say hi to your neighbor. Make a good first impression and the rest will take care of itself."

"Satch, this isn't fair. I'm in the form of Big Foot. It doesn't work that way!" He glanced in the direction of Ted's camp. "What do you suggest I do? You're way more morally compromised than me. I'm not good at being… well… a silver-tongued bastard who'd say anything for some pussy."

"Hey-hey." Satch sighed and after a pause, gave his friend advice. "Mistaken identity. It's gonna be your best bet and works like a charm most of the time. You act drunk and slide in the tent while she's asleep and do some hanky-panky and follow it up with the whole OOPS routine."

"I can't." Bif felt sick, he couldn't even picture doing it, let alone pulling something that dirty on anyone. "I just can't do that..."

"Look." Satch's voice lowered his voice, whispering. "It's not what you think you can and can't do. Morality is off the table, if I'm being honest, Bif. When I got stuck, instincts took over hard and there's nothing you can do when that kicks in and starts calling the shots. I wouldn't have dared to attempt the first time if it hadn't been for the..."

"Satch?" Yvonne's voice cut his words short.

"I gotta go man. Good luck." And the phone beeped.

"Son of a bitch." Bif shoved the phone back in his pocket.

The weight of it all crushing him, he turned back to the guitar by the wooden bench. He sat there, mind spiraling deeper as he plucked at the strings. There's only one way out, and he would have to find his own way to achieve the same results.

What did he mean "when the instincts kick in"?

6

CAMP DUD

Frankie woke to a loud skid and thud. The Bronco turned off, parked obscurely among some trees with just enough space from where the tent was set and the sun fading. The squeak and slam of the driver's side door made her stir, slow to wake up. She perked up, opening the door and stood, stretching her arms high. Walking to the back of the Bronco, Ted was taking stock of all the cameras he had brought for the trip. In a bookbag, he was loading trail cameras and more. She spun around, a portable table and laptop already set up for reviewing his footage beside the tent and she frowned.

It's happening... I'm losing to Sasquatch already.

If she didn't know better, he had a date with Sasquatch and not her. Spinning back to Ted, he grinned as he zipped the bag closed.

"Baby, are you planning to go on a hike or something?" Frankie watched as he slid the tub back into the Bronco and started to rifle through other supplies, grabbing a few bottles. "I just wore flip flops. I thought we would be setting up and just staying put. You know, you promised to fuck me till I walked funny?"

"I'm gonna set these cameras up and after that we'll have all the fun you want." He started to spray himself down with scent cover and the bottle after that made her gag and take a few steps back. There went the last of her sexual excitement and hope for a royal fucking this weekend. "Here, spray yourself down too."

"Oh hell no." Frankie crossed her arms and her brow lowered. "I hope you don't plan on being out in the woods all night playing Bigfoot Hunter."

"I prefer to call it Sasquatch, Baby." He was lugging the packed bag over his arms and his tone was serious. "It shouldn't take long to skirt the perimeter. The last time I was out here, I managed to record its call."

Is this a joke? Am I on some candid camera show? What the...

Frankie rolled her eyes, no words to possibly share with him at this point as her ire rose ever higher.

"All I got on camera were the sounds of him in this spot here. I think he's looking for a mate." Ted continued, unaware that she was disinterested and worse, pissed off. "So I'm hoping with double the cameras I might get a clear shot of a Sasquatch this time."

"Ted, I thought this was about *us* this weekend." She frowned.

"It is, it is!" He closed the back of the Bronco. "Since you aren't gonna cover your scent, Frankie, just wait here, Honey Bee. Don't want your scent to scare 'em off."

YOU'VE GOT TO BE FUCKING KIDDING ME!

"There's nothing exciting about that shit-smelling concoction that says we're going to be making love all night. Are you even going to be back before dark?" She motioned to the sky, tinged with the orange hue of the evening sunlight.

"I should be." He reached for a bottled water he had on the back bumper. "Get settled in, Baby Doll. Be ready when your Teddy Bear makes it back." He moved forward to kiss her and she backstepped, the scent overwhelming. "I'll rinse it off when I get back."

Frankie took another glance at the campsite. "Are you going to start a fire before you go?"

"Oh no, we can't do that." Ted gave her a bewildered look. "They won't come within twenty miles of a campfire."

Frankie gaped at him. "How are we going to make food? Stay warm?"

"We got some meals, ready-to-eat." Her scowl didn't faze him as he continued. "And I brought some extra blankets, there in the tent. It's not going to get too cold tonight. Maybe when I get back, I'll share with you how a Sasquatch in heat sounds."

Frankie covered her face. "You'd better be back by dark and make up for all of this."

"I will baby, I swear." He glanced down at his cell phone. "I gotta go, Sweet Pea. Time's running out."

Ted bounded off through the underbrush, and Frankie stood in disbelief. She knew he had been obsessed, but this was downright ridiculous. There she stood, half naked, ready to get completely naked, and her lover... well he decided Big-Sasquatch-Urban-Legend-Thing was more important. Bored and disappointed, she meandered around. Ted had taken the keys to the Bronco with him, and his laptop was locked with a password.

I can't even watch porn!

Lord knows he assumed Sasquatches might hack his system at the rate he was going. She didn't bring anything. There wasn't supposed to be any down time besides sleeping and fireside meals. The ride here had been promising but snuffed out in record timing. Stifling a yawn, Frankie decided to just climb into the camouflage tent and start sleeping. What else was she to do?

***

A chill brought her from her sleep. She had tossed and turned, kicking the comforter off. Rolling onto her back, she saw it was dark out and an orchestra of bugs sang the praises of nightfall. Scrambling around, she found her cell phone: it was 9:30 PM. Rolling to her knees, she unzipped the door to the tent. It was so dark, she could barely see the Bronco, but it didn't deter her from slipping on her flip flops and coming out to see if Ted was back.

"Ted? Ted!"

Silence.

She texted him, but the phone binged: No Service Available.

"Son of a bitch..." Muttering, she looked out to the forest all around with no idea where to look or what to do. "TED!"

Silence.

You fucking douchebag. It's been dark for over an hour, and you're still not back!

Frustrated, her stomach growled. She was hungry and the only thing he'd brought were MRE's. She opened the top hatch and climbed up on the bumper. Hunched over the tailgate, she began digging around. Under her breath, she continued muttering her complaints about Ted, camping, and even Sasquatch. Her Daisy Dukes' button was digging into her as she tried her hardest to reach the MRE's. Even her outfit was starting to betray her, and she unbuttoned them and let them slide down her hips some and went back for the long reach, high-centered on the tailgate.

The top hatch had slowly descended and pinned her. She tried to push herself onto her tippy-toes, but all she managed to do was wiggle until her shorts fell to her ankles. She froze, groaning. *It's not like there's anyone out here with us...*

Placing palms flat on the bed, knees and thighs tight against the tail gate, she attempted to push herself out. The glass and aluminum top hatch refused to budge. Shrieking, she cursed Ted's name to hell and back before falling silent. *How long will I be stuck like this?* Despair washed over her, and she looked down through the dark at the MRE packages.

Squinting and trying to shift so the aching of her pinned hip would ease some, she opened the MRE, unable to read the label with her phone lost in her shorts that had fallen from the bumper to the ground. Taking a bite, she gagged. *Is this, is this supposed to be Chicken Fajita? What the...*

"Fuck this! Someone give me a Jack Link's beef jerky stick." She abandoned it, looking at the packs in horror, wondering if they were all the same flavor. "How the hell does Ted eat these?"

Shifting against the tailgate, she tried again and nothing. She had gotten herself at the wrong angle, her toes numb from the effort to keep them on the bumper. A chill rattled through her. Wearing a string bikini to go camping at night had turned into the worst idea ever, right next to thinking Ted could let go of Sasquatch hunting long enough to fuck her. She slammed her palms into the tub.

I should have known when he packed this damn thing full of trail cams. I'm such a moron thinking I was going to have a weekend full of unfathomable sex! What am I thinking to come up with such wild expectations?

7

instincts

The alarm on Bif's phone went off. Night had fallen and the short nap only made him feel more annoyed. He had stayed in his tent, waiting for Ted to stumble into his camp on his ventures of setting up cameras, but he never did. He smirked. Satch called it. Crawling out, he stretched and yawned. Crickets chirped and the trees were still, like black sentinels in the waning moon. He took in a lungful of air and tensed.

Good gravy, I can smell her from here. Don't tell me homefry didn't come back and take care of business? This has got to be torture for the poor girl.

His curiosity peaked. Making his way to the edge of their camp, he squatted so he could blend with the underbrush. There were no signs of Ted, and from the smell of it, he hadn't been in camp since he left hours ago. Bif began to stand up in order to creep up to the tent when he saw movement. He ducked back down and watched as Frankie scrambled out.

Her face said it all. She had gotten nowhere in her attempts to have fun with her man. If he had a guess, she hadn't seen him since the scent-cover ordeal either. No amends had been made, and now that the sun was down, it was his time to try and come up with a way to sweep her off her feet.

"Ted? Ted!" Frankie called out, but no one responded.

Bif watched as she brought out her cell phone. Most folks couldn't get service out here and from the scowl on her face, she wasn't happy to discover this. He could, but when you're a shifter who spends once a month in the middle of nowhere and never knows what trouble you might find, it helps to have service. The despair in her body language was hard to watch.

"Son of a bitch... TED!" Frankie screeched.

Silence. Bif couldn't chime in, not while in full Big Foot form. She'd go from pissed off to terrified and all hope to get himself back to normal would go out the window. Granted, he felt bad for her.

What a fucking douchebag. Leaving a hot girl like that with no campfire either! And ready to go, just bust out your cock and get ready to fuck all night. Who passes that up?

Scratching his jaw, Bif figured he might as well watch her and see if maybe a chance to sneak in and pull Satch's OOPS routine might help. Fighting back a yawn, he watched her lift the hatch and climb onto the bumper. She leaned over the tailgate, the daisy dukes and bright pink bikini bottoms drawing his eyes to them. He could feel himself get hard watching as her ass wiggled, bent over the tailgate. The glass hatch above her started to drop, breaking his stare.

Wait, the stick... she forgot the stick!

He stood up to rush forward, but the glass hatch had pinned her. Panicking, Bif ducked behind a tree.

What the hell am I doing? If I get discovered, I can kiss my life goodbye.

After a few moments of frantic wiggling, her legs dangled in defeat. She was stuck. Bif snuck closer, curious what she could be doing in there. She didn't call for Ted for long, but... the smell of a MRE filled the air, and he covered his face. Every moment he spent watching these two made it more obvious how shitty her situation had become. He started to reach for the hatch to free her when his instincts made him freeze.

Oh hell, she smells like a hot peach cobbler, and all I want is a taste.

He licked his lips, staring at her ass. A sexual hunger flooded him, and he abandoned his aim. If Ted wasn't going to give her a little TLC, maybe he could at least make this moment stuck in the Bronco a little sweeter.

Just a little taste...

"Fuck this! Someone give me a Jack Link's beef jerky stick." Her voice sent chills across him.

Careful what you wish for, girlie.

He could feel his throbbing erection tight against his pants. As much as he ached to feel his hard cock inside her wet heat, the smell of her had been intoxicating. Grabbing her hips, he would give her a reason to wiggle and scream. A cooing and purring rolled out of him, and he lost himself to her growing arousal.

Peaches and cream...

8

TAILGATING

The heat of hands grabbing her ass cheeks made her tense.

"Ted?"

An odd chortle and coo responded.

"Are you pretending to be Sasquatch?"

He did say he would share the mating call with me when he got back...

Another chortle made her relax as the hands slid up to her hip. Fingers weaseled under the strings and her bikini bottoms fell away.

Finally! Some fun! The reason why I came! Wait... were Ted's fingers always that long and fat?

Frankie tried to shift to look over her shoulder, but the hands gripped her thighs and tilted her ass higher into the air. Before she could express her annoyance, a hot tongue licked over her clit and opening. A moan escaped her.

That's what I want.

Another pass, and she moaned louder, her toes curling. Lips started to suckle and kiss her, surrounding her clit and she couldn't keep her legs from shaking. In an instant, the pleaser had her panting and her body hot with want. Fingers dug into her thighs, fighting her desire to close them. With the Bronco hatch and tailgate making a barrier, neither of them was able to see or touch, other than the exposure of her ass and pussy. She wiggled and shrieked. The lips pulled harder on her clit and the tip of a tongue sent her legs jittering.

Reaching out, she pushed against the tub, her eyes rolling back. The night air invaded as he pulled away, chills rippling across her skin. Once more, the silken heat of a tongue travelled across her clit, licking her opening teasingly before venturing further. Fingers dove inside her, two digits thick and long as any dick could hope to be. She was so wet, they slid in and out with ease.

Since when did Ted become so good at...

Her breath caught in her throat. Fingers thrust ever faster, her legs shaking as she found herself coming. The stroking riding along the sweetest spot, not even she had realized how sensitive it could be at this angle. She gripped the edge of the container, her back arching as she came, gushing as the stroking continued. Shrieking, she lost herself. As her orgasm waned, the fingers left her, and she struggled to catch her breath.

Looking over her shoulder, she couldn't see where he had gone. Her legs felt numb as she wiggled, trying to get her feet on the bumper again.

"Dammit Ted! I'm stuck!"

Where'd he go all of a sudden? He's got to be...

"TED!"

"Good grief, Frankie!" The hatch lifted and Ted pulled her out of the back of the Bronco. His arms wrapped around her, a hand squeezing a breast and the other diving between her thighs. "Wet and ready!"

"Of course, I am!" His arms kept her trapped against the heat of his body.

Laughing, he bent her over, her hands catching on the bumper. At least her feet were on the ground and the sound of Ted's zipper brought sweet, sweet excitement.

A fucking dick! About damn time!

She wiggled her hips, anticipation building.

"Damn girl!" Ted's hands gripped her hips, making them ache. "You're hungry for dick!"

"Shut up and fuck me!" Frankie screeched over her shoulder.

Ted snorted. His hard cock pushed against her wet opening. She leaned back, wanting him to go in, to give her all of him. He pushed fast against her, entering his entire hardened length inside. She squealed, her back arching as a hand slapped against the Bronco hatch. Her eyes rolled back. She was still so swollen and sensitive from the first orgasm that she tightened around his cock. Fingers dug into her hip as he ground against her. Hard and deep, both moaning. Her breasts rocked and her face pressed against the tailgate.

Ted's hands moved off her hips, sliding under and gripping her breasts. He pulled her off the tailgate, her back arching into him. Ted sandwiched her between him and the Bronco. Frankie propped her knees on the bumper, straddling to let him grind deeper. Leaning back into him, she let her orgasm release. She could feel herself tighten around his cock. He squeezed her breasts tighter, moaning as he began peaking. Gripping her hands over his, she rocked, enjoying how he moaned over her shoulder.

Frankie began to squeal, and Ted covered her mouth. She bit his fingers, and he withdrew them.

"Dammit, Frankie," he grunted, finishing and leaning over her still. "You need to stop being so loud."

She shuffled him off, taking off her shirt to mop herself up. "There's no one else out here. What does it matter?"

"You'll spook Sasquatch." He tucked himself away, meandering toward the laptop. "Wonder if I caught anything on tape yet?"

"Are you kidding me?" Frankie tied her bikini bottoms then threw the damp shirt at him. "This was supposed to be our weekend!"

"Quiet down!" He punched in his password and began looking through trail cam feed of a billion bugs setting off the motion sensors. "It's not like I can fuck you non-stop, woman."

"Ugh, I'm going to sleep." Frankie marched past him and zipped herself into the tent.

Why am I even dating someone this obsessed over a damn urban legend?

PEEPING BIF

*L*eaning against a tree in the shadows, Bif rubbed his cock. He wanted her bad, but he had snapped out of his lustful playing when the smell of deer piss and doe in heat came into the clearing. How in the hell Ted didn't see him or question the state of his girl was beyond him, but to watch and hear her? Oh, he wanted to see more, despite his better judgment.

He moaned, stroking himself. The flavor of her still sweet on his tongue.

"Dammit, Frankie. You need to stop being so loud," roared the half-baked Ted.

Bif didn't care for the rough tone or handling of Frankie, but he caught her name again. What a unique name, something he wouldn't forget easily.

"Shut up and fuck me!" Frankie screeched over her shoulder.

I would gladly give it to you! Fuck Ted. He doesn't deserve a girl that hungry to make love to her man.

Ted bent her over and the air filled with her scent. Bif panted, stroking as he watched them fuck.

She wanted me, not him. That should've been me. I made her come long before your dick came…

Grunting, Bif came as Frankie's shriek filled the air.

He caught his breath, wide-eyed.

What the hell am I doing and saying?

Bewildered by the hunger of lust, he went back to camp and sat on the bench. Grabbing up his phone, he called Satch.

"Hey, don't you know people are asleep at this hour?"

"Shut the fuck up." Bif still sounded breathless.

"Oh hell, did you get chased?"

"No." Bif inhaled deeply and freed it. "What did you mean by instincts? Like what kind of instincts?"

There was silence. He could hear Satch leaving his bed, the room possibly.

"Satch, I need to know. I'm not feeling like myself." His heart pounded in his chest. "I'm making mistakes and bad calls. I'm gonna get myself caught or killed."

"Look, just fuck someone. Get it out of your system."

"Seriously Satch?"

"I don't know how to describe it." He was whispering, something unusual for Satch. "I lost myself to pure hunger."

"What kind of hunger?" Knots formed in Bif's gut.

"I was ready to fuck any girl on the planet. The slightest hint of arousal on the wind smelled like… like…"

"Peaches."

"Yea, man. And it tastes as sweet as it smells."

"It does." Bif leaned on his thighs, holding his head.

"Oh, you got in there?"

"Not really, the hunter showed up and ended it."

Clearing his throat, Satch had one warning. "Careful. You're going to start feeling territorial over her. Enough you might have to bury her man six feet under. Fuck her and get the fuck out."

"Come get me," Bif pleaded.

"I can't."
 The phone beeped.
"Fuck!"

Good Morning, Wood

Frankie shivered. The early morning air, humid and cool against her skin was enough to stir her from her sleep. At some point, Teddy had given up checking his laptop and laid down next to her in the tangled nest of blankets. She scooted closer, cuddling under his arm and against his torso for warmth. He grunted, but his arm pulled her tighter, rubbing her shoulder to acknowledge her need for heat.

She had nearly dozed back off when he gripped her hand and led it away from its resting place, under the covers and to his morning wood. She snorted. After being ignored and rushed through the main event of intercourse, the last thing she wanted to see or touch was his dick. She tried to pull away, but again he led her back to his raging hard-on.

Half-hearted, she rubbed the length with her hand, hoping maybe Ted might doze back off and she could escape the unspoken demand. He wanted a blowjob, a morning one at that. Any time this had come about, she would be left unsatisfied, let alone played with. After the sub-par start to what she had hoped would be sex-camping, she had zero interest in pleasuring him. He still owed her, by a long shot.

"Come on, Baby," he mumbled. "Daddy wants a wake-up kiss."

She pecked him on the cheek, and he grunted.

"Lower."

"Teddy Bear, I'm not in the mood," she whined, her handjob falling apart and making him shift his hips.

"But I am," he whined back in the same tone.

"What do I get?" She pulled her hand away, making him crack an eye at her.

"What do you get?" he echoed, confused.

"Yeah, if I get you off, what's in it for me?" Frankie flustered. "Anytime I give you morning head, I get left wet and wanting."

"Aw, Baby Doll, I promise I'll take care of you later. Anything you want." He was tugging her hand down, practically shoving her face to his crotch. "I promise."

"Like what?" She pulled the covers back to reveal his throbbing erection.

"Anything you want me to do to you." Another push, he wanted this blowjob. "I'll lick your pussy all night if that's what you want."

"Yes. Especially after last night." Frankie's tongue circled the tip of his dick and he moaned.

"Yeah, Baby Doll. Fucking you against the Bronco was hot."

She rolled her eyes, sucking tender and slow on the tip of his cock.

I meant that moment you were eating me out but, was it Ted?

Before she could ask him the question and panic built in her mind, Ted grabbed a fistful off hair and shoved his cock all the way in. She choked and gagged, not ready for it this time. It didn't stop him from pulling himself in and out of her lips, moaning. He grew harder with each pass and as soon as Frankie could feel herself getting wet... he came.

She swallowed, a death glare on her face as she wiped her mouth on his shirt.

"Hey, don't do that," he grumbled, tucking himself away.

"Not like I have my own shirt to use," she shot back, rolling over and covering herself in the blankets.

"Oh yeah, well, I'll give you one of mine, Sweet Pea."

With a grunt, Ted rolled up on his heels and was out of the tent. Frankie squirmed under the covers, a shiver rolling through her in the absence of his body heat. After a minute, the tent opening blinded her with morning light and a shirt slammed into her face.

"Ted!" She peeled it off, thankful the shirt smelled clean and not sweaty.

"I gotta go check on my gear and want to look for tracks." Ted let go of the tent flap. "I'll be back soon. If you're hungry, there's MREs in the Bronco."

"They taste like shit, Ted." She popped her head through the neck of her shirt, and he was gone. "You've got to be fucking kidding me."

She zipped the tent closed and flopped back into the covers, wrapping herself up. As much as she wanted to go back to sleep, her mind wandered back to being stuck in the Bronco. Thoughts of the way the mouth and tongue worked her over and the stroking of fingers. Whoever had satisfied her last night, she wondered if there was a chance to meet them again. It was sneaky, dirty, but so was the fact Ted had lured her out her with empty promises while he played Sasquatch Hunter.

Rolling onto her back, her thighs wiggled. She was getting wet just thinking about it. Never had Ted or any of her exes given her the bliss of an orgasm from oral. Her fingers slid under her bikini bottoms and started circling her clit. They dove inside her, slick and wet, returning to the circling with heightened sensitivity. The way he'd suckled there and later the sensation of a tongue entering her like that. It had been so erotic and lustful. He had been hungry for her; knew how she was starved to be played with until she came.

She could feel her nipples harden, pulling on the shirt and making her moan. Another dive of her fingers, *so wet*. Again, a moan escaped her trembling lips. Her back arched as she circled, faster and aggressive, *yes!* She peaked, sucking in a gulp of air as her mind recalled the fingers entering and stroking her with such determination. As the peak rattled through her, Frankie felt a want and lust. She needed to find the mysterious forest lover. *Fuck chasing Ted!*

Panting for a minute, her stomach growled, and she frowned. MREs were not her breakfast of choice. Sliding on her flip flops, she at last exited the tent. Ted's laptop was gone along with most of the things he had left out last night. He clearly had no intentions in being back in time for lunch. *Bastard!*

The Bronco had been left unlocked, so she began digging around. As the sun rose, she flustered further in the rising heat and humidity. There were no more snacks in her purse and digging around in the glove box only resulted in typical paperwork for the Bronco and mechanic receipts. Looking into the back, her eyes fell on the wretched MREs, and her stomach turned.

SHE'S GETTING HUNGRY

Bif couldn't help but come spy on the state of the camp. Instant regret slammed into him. They were both in the tent and from the sounds of his moaning, she was taking care of her man. Bif leaned against the tree, arms crossed. Anger and frustration boiled up inside him. Never in all his years had he felt so damn angry about... nothing.

Why am I angry? It's not like he's fooling around with my girl-friend in that tent!

Satch's warning echoed in his mind. Something had gone wrong in Yellowstone. He always glossed over it, never telling it in great detail, but he had been through this. Maybe he did find Bif in the woods and the moment he saw he hadn't reverted back, he packed up and got the hell out of Dodge. He knew the dangers and abandoned him because he was afraid.

A shudder rattled Bif's shoulders.

The tent flap opened, and the aroma of peaches made him tense. He watched as Ted, smiling with satisfaction came out to the Bronco and circled back. He smacked Frankie in the face with a shirt and Bif bit his bottom lip.

Why in the hell is she dating this asshat?

Ted let go of the tent flap. "I'll be back soon. If you're hungry, there's MREs in the Bronco."

"They taste like shit, Ted."

Frankie's golden locks mesmerized Bif. In the morning light, she captured his every want in a woman. Pulling the shirt on, her nipples pushing through her bikini made him lick his lips. His pants tightened, and he muttered to himself.

Satch wasn't joking, I just feel hungry ... for her. And she's not even mine to have.

Ted had vanished into the woods on the other side. More scent cover wafted over, and he turned away, heading back. The poor girl was starving. No fire, and no real food. He flipped open his cooler and smiled.

"Mama's bacon always did the trick; don't fail me now." He started gathering the supplies and the cast iron pan.

There was one bonus to the lifestyle he lived; he could cook like a pro chef on a single skillet with minimal supplies. Protein everything had been the staple for these things, so bacon and eggs it would be. Despite all of the smells, they did nothing to squash the scent of peaches in the air.

I bet she's messing with herself. Asshat got what he wanted and ran out to play Big Foot Hunter. Frankie's in there just trying to salvage what she can and oh, how I hope I get the chance to do her right. Fuck you, Ted!

He set the food in place on the bench. Scratching his jaw, he decided to leave a note. She had to have figured out that it wasn't her boy who had his way with her while stuck in the Bronco. He had been tender and soft with her, not the greedy harsh motions of Ted.

Happy with keeping it simple and short, he hid just out of sight. Plucking his guitar, he sang himself a song and waited. Never had he felt as much like a predator trapping his prey as he did in this moment. Frankie came into the clearing, and he stopped his plucking.

How can a man resist a woman so curvy and beautiful?

12

FOREST LOWER

Slamming the Bronco door, she hoped Ted could hear it and cursed his name over it. Two steps toward the tent and her nose caught the scent of something.

Is that ... bacon?

Her head swiveled and she began to wander toward the smell. Her stomach grumbled.

What the hell am I doing? Am I really desperate enough to invade another camp for food?

She paused, the sound of singing hitting her ears. *Is that the radio or is there a man out here who can sing like Dierks Bentley?*

She took a few more steps toward the smell and sound. Blinking, she saw a tent and a table laid out with a grand breakfast. Her heart pounded, the music stopped abruptly, and she stumbled into the clearing. Her stomach growled and she looked around.

"Hello?" Stumbling toward the breakfast, she spun once more. "Anyone here?"

Frankie furrowed her brow and realized there hadn't been a radio, but on a far tree, an acoustic guitar had been left behind. Her stomach growled once more, the bacon and eggs invading her nostrils. She turned to the table beside her and there she saw a note.

Dear Bikini Bottom Girl,

Enjoy.

B.F.

Frankie looked down to her bottom half. *Well, I think I'm the only moron who would camp like this, so they must be talking about me.* Her eyes widened. *Is this ... Forest Lover's camp?*

Her tummy tightened. Uncertainty rolled through her mind as she looked around.

I mean, clearly, he made breakfast for me... She sat down, slow and unsure. *It would be rude not to eat it?*

"It's ok." A deep, sexy baritone voice made her jerk. "I made it for you, seeing that all *he* brought were those shitty MREs."

"Who are you?" Her eyes scanned the trees, but she couldn't pinpoint where the man stood.

"A lonely man wanting to make a girl's day." He chuckled, and her mind flashed back to last night.

"Last night, that was you?" She swallowed. *Am I out of my mind!*

"Sorry, I was..." His words faltered. "I've gotten myself in a situation and I started to take advantage... it wasn't right. Hope the breakfast makes up for it."

She could hear footsteps leaving and it startled her, "WAIT!"

The steps stopped.

"I... Look, I don't know who you are, but..." Frankie's face was red, the heat of the thoughts rolling in her mind both embarrassing and brash. She started again. "Look, Ted made a promise, and he hasn't kept it. We're done."

"Oh?" He couldn't hide the intrigue in his voice.

"But you..." She searched for a way to phrase it. "Last night, when you..."

Another chuckle came rolling out from the woods. "Don't tell me your man has never taken care of you like that, Darling?"

She puffed out her cheeks, the blushing never-ending.

"No need to blush."

She swiveled her head but still couldn't seem to find the sexy-voiced forest lover anywhere.

"I'll tell you what: if you need me to take care of you, just come back here."

"Ok, deal." Frankie's internal screaming couldn't decide if this was crazy or amazing luck.

"Now, you eat up. I promise you'll need that energy for later if you come back." And the steps crunched away before she could think of anything else to say.

Turning to the food, she picked up the fork and took a bite of the scrambled eggs. It was amazing. The man not only could show a girl a good time, but he had cooking skills. Picking up a slice of bacon, she hummed with delight. Not overly cooked and with the right amount of crisp. This was the camping experience she had imagined for her and Ted.

Well, if Ted's not going to give it to me, at least Mr. Forest Lover was willing to do so!

Frankie felt like a starved orphan, scarfing down the food until she cleaned the plate.

"Hungry, huh?" His voice made her blush.

"You have no idea." She leaned on the bench table, lost in thought. "I... thank you. Guess I look like an idiot, no food, no proper clothes..."

"Na, if you ask me, that boyfriend of yours needs to take better care of his girl."

It made her smile. "You play guitar?" she changed topics.

"Yes, ma'am."

"May I listen for a bit before I go back?"

"Anything you want, you just ask." He went back to plucking, the sound of it melting away her troubles.

Dammit, this is what I imagined, this is what I wanted, and this is what I thought I had been promised.

Frankie had lost track of how long she had been sitting there. He hadn't shown himself, but the music had lulled her to sleep almost. Standing suddenly, he stopped. The silence held strong until at last Frankie cleared her throat and spoke.

"I'm exhausted, but again, thank you for the food and the music."

There was a chuckle, "You're more than welcome to come back for more."

Her cheeks ached with her smile, "I like that. I might just do that."

Wanting to hide the heat in her face, she left the campsite in a rush.

Dammit Frankie, you didn't ask him for his name!

13

TED'S CAMERAS

Bif paced back and forth, pondering on his dilemma. His thoughts took inventory of the facts, one by one. He was a shifter stuck in Big Foot form and the only cure was to do the horizontal tango three times. Satch recommended sneaking in, but he had tried that. Between the animalistic lust and the idea of consent, it had left him in a wake of self-loathing. Granted, by some twist of fate, she was a gorgeous blonde and seemed rather calm about the incident.

Shit, I must've done a number on her last night to forgive me so easily. She even got a little turned on thinking about it.

A smile bloomed on his face, and he couldn't let it go. If he played his cards right, he might end up with a new girlfriend at this rate, or at least the best damn weekend hookup ever. The main obstacle was her man, Ted the Sasquatch Hunter. Looking around, he grabbed up his ball cap and with a groan, pulled on his hoodie. He looked like a gorilla in a skater punk outfit, but it would at least obscure the fact he was indeed Big Foot.

He skirted the outside of Frankie and Ted's campsite. He could tell she was asleep in the tent, and he sat on a laptop reviewing trail cam feed. Spitting at the ground, Bif made his way around and started taking inventory of all the equipment on the trees.

Good grief, a deer hunter has more sense than this.

He tapped a trail cam with his foot, and it fell off the tree. Chuckling, he squatted down and pulled the SD card out and snapped it in half. Ted had run the plastic tie strips the wrong way and with just the slightest tug, the cams were coming loose.

Despite that, he had to be more leery of the wireless cameras he'd drilled into the side of the pine trees and firs. Granted, they gave themselves away with long lines of sap dripping down the side of the tree. Laughing again, he tilted them up and shook his head that the man didn't even try to paint the white casing black or green.

Is he a rookie at this? Hoping to return half this shit to Walmart when they get back?

Mapping out the cameras didn't take long either. Like Satch had suggested, Ted had managed to make a singular circle on the north side of his camp. Satisfied he'd disrupted most of the cameras, Bif started to back track to their camp to see what else he could sabotage just in case. Footsteps and broken branches littered the area. This hunter had been beyond sloppy.

You failed to please your girl in hopes of catching me on camera. Looking at your attempt at that, you're failing at that too, Captain Deer Piss.

Bif snorted to himself as he sauntered along.

"I think I found a print!" Ted's voice shot through Bif, and he stopped.

Where? My camp?

Eyes wide in alarm, he snuck closer as the couple began to argue. Bif dared to get close, real close, and there he saw Ted's sticks and bright caution tape.

Shit! Behind the Bronco!

"NOT LIKE THIS, TED!" Frankie's voice brought Bif's eyes up in time to see her burst out of the tent. "We're done."

And that means she's all mine to have. Good luck hunting with broken cams, Ted!

Heart pounding, Bif rushed back to his camp. Grinning like a fool, he shed his hoodie and sat hidden in the shade. He could still hear them arguing. There weren't many choices as to where Frankie could go, and after this morning and last night's interlude, he hoped she'd come his way.

Looking down at this guitar, he picked it up and started playing. At least he could pass the time and hide his excitement this way. Something about playing kept the animalistic lust at bay, but he wanted to take her, claim her as his.

If she's done with the hunter, then it's time to show her the animal.

14

Lunch Goes Long

Ted woke Frankie with a nudge of his boot, and she rolled to face him, frowning.

"You gonna sleep the day away?" He lifted an eyebrow.

"Well, I was hoping to fuck the day away, but you've been gone for most of this camping trip." She rolled back over. "How's the hunting going?"

"I think I found a print!" His excitement was ill-timed.

"Oh goodie." Frankie rolled her eyes, stifling a yawn.

"I need to check the trail cams," he announced, unpacking the laptop and various cameras and SD cards at the table. "It was close to one, maybe I caught Sasquatch on camera finally."

"Ted, this was supposed to be *our time together*." She sat up, glaring into his back through the tent opening.

"It is, Sweet Pea." He didn't even turn to talk to her.

"No, it's not. You're busy smelling like deer piss and hunting an urban legend."

"I thought you'd want to join me."

"NOT LIKE THIS, TED!" She burst out of the tent, her frustration peaking. "We're done."

"Wait, what?" He finally met her gaze as she towered over him, arms crossed. "Done?"

"It's over. This trip, this relationship, and us. DONE." She growled. "Over. Take me home."

His brow furrowed. "I'll take you home when I'm ready to leave."

"And when will that be?" she hissed.

"Tomorrow." He slammed the laptop closed and started packing up his stuff. "Since I don't have to worry about taking care of you, I'll go back to hunting."

"What? Are you kidding me!" He was marching out to the woods. "Dammit, Ted!"

She let him go, the scent cover and animal piss making her stomach turn.

Turning to the Bronco, she pulled out her cell phone. No signal. Letting out a frustrated scream, she looked around the camp. This was supposed to be the ultimate date weekend. Instead, she had been roped into it so he could run off into the woods but still get his share of blowjobs. Looking at everything, the image of him marching off, it hit her. He never intended to give her a minute of his time. The asshole had packed for a full production hunt and not one plan to get kinky with her in the wild. He figured she'd be a puppy dog that would sit and wait like a good girl for him.

"Fuck you, Ted!"

Looking at the time on her phone, it was pushing a little after noon. She looked down at her bare legs and bikini bottoms with disdain. She felt stupid. Naïve. And all she wanted was someone to love her physically and emotionally. Ted had proven he had aimed to have his needs cared for and had abandoned hers.

Silence fell on the forest and like a whisper on the wind, she could hear the plucking of a guitar and the humming of a baritone voice. *Forest lover... should I take a chance on a stranger?* She looked up at the dappled sky through the tree branches. *What do I have to lose? It'll make one hell of a story to share, I suppose.* She grinned. *I wanted a weekend of fucking, and I'm going to make that happen!*

Frankie marched toward Forest Lover's camp. Before she got close, his singing and playing had ceased. It made her freeze.

"You came back sooner than I thought." He spoke through the wall of trees and underbrush.

"Well, we got into a fight," she blurted.

"I heard it from here."

"Sorry…" She continued into the clearing and once more found herself alone, the guitar leaning on a tree. "Am I not allowed to see you or something?"

"Well, about that…" He seemed nervous. "It's about my situation. It may be best to not see me just yet."

"Are you horribly scarred or something?" Her face flushed. "I mean, not that it matters…"

"Scarred." He echoed as if calculating the meaning of the word. "I suppose we can call it that."

"So…" She tugged on the hem of her shirt, looking down at her feet.

Her eyes widened. One foot had landed within a bare-footed print and not one part of her flip flop touched the edges.

Damn, he's got a big foot! What is that, size fourteen? Bigger? She smirked, a thought from her teen years creeping forward. *You know what they say about a man with large feet…*

"Did you get hungry again?" His voice cut through her thoughts.

"N-no… well… in some way." Her determination and bravery crept forward. She had made up her mind before marching here so it was time to make the offer known.

"Hungry in what way?" The tone made it clear he had some inkling of what she came to offer him.

"Well, shit, I'm trying to ask this without sounding like a complete whore, but…" Closing her eyes, she puffed out her cheeks a moment before balling her hands into fists. "I came out here to fuck and if Ted won't deliver, I figured maybe you'd be interested."

Silence filled the air and her stomach knotted.

Was that too forward? I mean, isn't it every man's dream to be made an offer by some hot blonde in a bikini to fuck his brain's out on a whim while out camping? Good grief, this sounds like a bad porno film...

"I'm sorry.... I'll just leave..." Frankie spun on her heel, feeling like an utter fool.

"Wait." There it was; the bark of a baritone that made her weak in the knees. "Close your eyes."

"What?" She twisted around toward the sound of his voice but still couldn't see him anywhere.

"Promise me you'll keep your eyes closed until I tell you it's okay." His tone was deep and steady. He was serious.

"First, tell me your name." Frankie lifted her chin. *At least get the man's name beforehand, good gracious!* "I'm Frankie."

"I heard your name from your ... now ex." He scoffed, and with a sigh she could hear from where she stood, he let his name fly. "You can call me Bif."

"Bif," she echoed, trying out the name. "Ok, Bif. I'll close my eyes, but I can't promise during the deed if they'll stay that way."

"R-right." He hadn't thought of that, and she heard him rifling around. "I have a bandana. Will it be okay if I blindfold you? Just in case."

Kinky. Closing her eyes tight, Frankie threw her arms out. "Come blindfold me then! Eyes are shut tight. Promise!"

Footsteps came closer and Frankie swallowed. Excitement and fear tangled together as he circled her like a predator. A finger caressed across her arm, goosebumps rippling across her skin. As the finger rode over her shoulder, she could feel the heat of his body behind her. *Ted has nothing on this man!* He tucked her hair behind her ear. A shiver rattled her shoulders as the heat of his breath washed over her neck.

"I'm going to blindfold you now, Frankie." His baritone voice rumbled into her ear, and she ached for him. "I promise I'll make sure you'll enjoy every minute of this."

"Promise?" He tied the blindfold tight and Frankie bit her bottom lip.

"Let me know if I kept it after we're done," he teased, his lips kissing her neck.

Hands, large and making Frankie feel small, cupped her shoulders. They encouraged her arms to fall, to relax. She let herself lean back into him, his hard-on making her gasp. *Will that even fit! He's built like a horse!* His arms wrapped around her, pulling her tighter against him. He suckled at her neck, and she tilted her head to let him have more access. Thoughts of the Bronco last night flashed into her mind and her body heated at the memory.

A hand glided across the skin of her stomach, sliding under her shirt and bikini to cup her breast. She hummed as he kneaded her flesh and began kissing down and across her shoulder. The other hand found the top of her hip and snuck under her bottoms. Fingers dove between her thighs, finding her clit with precision and she jerked. The touch of him was electrifying and he giggled at her shudder.

"You okay?" he whispered into her ear.

She wiggled against him, the muscles in his arms hardening to keep her in place as his fingers worked.

"I... I can't help it," she breathed as her hands gripped at his arms.

His hard cock rubbed against her lower backside, and she could feel herself getting wet with anticipation. "I've barely gotten started and you're already..." Fingers teased, daring to dip inside her, and came back slick as they circled her clit.

Her breath caught. A jolt made her stiffen before her knees started to go weak. Something about his touch was like nothing she had experienced before. Her breath quickened with the rise of her heartbeat. With each circle, she let herself fall further into the bulk of his body. The sensation of his breath on her neck as he nuzzled her only added to the shivers racking her body from head to toe.

I'm going to die; this feels too good...

"Girl, you're falling down on me," he breathed, groaning as his cock throbbed sandwiched between their bodies. "Where you want to do this? I'll carry you anywhere you want."

Frankie tried to open her eyes, but the bandana obscured her view. The image of the wooden bench she had eaten at this morning flashed in her mind and she bit her lip. *Should I dare to make such a bold request? Fucking me out in the open, where Ted just might hear us, no... see us.* She grew a little wetter, her loins throbbing. *Fuck Ted! Let him see and hear what he could have had!*

"The bench," she whispered, unsure how Bif might take it.

Without another word, he spun her around and lifted her up by her ass cheeks. She straddled him, thighs on his hip and a monstrous erection under his pants rubbing against her... she moaned, aching to see what a big dick like that might feel like. He sat her on top of the bench, her feet on the bench seat as he pulled away from her. Hands free, Frankie wasted no time abandoning Ted's shirt and began pulling the strings of her top. She could feel Bif pulling the strings and unknotting her bottoms.

"Scoot further onto the edge," he breathed before the heat of his lips wrapped around her nipple. Arching her back, she shifted to where he needed her to be. She moaned, the heat of his hands sliding up her legs, shifting to finish their journey along her inner thighs. A thumb rode across her wet pussy and continued the work he had abandoned. She jerked forward, legs failing to close as her knees locked against large shoulders.

So much bigger than Ted... so big...

Blindly, she reached forward but his hand caught both her wrists. "No touching me just yet. Let me enjoy you a little longer. You'll need these in a minute..." He let go.

How scarred is the poor man? Screw it, the man is an amazing lover, and I haven't made it to the main course yet!

She rested her palms behind her, widening her legs. If he wanted to enjoy her, then she would open herself up and let him have all he could handle. The thumb began circling again and her legs shook. The other hand glided against her inner thigh and two fingers slid inside her. She groaned. He was slow and deliberate, pulling them all the way out before descending slowly back into her depths. She tightened on his fingers, and he seemed to growl in response.

I wanted wild hot sex in the forest ... and that's what's finally happening. Oh, but please, I can't stand this...

Frankie wiggled, grinding against his hand and knuckles on the third entry. "Faster."

"No. I'm still playing..." his voice obscured by a growl.

"Please..." she wiggled, impatient. *Surely having a hard-on for this long has to be driving him wild. Ted can't go a full fifteen minutes without shoving in me or in my mouth.*

The hands pulled away and she whimpered. Before she could say another word, his hands pushed her legs wide and the silken heat of his tongue sent a shocking wave of euphoria over her. She lurched forward. Fleshy lips suckled on her clit, and she teetered on the edge of an orgasm. Her shaking legs squeezed around his shoulders, and she arched her back, shrieking.

Fingers teased her with the threat of coming back inside her, the tips just passed the threshold, agonizing and exciting. She flustered, never had she felt so damn wet. Shifting her hips, she wanted more. His teeth threatened her clit, and she shrieked as he thrust his fingers in and out with uncanny speed. She folded on top of him, fingers gripping the hair on top of his head. She came, hard and wet.

It was the first time she had ever felt the rush of fluids in response to being toyed with so heavily.

Panting, her body shook from the orgasm, but was given no relief from the breathtaking pleasure. His lips left her clit with a pop of suction, earning another squeal. A deep inhale and the heat of a tongue gliding inside her sent her arching, releasing his hair to catch herself. She let herself lay across the wooden bench. A hand glided up her thigh, across her hip and abdomen before finding a bare breast. He caught her nipple between a finger and thumb, and she squirmed.

His tongue flicked her clit, and he sucked it once more. Fingers moved in and out again and before she could voice how over-whelmed with arousal she was, she came again. Breathless, he pulled away and she was quick to shut her legs, her inner thighs hot, wet, and throbbing. Frankie hummed as she rode out the second wave of delight. But she wanted more, wanted him, wanted that throbbing erection she had felt at the start of this inside her.

"I want you..." she huffed, cursing the bandana. "I want you inside me."

The sound of a zipper and pants dropping made her throbbing grow. "Open your legs and let me in."

Panting, she fought against her body and parted her thighs. The heat of his body slipped between them, and the tip of his hard cock rubbed against her opening.

"Are you sure?" His voice was husky and breathless with his own desire to be inside her. "If I'm too big..."

"Fuck me..." she blurted, crazed with want. "I'm wet for you, now fuck me."

At first, he was slow, her wetness making him glide in with ease. He moaned as he entered her. She ached and relaxed and tightened and at last her breath caught. Never had she felt so filled by a man. Hip against hip, he paused. He leaned down, suckling one breast then the other. Frankie's hands had found the edges of the bench and gripped them. White-knuckled, she started the grind, adjusting and loving how big he felt inside her. Every little motion made him throb and it sent waves through her, and she wanted more. The suckling of her nipples had excited him, the shift of her hip had made him throb, and now he started to stroke in and out, slowly.

Each time he slid back inside, her breath caught, and he would pause. She would tighten and loosen, and they repeated this teasing and cautious moment a few times. Frankie wanted to feel how big he was, and one hand slid between them. Both moaned; Bif throbbed, and Frankie moaned as her hand failed to complete the grip. The motion pushed him to speed up, both moaning as she grew wet with each stroke and his throbbing cock slid faster.

Her back arched, an orgasm beginning to peak. He leaned down sucking her breast and teasing her nipple with his teeth. She began to shriek as his growling pushed it over the tipping point. He began moaning and pushed hard against her as he came with her.

"Oh!" Frankie's shrill scream caught in her breath.

His throbbing erection sent her into a second orgasm. The hardness of his erection as he came only amplified everything that had become so sensual in the course of what had happened. Bif slid the bandana off, and she squinted up at him through the wave of ecstasy.

My God, he's fucking gorgeous!

15

A Voice Like Dierks Bentley

Bif wrapped his arms around Frankie, catching his breath. He was normal again, but the elation of taking her did the trick. Pulling away, he wanted her to see him, the real him. She had played along and as he throbbed inside her warmth, unwilling to leave, he wanted to slow down. Brushing the hair from her eyes, she looked up at him in wonder.

"I don't understand," She whispered, searching his eyes for the answer.

"Understand what?" he smirked, lifting an eyebrow knowing what she meant.

"You're gorgeous."

He throbbed inside her, before leaning down to whisper, "So are you."

Bif pressed his lips hard against hers. He had been so afraid to do so in his other form, but now he could open himself up to her wandering hands and eyes. Her warm hands rippled across his ribs and glided over his collarbone. She moaned as he pressed his hip against hers, grinding slowly and with skilled rhythm. Frankie's fingers tangled in his curly, blonde locks and her tongue thrust between his lips.

He let her in, both moaning as the sunlight beat down on them. Birds chirped, the fire crackled, and the bench creaked under their weight. He sucked on her tongue, and she struggled to take it back. When she broke loose, he chased it back into the warmth of her mouth. Twisting and rubbing against each other until she began sucking on his tongue.

Her knees rose higher, pressing against his ribs and opening herself further. Bif broke off the kiss to arch his back, pulling all the way out and sliding slow and steady back into place. Her breath caught in her throat; their eyes locked as he repeated the motion. Goosebumps rippled across her skin, and he could feel that low rumble of a purr escape him.

"How on earth could a man not make love to you, Frankie." It was a fact that fell from his lips.

She bit her bottom lip, and a look of uncertainty crossed her eyes.

"Don't you ever dare doubt yourself." He picked up speed, hooking a knee over her leg and shifting the angle of his cock as he stroked. "You're gorgeous, you're strong, and..." Her back started to arch as her heat tightened around him and he ground against her. "...I would love to make love to you all day and all night, Darling."

Her fingers dug into his arms, egging him on. Bif abandoned holding her leg, the pink nipples tempting his lustful appetite. He dove his arms under her and pulled her up to him, wrapping his lips around her nipple and began sucking. Frankie only clawed at his shoulders more, moaning and rocking in sync with him. Again, the growling purr rolled out of him, and he let it.

She's as sweet as any fruit plucked in its prime. I could do this all day just to hear her moan, feel her cling to me, feel how tight she is around my cock.

"Frankie…" He moaned her name, licking across her collarbone and up her neck. "Frankie…"

"Oh, you have a voice like Dierks Bentley," he sucked on her earlobe. "I could listen to you coo my name like that…"

Her breath caught as she lay on her back, Bif's body swallowing hers. "Bif!"

"Frankie… I've fallen for you."

She shuddered and a shriek of ecstasy erupted from her. He moaned. The pulsing heat brought him over his own edge. He pulled her close with one arm and propped himself up with the other. Her arms gripped him, and they held each other, panting.

No man can go twice like that… that part's all thanks to being a shifter. Wait, does this count as one round or two?

He eased her back and pulled away. Grunting, he looked for his cargo shorts. As he put them on, he reached into his tent and pulled out a blanket. Frankie was still humming and laying on the bench table and he couldn't contain his chuckle. As she sat up, he wrapped her up in the blanket.

Bif leaned down and picked up her bright pink string bikini. "You seriously didn't pack anything else?"

Frankie's eyes darted away. "I had other plans … that were more on par with not wearing anything at all for the whole weekend."

Bif's smirk came back. "I can help you with that too."

Her eyes met his and he gave her a wink.

"Hold up, I think I can take care of the other issue too. I camp a lot, so I know the value of some extra clean clothes." Bif dug into his backpack, pulling out another pair of shorts and a long-sleeve shirt. "They might be a little big."

"It's more than what Ted packed." She wiggled off the bench, pulling the cover tighter around her. "I'm sorry…"

"Sorry?" Bif let her take the clothes from him and gauged her expression. "Girlie, there's nothing to be ashamed of."

Again, Frankie darted her eyes away. She grabbed the clothes and turned. Taking a step, she halted as if unable to make a decision on how to perform the task of getting dressed. Bif's heart swelled, aching against his chest. She jolted as his arms wrapped around her from behind. His lips tickled at her ear, and she leaned into him.

"My things are your things. You can dress and rest up in the tent and I'll make us something to eat."

A long sigh escaped her, the tension leaving her body. "I'd like that, Bif. I'd like that a lot."

He nuzzled her neck and kissed it. "Has anyone ever told you, you smell like the sweetest batch of peaches?"

She laughed, spinning around to kiss him. "No, but I'll take your word for it."

Bif let her go and she climbed into his tent. Taking in a deep breath, he turned to the cooler. There wasn't much to choose from as he shifted the items around. A slab of ham and a chunk of Cuban bread would have to do the trick. Throwing a few logs on the fire, he coaxed it back to life so it could heat the cast iron skillet.

He could hear Frankie rustling around. The smell of peaches filled the air as the blanket fell away from her bare skin. A shudder rolled through him, and he tried to focus on the task at hand but failed. As the clothes baring his scent covered her, a wave of arousal took his breath away. It was like marking what was his and it startled him.

Pulling his cell phone out of his pocket, he cursed under his breath. The battery was getting low. Despite it, he texted Satch.

[Bif: How territorial are we talking about?]

Bif tossed the ham on the skillet, the smell erupting and cutting his agony short.

I can't believe how strong all these animal instincts are getting. Normally this sort of thing happens in shift but... I'm normal now.

The cell phone buzzed.

[Sasshole: Very.]

[Bif: wtf does very mean?]

[Sasshole: Throw a man through a tree or tent very.]

[Bif: I need you to get me out of here. I'm gonna kill a hunter at this rate over a girl!]

As Bif hit send, the cell phone beeped and starting the shutdown process.

"Shit." His heart pounded against his chest, deafening his ears. "What the hell am I going to do?"

Throw a man? Really, Satch? Is that the reason why the fuck you abandoned me and haven't been back? You dick. You know what's happening to me and you're just going to let me blindly fumble through it all. Fuck! I don't even know how long I have before I change back!

"HEY!" Ted's voice echoed through the forest as he came bursting through the underbrush.

Bif tensed, the sizzling of meat on a skillet filled the space between them. His foot stepped onto the pink bikini bottoms to hide them. It was one of the few moments in his life that he was thankful for his monstrous footprint. His eyes darted about, looking for the top but spotted it tangled in Ted's shirt on the other side of the tent. At least from there, as long as Ted didn't walk any further forward, he'd never see them.

"Have... Have..." Ted panted, out of breath from the burst of energy he had exerted.

Steroid junkie.

Bif snorted, flipping the ham on the skillet and eyeing the tent. Frankie seemed more like a rabbit caught in the open. He couldn't let him have her. Fear came off her in waves, thick enough Bif could taste it on his tongue. He shifted, trying to swallow down the rising anger. For any man to make a woman feel that afraid...

"Have you seen a girl out here?"

Bif laughed. "Yours or mine?"

I was never good at lying, but clever with my words.

Ted made a face. "Mine, you Jackass!"

"In that case, nope." Bif shrugged and nodded to the tent. "Look if you don't mind, my girl's sleeping and I'm still making lunch."

"R-right." Ted backed away, throwing up his hands. "Sorry, uh, if you see a girl in a pink bikini, just let me know. I'm just on the other side of this batch of trees." He spun on his heels and jogged back from where he came.

Bif slumped forward on his knees, blowing out the breath he had held. Eyeing the tent, Frankie opened the flap, trembling.

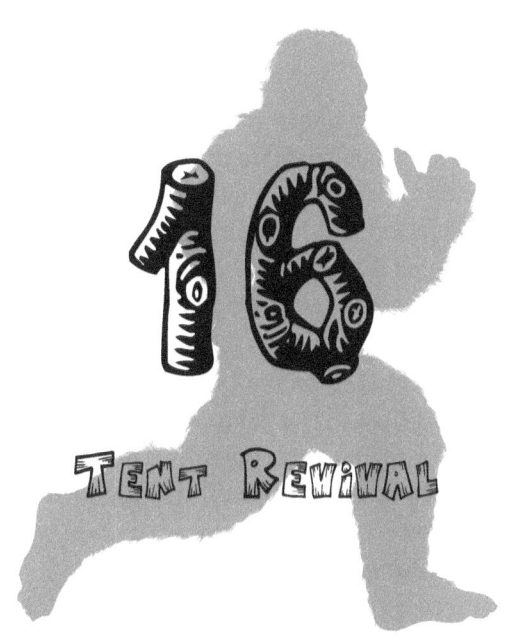

16
TENT REVIVAL

Frankie crawled into Bif's tent and zipped it closed. She sat there, her body still buzzing from one of the most fulfilling sex sessions she'd ever had. On the other hand, her emotions were causing chaos in her mind. She looked down at the clothes in her hand, unsure whether to be relieved or frightened.

What the hell am I doing? Really, Frankie? Rebound sex right after a fight and with some stranger in the woods! Have I lost my mind?

Looking over her shoulder, the silhouette of Bif made her heart ache and her body excited.

What do I have to lose? I've only known Bif less than... Her stomach knotted. *Twelve hours tops. Dammit, that man out there has shown me more compassion than Ted has in weeks. Made me breakfast, is making me lunch, and he even gave me clothes. I don't know why he's out here camping alone, but I take it as a sign.*

She let the blanket slide off her shoulders and started pulling on Bif's clothes. They swamped her, a little bigger than Ted's even. The shorts were sliding off her hips and being commando didn't make it feel any less awkward. Looking around she realized her bikini was outside, thrown to the wind in their moment of passion. Tugging on the pants, she reached to unzip the tent.

"HEY!" Ted's voice made her fall back on her ass.

He sounded pissed and Frankie froze.

What am I going to say to him? He's not exactly known for being levelheaded and even-tempered. Oh no, Bif is out there. What if he tells him I'm here? Would he do that? He wouldn't, would he? What does it matter to him? He got what he wanted...

Frankie bit her lip and started to shake. She had never been in the crossfire of two raging bulls, but at this moment, she saw horns pointed at her from both sides. Her heart pounded in her ears and fear shook her body.

Oh my God, what have I gotten myself into?

"Have you seen a girl out here?" She cringed at Ted's question.

This is it. You reap what you sow, that's what Mama always said. Here it is...

"Yours or mine?" Bif laughed and it caught her off guard.

What kind of question is that?

"Mine, you Jackass!" Ted sounded furious.

Who else would he be looking for?

Panic filled Frankie. Her situation wasn't exactly peachy, and now it just seemed to be getting worse.

"In that case, nope." Bif's words came in a wave of relief to Frankie.

Was he testing Ted? Is Bif shielding me from him? Wait, is he implying I'm his girl now?

Frankie looked down at the baggy shirt and shorts. They smelled like Bif, and a revelation hit her. She didn't once relish Ted's scent. Not when he tossed the shirt in her face, or any time before this awful weekend hit.

Why am I with Ted? So what if the sex was great... Her thoughts faltered. *Well, after Bif, it's subpar at best. Always focused on him getting off and leaving me put away wet. What kind of miserable sex life is that?*

"Look if you don't mind, my girl's sleeping and I'm still making lunch." Bif's words made her smile, and though she still shook with fear, she knew he wouldn't let Ted touch her unless she indicated otherwise.

She held her breath, waiting for Ted to stomp off. After his footsteps faded, she unzipped the tent. Swallowing, she forced herself to look up at Bif, unsure if he would be angry or frustrated with her. Her breath caught. His blue eyes bright in the sunlight and his toothy smile greeting her. And it made her heart ache.

Ted has never looked at me like that. Not in a way that says 'he loves me' or even made me feel wanted.

"Who are you?" The words fell from her lips as she held his pants up on her hip.

"Besides my name being Bif?" He lifted an eyebrow at her.

"Sorry, that was rude..." She searched his eyes a moment. "Thank you."

"For what?" He snorted, turning back to flip the ham once more. "It's no big deal to cook lunch for two."

"Not just that." She came closer, sitting on the bench so she could hold her arms. "What you did there, with Ted."

Bif stayed silent, eyes locked on the skillet.

"I didn't realize how scared he makes me feel until..." She gripped Bif's bicep, calling his eyes to hers. "This might be brash, but I think I'm falling for you. It's wild, and insane... But the way you make love and look—"

His lips locked with hers. She moaned, cupping the chiseled jaws and dove deeper into his mouth. Sucking on his tongue as it dared to push back into her mouth, he moaned. Frankie wanted him, wanted him inside her, wanted to go home with him, and most of all, wanted him in her life. This was a man that rarely could be found, gorgeous and passionate. She broke the kiss.

"I'll need to sneak back and get my things. I want to go home with you." If it hadn't been clear she'd cut ties with Ted, it was clear now.

"One problem." Bif sighed, tucking a strand of blonde hair behind Frankie's ear. "My phone died, and that means my ride won't be here any time soon."

Frankie collapsed on him, laughing. "Is that why you're out here? You're stranded?"

"You can say that." Bif wrapped an arm around her, chuckling. "Let's eat lunch. Satch will eventually make it out here."

"Satch?" She scooted over as he placed the ham on bread and began cutting the sandwich in half.

"A good friend of mine." He handed over her portion. "Sorry, it's just bread and meat, but it's at least filling."

"It's better than Ted's collection of Chicken Fajita MREs." Taking a bite, she relished in the fact she had been given real food twice now by this amazing man before her.

"Wait, isn't that in the top ten worst flavors?" Bif paused before taking a bite. "You don't think he bought them up because they were on sale at the army surplus store, do you?"

She swallowed her food. "They probably offered them to him for free. It was horrible, I gagged on it, but he eats them up. I swear the man has no taste buds."

Bif started laughing, trying not to choke on his food. "You might be onto something."

They ate in silence for a while. Bif finished first and began cleaning out the skillet and she had taken her last bite, unable to finish. She stared at the sandwich for a while before turning to watch Bif for a moment. Her self-esteem wavered once more and as if he could sense it, he turned to her with a confused look on his face.

"You ok, Frankie?" Bif sat up, giving her his full attention.

"You must think horribly of me," she muttered, her chest stinging.

"Why would I?" His distraught expression went through her, but before she could continue, he scooped her into his arms. "If anyone should be horrible, it's me. I mean, trying to sneak in on another man's girl like I did but... but..."

"I was the one who came marching into your camp, eating your food, offering myself up like some prost—" He squeezed her tighter, cutting her words off.

His voice was low, rumbling in her ear. "Did you mean it when you said you wanted to go home with me?"

She clung onto his bareback, never wanting to let go. "Yeah, I did."

"Let's get your shit from Ted's camp then." He kissed the top of her head and her heart leapt to her throat. "You're my girl. Let me show you how a man should treat his girl. Let me take care of you, Frankie."

Tears welled up in Frankie's eyes.

"Uh, but we still have the issue of being out here until my friend arrives. Hope you like camping." She started laughing, sniffling. "Unless you have some way to charge a phone."

"I do!" She pulled away, wiping the tears from her cheeks. "But we'll need to wait for Ted to leave camp."

"Well, he's now out hunting Big Foot and you, so I don't think he's gonna be staying in camp much." Bif wiped a remaining tear off her face with his thumb.

"Is it a micro-USB?" She stood up, tugging his pants up. "The Bronco is unlocked, and my charger is in there."

"Perfect." He stood and began heading toward camp.

She paled, "Wait, he just left here."

"Oh, he's back fix... um, checking his trail cams," Bif corrected himself and Frankie furrowed her brow at him. "It's now or never, Girlie."

"R-right." She caught up to him, curious now. "But how do you know?"

He gave her a nervous side glance. "I've been camping for a long time; you catch onto these sorts of things."

Frankie wasn't buying it. "Hold up." She managed to run ahead and stand in his way, palms flat on his bare chest. "I can't help but think you're hiding something."

Bif's eyes widened. "Like what?"

"Why you're really out here." Frankie gave him a serious glare.

"Look, I got shitfaced during our campout, and they thought it funny to leave me behind," Bif confessed.

"Oh." Frankie lifted her hands and let him pass her. "But who doesn't get shitfaced at a party?"

"It's not the normal routine for me." They came to the clearing and as he had predicted, no signs of Ted.

"Oh?" Making it to the Bronco, he slid into the driver's side and she the passenger seat. "Why is that?"

Bif flinched, pausing a minute before pulling his phone and plugging it in. "I recently broke up with someone."

Frankie's mind spun. *What were the chances of two heartbroken people meeting in the woods and hooking up?*

"Look, I'm not hooking up with you for a rebound." His tone and expression were serious. "She was bad news, and the sort my friends warned me about. I should have listened. To her, I was a free ride until she found what she really wanted, and that happened a few days ago."

This must be fate... Frankie sighed, the last of her tension and doubts melting away.

17

Bronco Fun

Bif waited for her response, but Frankie gave him a tender smile. Her eyes said it all. She felt bad for him and could relate. She had just broken it off with Ted after all, but to know he was in the same situation made them closer somehow. The muscles in her body lost their tension, and in turn, he could let his own fall from his shoulders. Looking back to his phone, it was charging at last, with fast charging initiated.

"How long will it take?" Frankie had changed topics.

"Says an hour and seventeen minutes if I keep it turned off," Bif announced.

"Okay." Frankie bent down to gather the things on the floor. "Dammit, Ted."

"What's wrong?" Bif furrowed his brow.

"Asshole dumped my purse out." She shifted her position to better reach the floorboard.

Watching her, she was on all fours on top of the bench seat. Ass staring at him, her head and hands scrambled to gather her things and place them back into the large satchel purse. Bif licked his lips, his pants tight as his cock grew hard. He panted, hot with arousal, shifting himself in anticipation of what he wanted to do with her. Reaching out to grab his pants off her hip, he watched his hand shift from normal to hairy.

FUCK! NOT NOW! I'm in the fucking Bronco with her and if she turns around, I'm so fucked!!!

The smell of peaches brought his attention back to Frankie's ass. "Don't move. Stay there and don't look."

"Wait, what?" Frankie banged her head on the dashboard, her eyes squeezing shut.

"I can't stand watching you wiggle your ass in my face like this," he breathed, tugging his shorts off her ass and to her knees. "Just a taste..."

"Bif!" She braced herself on the floor. "What about Ted?"

"Better keep your head and voice down." He relished in the heat of her skin under his hands. "You think you can keep the screams in?"

"Oh god..." Frankie's arousal rattled through her, and Bif could sense the heat in her body rising. "You're seriously going to fuck me in Ted's Bronco?"

His fingers slid over her fold, already wet and hot. "Yeah, because I doubt he's ever finished the job."

Frankie's heart sped up, her anger rising. "How would you know?"

Bif purred, "Because Ted's that kind of douchebag to finger a girl just long enough to get head."

That one hit a nerve. She tensed up, even white knuckled. I called it.

Frankie shifted, straddling her legs to give him better access. "You're assuming you can make me scream."

Bif laughed, unzipping his pants to relieve his hard, throbbing cock. He could see the shudder roll through her, the excitement growing between them. A smile filled Bif's face, and he wondered what he wanted to do first. Even knowing the quicker he came the faster he changed back; he didn't want to shortchange her in pleasure. His fingers slid from her knee and up her inner thigh. The prickling of her skin and the growing smell of peaches let him know she was growing ripe with want. Gripping her hips, he slid her across the bench seat quickly, making her yelp.

"You've lost." His hot cock rubbed against the opening of her pussy. "I think that's a record for me."

"That's not fair." She squirmed and his cock throbbed against her. "Dammit you're so hard and big."

Bif leaned over her, his hands sliding from her hips and finding her breasts. He enjoyed how her curvy body fit into his own like a lost piece of himself. Her breasts soft, nipples hard, and the dripping of her onto his dick were intoxicating. Frankie's head started to turn to look back and Bif panicked. He slammed his cock inside her, forcing her to focus on keeping herself from faceplanting on the floor. She whimpered but bit her lip.

Oh, she's so tight and hot right now! Smells like a peach cobbler on a summer day, and I want it all to myself!

He squeezed her breasts harder, twisting her nipples. Again, a muffled whimper. Rocking his hips, long hard strokes earned shaking of legs and muffled screeches. Bif wanted to make her scream. One hand abandoned its breast, snaking down the middle of her torso and diving between her thighs. She squirmed and he could smell the mixture of panic and excitement. This would be hard for her to keep quiet.

Pulling out, he plunged a finger inside her, coming back to circle her clit with ease. She let out a gasp, as if coming up for air before diving back to silence herself. Her legs started to close, and he threw his knee between them, nudging them back open. The shudder that rocked her body egged him on. Teasing, he rubbed the tip of his dick on the opening. Again, she tried to close her legs, moaning in a wave of agony and pleasure. He rushed forward, thrusting his length into her.

Frankie arched her back, but his reflexes had been quick. Abandoning the breast, he gripped her shoulder to keep her from banging her head on the dash. Bif cursed under his breath, shifting back to normal as his peak slammed into him. The break in focus made him moan, his other hand abandoning her thighs to grip the seat. He started to come. His cock was hard as she tightened more around him. Frozen from the hard hit of his orgasm, she began grinding against him and he moaned. His hands came back to her hips, wanting to rock in tandem with her.

"What if I make you scream?" Bif realized she had been watching him, though unaware if she had seen the shift. "You seem to be the noisy one."

"Ha, I didn't almost bang my head on the dashboard twice." He swallowed the uncertainty down.

She managed to pull her top half back out of the floorboard. She rolled back on her heels, and he relished that she sat on his lap, never letting him slide out of her. She began rocking, playing with herself as she ground in his lap. Again, a moan and purr rolled out of him.

"I love it when you make that sound," Bif's face flashed red.

If only she knew I wasn't doing that until I met her...

He slid his hands across her body, wanting to feel every muscle at work. The way she rocked, the shaking in her legs, and the firmness of her breasts. She hadn't come yet. He hadn't won the contest though the Bronco's rusted suspension had started creaking from all their fun. She moaned, and he could feel her tighten on his dick and a shudder rolled through her. He hated seeing her agonize on the edge of orgasm.

"Turn around," he muttered.

"I thought you didn't want me looking at you?" She pulled away; the cold air unbearable compared to her heat. "You're such a strange one, Bif."

"I could say the same about you, Frankie." She smirked, spinning around to mount him, his cock sliding deep inside her.

"Is this what you wanted?" Their eyes locked and he started to grow hard again. "I take that as a yes."

Bif wanted more. His hands slid his shorts off her body so he could see all of her. Again, his cock throbbed, and she tightened in response. She leaned down and kissed him deeply. His arms wrapped around her, fingers riding in the divot of her spine. Tongues lashed at one another, taking turns chasing. Frankie began rocking once more, moaning into his mouth. He broke the kiss, wanted to watch her work, shifting them both so he could slide deeper inside her.

"I can't play with myself like this." Her cheeks flushed; her orgasm so close yet too far to reach. "I want to come so bad..."

"Why would you need to play with yourself when you have me?"

Pulling her into him, his lips wrapped around a nipple. Hard short sucks sent her body into a shiver. His other hand rode her spine down, gripping her ass hard. She tightened. He began thrusting in and out of her fast and hard. She whimpered. A yelp started to form. Swallowing only made her whimper. An orgasm like no other peaked. Desperation took hold. Frankie lunged forward, her teeth biting into his shoulder. It muffled a scream and he moaned.

My god she's like an animal and I want to drink from it all day!

She came, a gush of fluid escaping her as nails and teeth dug into him. It did nothing to slow him. He wanted her to come hard, he wanted her to scream his name. He pulled her off, and before Frankie knew why, she found herself on all fours on the bench seat. Without wasting time, Bif was inside her, fucking her doggie style. The deep hard strokes made her breath catch as she gripped the door's arm rest. His hand rolled over her hip, playing with her clit and she yelped.

Close, but I want to hear that scream!

18

Left Hanging

Frankie's eyes were wide. She had wanted to be fucked in this Bronco for so long and at last it had happened. The only odd thing, it wasn't Ted grinding away at her backside or playing with her clit. Nor would she change a single thing of what had unfolded. Her breasts swayed with each powerful thrust from Bif, and she would start losing the game of keeping quiet. Granted, she had noticed how he moaned when she tightened.

He feels so fucking amazing!

Moaning seemed to be neutral ground, but the man had moves and a cock to back it. Her thighs were wet, her body wanting him more. A shiver shook her, the arousal still climbing under the heat of his body. Her eyes fell to her purse and there she saw her secret weapon: high dollar lubricant. She reached down, moaning as his dick rubbed inside her in a way that made her legs numb. She gave herself away, and he made his thrusting slow and strong. It was enough to almost make her forget why'd she'd shifted her body. He picked up speed and she held her breath.

I can't lose! I want to hear him scream my name this time!

Desperate, she tossed it behind her. Bif halted his barrage when it hit him in the chest. The cold bottle fell, resting on her ass cradled where they joined. He picked it up to read the label. Confusion struck his face and she smirked. Frankie saw how he flushed; he was starting to lose ground already with that face.

"You ain't dry, so are you proposing what I think you are?" One eyebrow arched high as he wiggled the bottle in his hand. "Didn't think you were that kind of gal, Frankie."

"One of us will be screaming the other's name before we leave this Bronco." She wiggled, tightening to make him moan. "And it's not going to be me, Bif. I already lost once."

He narrowed his eyes at her, reflecting the playful smile she gave him. "Are you sure about that?"

Frankie went to wiggle again, but he pulled out. He had evaded her next attack. A yelp escaped her as Bif flipped her over on her back. The bulk of his body weighed down on her and she found herself nose to nose with him. She searched his eyes and he seemed to be doing the same. She moved to kiss him and lifted his face away, denying her.

What was that? Lure me in with those baby blues and denied.

"What's wrong?" she whispered, her voice barely audible over her own heartbeat.

Is he against it? Was I too bold? I didn't think... I mean, I barely know the man and I'm assuming...

"You don't have to go so far to please me." His voice rolled into her ear in a deep, low grumble. "I'm not him, I..."

He thinks I'm trying to please him! Normally, it would be a yes but this time... this time...

"It was in my purse for me. I want ... it," she confessed then bit her lip.

Am I out of my mind? Why'd I let the cat out of the bag so bluntly?

He closed his eyes. "You really were looking for a weekend fuck-fest with your man. How'd he not know?"

EXACTLY!

"It was his idea originally." Frankie couldn't stop her face from turning red with embarrassment and frustration.

"Oh. I guess he forgot but..." He leaned in, the heat of his breath on her ear. "Good thing I'm here. I'm more than happy to take care of you."

I would die happy to hear his voice whisper in my ear like this every night.

He began kissing her neck and working his way down. Pausing at her collarbone, he sucked on it until he left a hickey before trailing down to her nipple. There he sucked long and hard, teeth teasing her before he let go with a pop. Frankie watched him as his lips travelled across the hills and valleys of her body. Those piercing blue eyes magical as they stole glances, meeting her eyes at key moments. Her skin pimpled as he pecked across her abdomen, a barren land often left out in intimate times.

Frankie's breath caught. His head dove between her thighs.

Oh no! Not after...

Lips and tongue hot around her swollen clit. She arched, whimpering to keep in the scream that pained to be released. The purr and moan from him made her knees jerk high, his shoulders keeping her legs from closing around him. She couldn't recall ever getting oral so far into a fuck session, but oh how sensitive it had become. Her fingers gripped his hair, trying to pull him from her. At this rate she would lose their contest of endurance. Her teeth dug into her tongue, denying the need to scream, to beg Bif to stop, beg him to do more, beg him to... It only coaxed Bif to take a long lick across her throbbing pussy before suckling on her again. The shaking in her legs made it impossible to hide how amazing he felt. She panted, trying to catch her breath from the waves of exhilaration filling her.

I'm drowning in pleasure!

"It's no fair..." She pleaded, hiding her face under her forearm. "You've broken that part."

The suction broke, making her jolt. "And you think what you offered was fair, Darling?"

"It was even ground."

"Is that so?" A finger dove inside her pussy, stroking in just the right angle. "You're telling me you like this as much as…" It slid out and into her ass and she gasped. Her back arched and she moaned. "Oh, I guess I'll take that as a yes."

"Please…" She peered down at him, and he narrowed his eyes once more. "Please give it to me."

"Oh, that's just playing dirty, begging me like that while wearing a face I can't say no to."

Bif grabbed the bottle and began rubbing down his long, hard cock. Frankie's heart raced, her breath quickening. Another squirt of the bottle and he pushed two fingers inside her ass. She wanted anal; her last boyfriend failing, and the one before that ruining it for her. It excited her to orgasm to have a man not take her once, but twice. Normally she offered it to the men in her life she hoped would be around for something longer than a one-night stand, but with Bif…

I can't leave here without knowing what it would be like to be fucked by this man in every way possible. Is it wrong I want to go home with him and not Ted? A fucking stranger I met in the forest has been…

He leaned forward, the tip of his dick pressing against the slick opening of her ass. "Are you sure? I ain't small, lady."

Frankie wrapped her arms around him, pulling him forward. It was enough to make him enter her. They moaned as he slid slowly, deeper into her until he was all the way inside. Frankie lifted her knees, giving him better access. He leaned down, kissing her deep and hard. Again, their tongues chased one another. Frankie would suck on his, holding him captive. Both moaned into one another's mouths as he began to rock his hips. They were holding back their screams of pleasure as they refused to break the kiss.

The glass hatch of the Bronco creaked open. Bif let most of his weight fall onto Frankie, and he signaled for her to be quiet.

"Fucking Frankie. I bet she trashed these cameras. Dammit, when I get my hands on her…"

They were far enough down to be covered by the bench seat.

The sound of equipment being thrown into the bed of the truck. "And just when I was seeing signs of a Sasquatch in the area. I need to get that asshole and his girlfriend next door out of here."

Frankie lipped, "I'm your girlfriend?"

Bif made a goofy face, "Why not?"

"Maybe I should throw their tent on their fire." Ted threw more cameras in the back. "I could hear them fucking this morning … and I'm sure they spooked Sasquatch with the way his girl was screeching."

Frankie's brow furrowed; anger written across her face. "Asshole."

Bif lifted his eyebrows high, "Don't look at me so angry."

As the blood rushed to her face, she lipped, "Fuck Ted.'"

A hand slid across her hip and gripped her ass cheek. Bif had a sparkle in his eyes. He leaned on her, starting to rock his hips once more. Her fingers dug into his shoulders. The speed of it increasing just enough to keep her in a never-ending arch without making the Bronco rock. She heard more equipment slam into the back of the truck, and she tightened on Bif's cock. He grunted. She opened her mouth to tell him to stop, but he tucked his face into her shoulder. Shivers shook her as his breath hit her neck like hot wax.

Bif whispered, smooth and sultry in tone, "Fuck me."

The glass hatch slammed close. "Frankie! Where the fuck are you!"

"Harder," she breathed.

"As you wish."

The Bronco started to rock, though slightly. Bif pulled up, looking out the windows. A big smile stretched across his face. Sitting up, she loved how he looked down at her naked body like a hungry beast. Her body shuddered, cold without him on top of her, without her breasts against the wall of muscle. His fingers dug into her hips, and he banged her with renewed vigor, the Bronco threatening to squeak as it had done at the start of this game of theirs. She arched, her hands only able to clutch his arms, nails clawing. He began moaning, his cock hardening inside her. An eruption of heat filled her as he came inside.

She lost her composure, "FUCK ME BIF!"

His fingers let go, trailing between her thighs. Fingers dove inside her wet, swollen pussy as he still throbbed inside her ass. She squealed, wiggling as a thumb circled her clit and fingers thrust in and out.

"BIF!" At last, she lost.

Her warmth tightened on his finger, on his cock, and the gush of her orgasm sent her heart aching against her chest.

My god, I've never come so hard in all my life.

Her breasts heaved as she fought to catch her breath. A tune caught their attention. Bif's phone booted on as it hit full battery. Pulling away from each other, Frankie gave him Ted's shirt to clean up with, and they laughed.

19
Camp Disaster

Bif zipped up his pants and grinned at Frankie. His secret nearly blown, yet neither of them realized how far they would go even when Ted came back. Wiping sweat from his brow, he looked around. There had been no sign or scent of Ted. Unplugging his cell phone, Bif started his text to Satch. He hit send and watched as Frankie tried to wiggle back into his shorts.

[Bif: Come get me.]

He yanked the backside up and she laughed as they slid on at last. Her face flushed and she hid away, putting on his shirt. Bif shifted and pulled the bottle of lube out from behind him. He nudged Frankie's arm with it. Puffing out her cheeks, she grabbed it and shoved it into her purse. Bif's phone vibrated in his hands, and he turned his attention to the screen.

[Sasshole: Why?]

[Bif: Look, the hunter guy is hot on my tail, and we're stranded out here. COME GET US!]

[Sasshole: Us?]

[Bif: Me and my]

He paused and looked at Frankie as she took inventory of her things. She blinked and looked over at him, confused.

"Is there something on my face?" She dug through her items. "Where's that compact mirror?"

"No, you're fine." Bif rubbed the back of his neck, looking at the unfinished text. "Did you mean it when you said you wanted to come home with me?"

Frankie froze and inhaled deeply. She held it there for some time before meeting his eyes. Bif swallowed. Her face so stern, eyes bright, and she gripped her purse tight. He raised his eyebrows as the anxiety built between them, both wearing a face asking themselves an array of questions. Doubts building, Bif opened his mouth, but she slid across the bench seat, the heat of her body and smell of peaches pulling at the Big Foot inside him.

She whispered, "Did you mean it when you told Ted I was your girl?"

He smirked, "You heard that?"

She nodded.

"I meant it as long as you want the title." He brushed a lock of hair off her forehead, clearing his view of her face.

"I want it. I want to be your girlfriend." Her cheeks blossomed red. "It sounds so stupid... we've barely met and... and..." Tears were building in her eyes.

"Stop that." His voice, low and soft. "I came on to you. Even though you were clearly with someone. You don't have to come home with me. I can give you a ride home, so you don't have to deal with that douchebag Ted."

"No," she looked pained. "I think I really do want to go home with you."

"Okay." He kissed her forehead.

Turning back to his phone, he finished the message he had started.

[Bif: Me and my girlfriend.]

Hitting send, he opened the Bronco and helped her out. They started working their way back to their camp when they heard a commotion. The sound of grunting and huffing, like a wild animal, startled them. Bif and Frankie squatted in the underbrush. There in Bif's camp, Ted was running a hunting knife through the tent. He turned and kicked over the cooler. Reaching into the torn apart tent, he gripped a bright pink bikini top. His face turned purple with rage.

"Oh no." Frankie started to shake. "He knows! I'm so sorry Bif... I..."

Growling came out of Bif, angry like a rabid dog.

"Are you okay?" Frankie's hands wrapped around his arm, and he regained his focus.

"Fuck." The territorial rage had blinded all rational thought.

Bif lifted his cell phone and snapped a photo as Ted threw Frankie's bikini on the fire. As he texted Satch, he pulled Frankie along behind him. Ted would be shredding his camp for a while. The only relief is the ground rules all shifters had on the night of a shift; don't bring any forms of identification. Ted could look all he wanted, but there wouldn't be a single clue as to who he was or anyone who had camped there a few night before.

[Satch: Is that dude throwing a pink bikini in the fire?]

[Bif: WE NEED A RIDE NOW!]

[Satch: FUCK! On my way... what the hell did you do?]

[Bif: I fucked the Sasquatch Hunter's girlfriend and she's coming home with me!!!!]

[Satch: Dude, I've told you before, fucking a girl doesn't make them your girlfriend.]

[Bif: COME FUCKING GET ME! I'M GETTING TERRITORIAL!]

[Satch: ... eta a few hours.]

They came out into the opening where the Bronco sat. Frankie started pacing, holding her head. Bif mind spun circles. Normally dealing with something like this wasn't no problem, but with newfound animal instincts overriding logic, he'd have to keep his distance.

"Shit, shit, shit!" Frankie had tears running down her cheeks. "I'm so sorry, Bif."

"Calm down." He wasn't sure if it was meant for her or himself. "We have a few hours before my ride will be here."

Frankie looked at him with dread. "Hours? It'll be dark."

"Yeah, I know."

"FRANKIE!" Ted's voice made them both flinch.

Bif grabbed her hand, pulling her into the woods opposite the direction of his camp. They turned and twisted until he found a small clearing with a downed pine tree. He eyed the area, seeing no signs that Ted had ventured back there as of late. Frankie squeezed his hand hard as a shudder rattled through her. He turned to her and hugged her tightly against him. Hot tears hit the bare skin of his chest and anger rose up inside him.

Ted will pay for this ... somehow, some way.

"I'm sorry I dragged you into this," she sobbed, pressing into him more as if hungry to take in all the protection and security he had to offer. "He's always been an asshole but to see him coming unglued..."

Bif shushed her, rubbing her shoulder as he kissed the top of her head. "It's okay! You did nothing wrong. You came out here to spend time with someone you love..."

Bif choked on his words, flashes of Bethany from last month sneaking into his mind.

Wasn't this me just last month? Wanting to just have a good time and be intimate and she blew me off even at camp? Am I any different than Frankie?

"I thought I loved Ted." Frankie's words made his heart flutter. "But then I discovered someone I wanted more, that I didn't think existed at all. I know I've been a complete whore and brash but, but..."

He chuckled, rocking her to calm her down. "To be fair, Frankie. Just last month I was in your boat... out here in fact. Thought she was the one or at least someone I'd be with for a while. In the end, I felt used, hurt, and broken even just a few nights ago. I sat there at camp feeling sorry for myself. Good thing my friends left me out her, or we'd never have crossed paths."

She laughed, pulling away to look him in the eyes. "Maybe life just brought us together when we needed each other the most."

He smiled. "I like that idea."

In the distance, they could hear Ted calling her name. She rushed forward, hugging him, and he held her a moment. Heaving a sigh, Bif had to do something. The evening sunset sky overhead began shifting into purple and orange hues. If he could just mislead Ted and get him spun around in the woods, it would buy them time to grab some things from his camp and make their way to one of the side roads.

"Look Frankie. I'm going to mislead Ted. You stay here. I'll see if my bag is still in camp; since I don't keep it right in the camp area, I might have it intact."

"What if you get lost?" She broke away, pacing and tugging on the hem of her shirt. "How are you going to find me out here? In the dark?"

A toothy grin crested between his lips. "I grew up in these woods. Trust me when I say I've had to walk out of here by myself with no ride a few times."

She searched his face for a moment and relented. "Okay, Bif. I'll trust you." She reached into his pocket and grabbed his cell phone. "But let me give you my number just in case."

The arousal waving through him at the sensation of her fingers in his front pocket made him hard again. He cursed under his breath as he struggled to unlock the phone so she could put her number into the contact list. In all the years he had been shifting, this would be unforgettable as to how much he struggled with the inner animal side. There had been stories, plenty of bullshits called, but now he had one to add to the pile.

"There." She handed it back with a half-hearted smile. "My phone doesn't work out here, but…"

"Most don't," he muttered, shaking the thoughts from his head. "Sit and wait for me. When I get back, we'll have one last romp in the woods while we wait for our ride."

He leaned down and kissed her deeply. She moaned against his lips, and he purred. Pulling away, denying the animalistic urge and the want to bend her over and have his way with her, he set his aim for Ted. The Sasquatch Hunter had proven on more than one occasion how terrible he was at navigating the woods during the day, let alone at night. He would send him in a direction he hadn't been and abandon him just far enough for him to spin in circles for a while.

Looking over his shoulder, he watched Frankie sit on the fallen tree, hugging her arms.

She's mine and I get to take her home. I promise you'll look back at this night and only remember the good, Frankie.

20
CAUGHT ON CAMERA

Frankie watched Bif disappear into the trees. It startled her how fast night had fallen on them, and now she felt crazy. Here she was, waiting on a strange man with the biggest dick she'd ever had while her now ex-boyfriend, the Sasquatch Hunter, started to lose his shit like a mad man. She laughed. It all seemed like a bad B-rated porno movie at this rate. She looked down at her phone and cursed under her breath.

"I didn't get his number. Fuck."

She turned on the flashlight feature and took a look around. The small opening had very little to offer besides the downed pine she sat on. Her light reflected something at the base of a nearby tree. Curious, she wandered over to it and knelt down. Her eyes widened. It was a trail cam with "TED" etched into the side. She puffed out her cheeks, seeing red. Opening the device she found no SD card remained. Looking around she found it a good distance away.

"Thankfully they're red."

She looked at the items in her hand: a trail cam belonging to her ex and the SD card. A grin spread across her face as a vengeful thought came across her mind.

If I set this up to run again, then when Bif comes back...

Looking at the downed tree, she began looking for a good angle. She would want to keep it low to the ground in hopes of keeping Bif's face out of the shot. Her imagination pondered on what they would do, where Bif would bend her over and if she could glare into the camera and make sure when Ted reviewed the footage, he saw what he could have had.

Here should work. At this angle, I don't think Bif will notice, but if I make him stand over there to... yeah. Yeah, Ted will have a front row ticket to the show.

Snapping the SD card in, she flipped the switch and rushed back to the fallen pine. She checked her phone, but it beeped at her: *battery low 10%.* Soon she wouldn't even have a flashlight. All around she could hear the crickets and a whip-poor-will in the distance. The night air had cooled, moisture rising and making her skin pimple.

Her phone died at last, and she lost track of time. Part of her was drowsy, exhausted from the day's events, but the other part of her waited with wanton want. The idea of having his hands, his lips, and his tongue exploring her body again, just thinking of his hard cock inside her again, made her wet and her loins throbbed with anticipation. Her body heated at the idea, growing wet recalling the last few times and the sensations he had wracked her body with. Her hand slid under the waist of the shorts.

These clothes are his. Even the shirt has his scent still.

Her fingers dove between her thighs. She gasped.

Just thinking about him makes me so damn wet!

She began to play, her finger circling her clit. A moan escaped her, her nipples growing hard. They brushed against the fabric of the shirt, adding to her excitement. Her breath quickened. In her mind, she pulled those peaking moments forward. She peaked.

Breath catching, she leaned forward moaning. Her eyes shot up to the trail cam, and she laughed. In the moment of thinking of Bif, she forgot about the idea Ted would be seeing everything that unfolded tonight.

In the distance, she heard some footsteps. She paled. Biting her lips, she waited to see who would break through the trees. After several minutes, nothing happened. She looked to her phone and cursed. A growling sound came from the underbrush and her heart skipped a beat.

Bif's going to come back to find me mangled by a wolf or bear. Shit!

She stood in alarm. Her eyes wide and searching.

"It's me."

Instant relief washed over her to hear Bif's voice. "Oh, thank goodness. Did you lose Ted?"

"Yeah." He sounded nervous again. "And I did find my bag in one piece."

She stood again. "Then let's go. Let's get out of here."

"First, I have a promise to fulfill." He paused. "But I need you to close your eyes."

"This again?"

Frankie snorted, bewildered by the request once more.

Good Lord, we've fucked every way to Sunday, and he still needs me to close my eyes on the start?

"I'm sorry. I'll explain later, but this should be the last time."

"Fine." She closed her eyes and crossed her arms.

His footsteps left the hidden spot in the trees. The heat of his body close and the amazing scent of his musky cologne filled her nose. Bif's finger brushed a strand of hair behind her ear before trailing down her neck, across her breast and torso, and stopping at the button on the shorts, unsnapping them. She gripped his hand, and he froze.

"Not yet." She whispered. "It's my turn to treat you."

"But…"

Frankie licked her lips, "I want you... I want to play with your cock like you played with my pussy, Bif. I promise, no hands."

She opened her mouth, her tongue like a red carpet inviting him to come inside. The pause lasted longer than expected, but before she could close her mouth to say anything else, the tip of his cock tapped her tongue. She fought the urge to reach up and grip his throbbing erection. Her tongue circled the cap and he moaned. He was hard and it throbbed every time the heat of her tongue slid across the bottom side.

Pausing, she suckled at the tip and another moan escaped him. He leaned forward ever slightly, and she knew she had made him weak in the knees for a moment. As he straightened his stance, she leaned forward. Slow and tongue wiggling, she took him in. The tip of his throbbing cock pressed against the back of her throat. Bif grunted, the lean in his posture letting her know what he wanted. She swallowed, deep throating him a little farther and again, he moaned.

Calculated, the tip of her tongue pressing hard against the base of his dick, she pulled herself off. When her lips left the tip, they came off with a loud pop. She began kissing the tip and suckling her way down his shaft and back up again. Each one earned her more vocal purrs and elated moans.

Ted was never this vocal and it's making me so wet hearing Bif.

She began sucking him in and out, taking him all the way in to the back of her throat and back to almost leaving him. His fingers tangled in her hair, thrusting along with her. Her tongue wiggled, enjoying how hard he grew, how often she could make his erection throb. She began sucking harder and holding it longer. At last, the sensation she had been waiting for, when a cock became rock hard, the ridge of the cap firm, and the tip riding the roof of her mouth.

She broke her promise, grabbing the back of his shorts to pull him all the way into her mouth. The moan as she deep throated and swallowed was enough to break the peak. A rush of heat slid down the back of her throat and she heard Bif gasp.

"Frankie!"

Inside, she smiled.

Finally, got him to scream my name!

Another gush and she swallowed all that he offered her before pulling away and off. She looked up at him and he panted, leaning forward and catching himself on the pine. For a moment, looking like a giant monster, but in a blink of an eye all seemed normal. Wiping her mouth, she had made him weak in the legs and he looked at her baffled.

"First time with baby deer legs?" she teased.

"I've given my fair share, but never received them."

A sparkle flashed in his eyes, and he rushed her. Arms strong and thick invaded her clothes, conquering her body. He spun her around, jerking the shorts off her ass. Gasping, he thrust inside her hard and fast. He hadn't even checked to see if she had been wet enough, but she had been drenching her own thighs as she sucked him off.

How could he still be this hard after coming!

She began shrieking, hoping somewhere out there, Ted could hear her pleasure. Her back arched. Bif's hands slid across her torso, each hand squeezing her breasts. Fingers pinched her nipples, and she tightened around his hard erection as it thrust in and out of her. She came, hard and wild. Her scream was visceral as it echoed through the forest. A rush of heat filled her. Bif had come again, purring and moaning into her ear. She rocked her hips against him, riding the orgasm out as long as she could.

The camera!

Bif pulled off her, but she grabbed his arm. With renewed vigor, she pulled him to sit on the log and she straddled him. Staring at the camera over his shoulder, she gave a toothy grin. Pulling the shirt off, she threw it off to the side. As if reading her mind, Bif took a nipple into his mouth, sucking long and hard. She pulsed her hips, marveling over how long the man could stay hard with no down time. A girl could break herself with a man like this, and she would gladly be first in line.

He moaned into her breasts, his arms wrapping around her as he thrust in rhythm with her own rocking. Gripping a fistful of his hair, she could feel another orgasm rising. She held him against her tightly, his teeth teasing her nipple making her shriek. It was enough to make her tighten on his cock, and he picked up his speed. Another squeal of delight escaped her. What he didn't see was that she never broke eye contact with the trail cam as she came once more. Another wail of passion echoed in the woods as she peaked. He leaned back, coming with her, arms tight around her to dive as deep as he could.

Panting, she collapsed forward on his shoulder. He started to laugh, kissing her neck.

"You were hungry to fuck me again, huh?"

She started to laugh. "You could say that."

"I'm not used to a girl who can keep up with me." She realized he struggled to catch his breath.

"How can you keep going after coming so hard?"

Another chuckle rolled from his chest, "It's a family secret."

"Holy shit, I could hear you two a few miles back." Satch strutted into the open.

Frankie folded into Bif who shielded her from his friend. "Dammit Satch! Don't fucking scare me like that!"

"Sorry, sorry!" He spun on his heel; hands high in the air. "Find your clothes. I won't peek."

Bif grabbed the shirt and handed it to her and gave her a moment to find the shorts she had abandoned. She reached over and grabbed her purse and nodded.

"I'm ready to go."

"Let's get the hell out of here." He grabbed her hand, fingers entwining. "Satch, let's go."

Satch shifted, eyeing Frankie from head to toe before offering a hand. "I'm Satch, Bif's best bud."

"Frankie." She shook his hand, taking note of the formal attire and loosened tie still around his neck. "Bif's girlfriend. Thanks for leaving your event to come get us."

"Event?" He looked down and covered his face. "More like escaping the Spaghetti Monster."

"Oh?" Bif lifted an eyebrow as they started to follow Satch through the woods. "Did Yeti Spaghetti find out you were dating Yvonne?"

"Oh yeah. At the family gala and let's just say it was cancelled a tad early when he shoved over an ice sculpture and flipped the buffet table."

"No joke?" Bif marveled, pulling Frankie closer as she soaked in the insane story. "Half pint has some hidden strength in those tiny limbs after all."

"Yea, Yvonne broke up with me because I wouldn't fight him for her." Satch shrugged. "What can I say? I'm a lover, not a fighter."

What kind of people have I gotten myself involved with?

21

EPILOGUE

It took Ted all night and half the next day to find his camp and Bronco. When he did, the tires had been slashed, his equipment destroyed, and his tent shredded. A Sasquatch had been there. The prints everywhere. Luckily his phone and laptop had come with him, and he reviewed the footage of the trail cams that hadn't been torn apart or sabotaged. Another truck pulled up and he climbed in. As they abandoned his Bronco for the time being, he flipped open his laptop to review the footage.

"What the hell happened to you, Ted?" Jay furrowed his brow.

"Sasquatch attacked the camp. Spent two days chasing the son of a bitch."

"No way." The truck turned down the dirt road leading out of the forest. "Never seen one that active. Wait, where's your girl? Thought you took her with you this time?"

"She fucking left with some guy camping next to us."

"Holy fuck." Jay scratched his beard. "You've had one fucked up camping trip."

"Tell me about it. I just hope I caught something on camera."

As he flicked through footage of insects triggering the motion sensor, he suddenly came across a shot of Frankie's face. He swallowed. As he reviewed the footage, wishing he had bought the trail cams with audio recording, he endured. The next video he watched as she masturbated in clear view of the camera. How he hated seeing the rebellious glare on her face. She was pissed.

Clicking on the next video, he paled. There he saw what he had been searching for but also... He covered his mouth watching Frankie suck the dick on Big Foot and as he came, he shifted into a man. From there he grew ill. The way he made love to her made him jealous and they changed positions. From there, it was as if he locked eyes with Frankie as another man, no BIG FOOT with the BIG COCK, fucked his girl the way she had wanted him to fuck her. She flicked a bird, grinning wildly before she arched and came. He recognized her body language.

"Ted, I said did you get anything good?" Jay's voice cut through at last.

"No." Bile rolled into Ted's throat. "All I caught was my girlfriend sleeping with Sasquatch."

THE END

Cuddling
WITH
CHUPACABRA

HONEY CUMMINGS
URBAN LEGEND EROTICA COLLECTION

TABLE OF CONTENTS

DEDICATION

To Brandye
Thank you for helping me cook up a wild child
like Clara and a Sheriff to match!

XOXO
Honey Cummings

1

THE BAD DIVORCE

Clara Worcestershire bit her lip, aroused. Her eyes scanned the text message, making her shift her hips in the driver seat. Pulling a lock of dirty-blonde hair from her ruby lips, she inhaled deep. She slid the seatbelt over, hating how it cut into her c-cup breasts and throat. Clara was the curvy, cute girl from next door and returning to her hometown filled her with memories of wild nights.

Oh, how I've missed partying after a good rodeo.

Daisy dukes, cowgirl boots, and shirts tied up to bare as much skin as possible were Friday night requirements. Bleach-blonde hair crowned her head, topping tanned skin and blue eyes; she never had a dull moment. Which meant helping a bull rider rock his pickup truck on occasion. Again, the arousal washed over her as she recalled her bachelorette party. Umber skin taut over muscles and eyes that glowed gold. Even now, the sensation of Jakob Regadera grinding against her made her throb with want. She found herself back in the land of bronco and bull riding. The possibilities for real physical fun excited her.

A loud noise forced her from her reverie, an oncoming truck slamming on its horn.

Shit! She jerked the steering wheel. *I'm in the wrong lane!* She ran off the edge of the road before pulling it back onto the asphalt.

She didn't want to destroy the one decent thing she'd won in the divorce, the whole settlement a complete farce if she was being honest. Her cheating ex-that-shall-not-be-named husband had runoff with anything of value, leaving her only a collection of junk from an old estate and the Mercedes she had almost wrecked.

The phone buzzed again, and she bit her lip, fighting the temptation.

I can't sext and drive, or my libido will get me killed.

She was sexting with a twenty-year-old college student. Age wasn't a factor for her husband when he chose to explore his secretary's pussy for fun. In fact, her replacement was her first female friend when they'd moved to the Big Apple. *We were friends, or so I thought.* Granted, she had never learned her age nor how long he'd been cheating on her.

She grabbed up the phone again, texting a naughty response because, *equality and all that shit.*

[Clara: I unzip my dress.]

[Tommy: I take off my shirt, licking my lips. <PICTURE>]

Up ahead, a gas station came into view. She wiggled in her seat, aroused by the pic of a bare muscled torso. She did need fuel, but she also needed some fun without wrecking into oncoming traffic. The old country store had a worn-out sign reading *Scruffy's Quik-e-mart.* Inside, it seemed Scruffy was trying to sell far too much with the tiny square footage.

"Gas station, convenient store, and bait shop?" Safely stopped at the pump, she reached for her phone again.

[Clara: I moan and my hand travels up your inner thigh to...]

[Tommy: My cock is growing hard]

A knock on her window made her jump, interrupting her reading. Annoyed, she rolled down her window.

"Hiya, Ma'am. You in need of a pit stop?" The older gentleman grinned at her. He had lost more teeth than he currently had.

What is this craziness? Since when do people just come up and speak to you?

She glanced at her phone and smirked. "Sure am."

The old man nodded, giving her a key attached to a wood block.

What the hell? Was he just waiting for a chick to swing in and piss?

She eyed the man as he walked to the back of her car. She popped the gas tank and took the key around to the side of the building, an arrow with *restrooms* guiding her way. She opened the dented metal door and locked it behind her. Her eyes took a moment to adjust to the green glow of the florescent lights. A cracked mirror was the only thing on the wall behind a small pedestal sink. Despite the cracked tiles and peeling paint, it was clean.

Finally, some privacy.

She looked down to finish writing the text she'd nearly died over.

[Clara: My dress falls to the ground.]

[Tommy: I lean down to suckle a nipple.]

[Clara: I grip the bulge in your jeans.]

Scrolling up, she pulled his picture back up on her phone, while she waited for his response. Humming, she took in all that tan skin and those hard planes. She didn't know his real name, just defaulted to Tommy, but she couldn't forget that body. Blue eyes and sandy-blonde hair, he was a dead ringer for a young Brad Pitt.

[Tommy: I bite your neck and fondle your breasts.]

A flash of provocative want washed over her again. How she wished it could be the real thing and not a virtual tease. But it was better than nothing. At least she knew what how it felt when a man could handle her body.

Reaching up, she fondled herself, twisting a nipple as she imagined him nibbling her neck. At last, she took her turn.

[Clara: I unzip your pants and take your thick, smooth dick in my hand.]

The thought just made her blood boil. A rush of youthful vitality had her reaching down the front of her own pants. Her breathing deepened, and she pushed her underwear aside, imagining a wild fantasy.

The phone buzzed.

[Tommy: Yes, baby. Stroke me.]

Her finger circled her throbbing arousal, praying for release. She slid her thumb to text her next desire. Her body hot with want. A moan escaped her.

[Clara: I run my tongue across...]

A loud knock landed on the bathroom door, startling her. The fantasy shattered.

Damn it.

She looked at the ceiling.

What do you have against me?

"Just need to use the bathroom." A lady's voice came through the door.

Shit, the door's that thin? Could she hear me?

"Just a minute." She flushed the toilet to reduce questions, then washed her hands.

When she opened the door and emerged, a woman with one child tucked under her arm, the other doing the potty dance, appeared. Clara held the door open for them; her cheeks flushed with guilt as she noticed the desperation on the little boy's face.

The lady hauled her two nagging children into the bathroom. "Much obliged," she said as Clara handed her the key.

The sight of them had flushed her fiery libido and sultry mood into the toilet. She sighed, opting for a drink instead. She exited the sexting session, bitter to abandon her fun. Checking her GPS app, she was only four miles shy of her destination. Taking a water from an iced barrel, she headed for the counter to pay.

An old woman gave her an appraising look. "You from out of town?"

Clara just nodded. She hadn't wanted to make this trip, and she didn't want to make it worse by explaining to strangers where she was going and why. After all, there's a reason why she'd escaped the small-town mentality. *Everyone's always up in your business... gossip city.*

"Where you headed?"

And there it is. Clara tapped her credit card on the counter. "Worcestershire Estate."

The old lady scanned her water. "Why the hell would you go there? It's cursed land. Nothing there but a barn and an old, abandoned house."

"Cursed?" Clara didn't remember hearing such rumors. *Is that why he wanted to leave it behind? Fucking dick. Giving me a haunted piece of shit.*

The old lady nodded. "Pump two, right?"

Clara nodded again.

The old lady punched in some numbers on the old register. "$48.23."

Sliding her card over, she asked again, "What do you mean by cursed?"

Swiping the card, the old lady gave her a long stare. "For generations, something evil has preyed on the cattle there, killing them in mysterious ways."

Clara laughed. *Why am I letting these hillbillies scare me with their silly superstitions?*

"She ain't kidding." The old man from earlier appeared, wiping his hands on an oily cloth.

Clara reclaimed her credit card and swiped the water bottle from the counter. Smirking, she gave him a skeptical expression, remembering the silly local urban legend she had ignored in favor of chasing boys and fuc...

"All the livestock dies from blood loss, sucked dry by that damn Chupacabra." He shoved the dirty rag into his overall pocket.

"Don't speak its name!" the old lady snapped, forming a cross over her chest.

"It's only fair to warn her about the shapeshifter," the old man defended. "Old man Baker claimed the beast could walk like a man when it turned."

Clara laughed. "Thank you, but I'm sure I'll be fine. I'm not the superstitious type."

The man gave a disapproving grunt.

As she stepped out the door and returned to the comfort of her car, she was glad to be back on the road, following the GPS. It won't be long before this disastrous trip was over. Thoughts of her cheating ex-husband, her sexting buddy, and the crazy superstitions intertwined her thoughts as she drove.

What kind of life have I made for myself?

2

THE FAMILY CURSE

Sheriff Jakob Regadera sat in his patrol truck, glaring at himself in the mirror. Grabbing an old fast-food napkin from the seat, he wiped away blood from the corner of his mouth. He hated how he had lost control. Frowning, he put the aviator style sunglasses on, hoping they would temper his unpredictable ability. Being a Chupacabra shifter had its pros and cons. One look into his eyes, and he could charm the pants off any woman or man. Granted, he'd cheated the system, using his ability during investigations, but lately, there was no way to turn off the switch.

I can't believe what I did this morning. Turning up the CB Radio, he waited for the inevitable call. *Any minute, Mr. Baker will make a complaint. I'm shocked it's taking him this long.*

The full moon was only a few days ago. The new moon was his trigger, unnerving him. Last night, he had been monitoring local coyote activity when he felt the shift, abrupt and unnatural. He swallowed, still tasting the metallic tinge of blood on his tongue.

Cracking open a Monster© energy drink, he guzzled it down, swishing the unwanted flavor from his mouth.

After gulping it down, he checked his teeth in the rearview. *Christ, I have fangs almost as long as a vampire's canines. What the hell is happening to me?*

Both his parents had been of Mexican descent, thus his umber tanned skin had been a blessing and curse. Dark black hair and a permanent five o'clock shadow on his chin and jawline made him rugged. He maintained a crewcut so he didn't have to stress about getting it caught in rope during his side gig as a bull rider. The rest of the small-town law enforcement were far from being as in shape as Jakob. His large biceps were tight in the sleeves, and even in an extra-large shirt, the buttons strained across his chest.

Every muscle is itching just to strip naked and run wild across the pasture.

"We have a situation down at Baker's Ranch. What's your 20 Sheriff Regadera?" The CB Radio crackled to life with a woman's voice and Jakob sighed.

He picked up the receiver and pinged back. "10-4. Grabbing donuts and energy drinks at Scruffy's Quik-e-Mart."

There was a giggle before she continued, "Coffee's better. Anyhow, Mr. Baker wants to file a report. Can you do an in-person report this morning?"

He took another sip of his drink and glanced at his fangs one more time. Dipping his sunglasses down, he groaned. His irises flashed yellow with reptilian slits for pupils. Blinking a few times, they faded back to brown, and he shoved the glasses back in place. For now, he wouldn't be taking them off in public. Cracking his neck, he watched as a trailer of bulls pulled in to fuel up.

His stomach growled with hunger. He could hear their hearts beating, the blood rushing in their veins, the taste...

"Did you copy, Regadera?" the radio screeched, bringing him back, and he cursed under his breath.

"10-4. Yeah. I'll go meet him at his house." Hanging the CB receiver on its hook he put the pickup in drive.

Licking his lips, he gave the cattle one last lingering look before ignoring his hunger. He was about a thirty-minute drive from the Baker's ranch, a fact he only knew since he'd just come from there after eating the livestock. Normally, the need to feed was stronger during the full moon. To curb the appetite, he'd buy a goat or two and set up shop in his barn so no one could see their fate.

They'd ask and he'd tell the half-truth; *I ate it.* Goat meat wasn't frowned upon, but what he didn't share is he'd had no desire for that part. Instead, he sucked them dry of their blood. During big events, he'd invest in a cow. Or an old mare fated for the glue factory.

But whatever happened last night, he wasn't prepared for, almost shifting the entire way.

Picking up his cell phone, he called his father. He hadn't spoken to him for years, but this wasn't the time to rage about the past. When his mother died, they'd gone separate ways, and he'd started a new life.

"Hello?" Jakob tensed at the sound of his father's heavy Mexican accent.

"Hey, Dad. It's JR."

There was silence. The last time he saw his father was after he'd eaten his father's prized Thoroughbred out of spite. He hated that the man gambled and worked the circuit. The way he treated those horses was damn near inhumane. And when that horse broke its two front legs, someone needed to put the poor thing out of its misery. His father was going to milk him dry for the semen and breeding stock.

"Look, I just need to know if there's someone that I can talk to about ... my condition." He inhaled deeply, holding his breath.

"You didn't seem worried about it when you ate Hercules."

There it is. Still pissed about the fucking half-dead horse.

"Fine. I'm sorry. I was young and reckless." It was an empty apology and they both knew it. "I'm having ... issues."

Another painful pause.

"Dad, I shifted last night," he confessed.

"How the hell did that happen?" The tone in his dad's voice quickly shifted to concern. "Were you caught? Do you need a place to hide?"

"N-no. I just need to talk to someone. See if this is ... normal." He struggled to get the last word out, shifting in the driver's seat. "I have fangs like a fucking vampire and my eyes won't stop shifting. It's bad."

"Jakob, your mom never really discussed the family curse." It was the worst news ever. "But what I do know, is that there are others out there. Shifters, that is. Find one and they might know something. I can do some digging on my end. Maybe there's something in her things."

"You still have her things?" His chest ached at the idea, *I thought he said he got rid of it all.*

Another pause. "Yeah. I kept it. Every piece."

Now's not the time to talk about that. Jakob took a left turn down an old clay road. "I've got to go. Let me know what you find."

"JR. Be careful."

He pushed end. Whether that was all his father had to say, he didn't want to know or hear that he loved him. There were still too many bitter memories drowning what few good ones lingered.

As the truck came around the bend, Mr. Baker stood waiting for him, a shotgun in hand, giving a mean stare.

Jakob cut the engine and pulled himself from the truck. "Morning, sir."

The old man spat tobacco at his feet. "Morning nothing!" he yelled, pointing his gun. "Something ate my goats, including old Bessie."

Jakob licked his teeth, recalling the flavor. "R-right. You want to show me where?"

"The barn, JR." Scoffed the old man, hobbling ahead of him. "Where else would they fucking be?"

Jakob rubbed the back of his neck. "Not everyone is as diligent as you are, old timer."

"Coyotes have been lurking along the fence line." He stopped, pointing at a trail of blood. "But this wasn't a coyote, JR. That's the work of the Chupacabra."

"Mr. Baker." Jakob inhaled deeply, enjoying the scent of blood in the air. "That's an urban legend. There's no such thing."

"I saw it," declared Mr. Baker, his voice shaking. "Some sort of lizard thing."

Paling, Jakob walked up to the old cow's body, squatting with his back turned to Mr. Baker. "I'm telling you, it's a myth. I was out here tracking a pack of coyotes or wild dogs. They must've found a way in the fence. Maybe they've got mange, makes their skin scaly."

"JR, that thing had yellow eyes and scales like a snake." Another splatter of chewing tobacco hit the ground behind him. "Squatted just like you are now. Just sucking her dry."

Jakob's heart quickened. "Is that so? Maybe it was a cougar?"

"No. No fur. Too big for even that," Mr. Baker muttered to himself.

Looking at the cow, he could see the fang marks he'd left on her jugular. He saw the whites of her eyes for a split second, but the charm of his golden eyes had calmed her. She laid down, willing as he sunk them in. Blood hot and thick, but he hadn't been satisfied with the two goats in the stall beside her. The flesh had been torn away, still attached. Guilt filled him. She bled out. He had aimed to take just enough to let her live, but when the old man swung open the barn doors and fired a warning shot, he ran.

"I'll put it in the report." He stood up. "Should I send someone to help you with the carcass?"

"Yeah," the old man said, then sighed deeply. "Look, JR. Just put down coyotes did it."

He swung back to the old man, confused. "Are you sure?"

"My sugar, you see. It was high when I checked it last night and again this morning." He rubbed his forehead and sat on a nearby haybale. "I don't know what I saw."

A weight of relief washed over Jakob. "I see. I'll send some folks over to help you clean this up. If your diabetes is acting up, might do you some good to rest and let someone else do the work. I'll pay. You've lost enough today."

"R-right." They met eyes and Jakob was thankful he had aviators to protect his secret. "You're right, Sheriff."

He patted Mr. Baker on the shoulder. "Maybe I can get you a new cow. Even a goat or two."

Mr. Baker shrugged, still glaring at his Bessie. "I won't say no to that either. Long as you set things right, I can't complain."

Making it back into his pickup, Jakob could breathe again. Another stolen look to the rearview made it clear his eyes were still golden. He was reaching for his cell phone when the CB radio cracked. Abandoning his aim, he turned it up and grabbed the receiver.

"Repeat that last message, Suzie. I just got back to my truck."

"There's smoke coming from the old Worcestershire Estate," she repeated. "Do you copy?"

"10-4." Jakob licked a fang and furrowed his brow. "I thought it was abandoned?"

"That's a negative." There was a pause, but he knew Suzie craved gossip. "Rumor is Clara's back in town and they're going through the big 'D', and I don't mean Dallas. And he got the palace and left her the shack."

Good lord, when was the last time I saw Clara? High school? No, her bachelorette party when… shit.

3

The Fuel

*C*lara had just turned on the radio to calm herself when her cell phone rang. Excited that it might be her sexting buddy still wanting to finish off live on the phone she answered too quickly.

"Hey," she said with excitement.

"You're late." Her ex's cold voice rumbled through the speakers.

Her body flooded with the wrong kind of warmth this time. Her pulse quickened with anger, and she retorted, "Which wouldn't have been an issue if you hadn't hidden half of my belongings in the middle of nowhere!"

"Don't make me call the sheriff. I doubt he'll tolerate your disrespect by wasting his time with your bullshit," he drawled.

"How considerate. I wish you gave that much consideration when you decided to *fuck* my best friend." She turned down a clay road, a broken sign saying Worcestershire leaning against a tree. "How dare I waste *your time*, because wasting ten years married to you was…"

Her ex gave an exaggerated sigh, just to ensure she heard over the line. "Don't be crass, Clara. Have some dignity. You've already lost the divorce. It'd be a shame to have you handcuffed in the backseat of the sheriff's car."

"Taking the high road now, are we?" she laughed. "Well, I'm on this road to this cursed farm of yours."

"Cursed?" She wouldn't have noticed the raised note in his voice as panic if she hadn't lived with the man for so damn long. "Who says it's cursed?"

His voice sounded defensive. *How odd.* "The locals."

"How foolish of you to believe local superstition."

There it was...

His defense mechanism. He'd used it before when she'd suspected him of the affair. At that point, he'd denied it before accusing her of some fault. It took a private investigator to uncover proof of his dirty deed, and even then, he'd accused her of causing him to cheat. She decided to push him, instead of just letting it go. It became a game, setting things up for the fun of it, sometimes out of curiosity. At the end, it ruined the divorce process, but she regretted nothing.

"Naïve enough to walk on a farm where a Chupacabra has been eating the livestock? Is that why it failed? You were sucking your cattle dry and ran the family business down like you did me and our marriage?" A grin came to her face; she could still play the games.

A nervous laugh came over the speaker. "No one would believe that," answered the sinister voice.

Concern drew her brow together as the wrought iron gate came into view. It leaned into the brush and overgrowth. There were no signs of anyone ever living there when she'd let him sweep her off to the city. She hadn't planned to be in Gandersville for long, but she didn't have the money or means to go anywhere.

Was this some great divorce joke or something? What creepy hell was this?

"I'm here," she said, ending the call. He had started whatever snarky retort he had for her, and she smiled.

She stopped in the middle of the driveway and looked around. For miles, there were rolling hills of vibrant green grass and driveway asphalt that had become gray with wear. She got out of the car and a breeze caught her hair, the sun high in the sky. The crisp white paint was a stark contrast to the green lettering on the sign reading *Worcestershire Ranch*. It had lost its footing now, rust painting it as it leaned against the wrought iron gates. She could see buildings at the end of the long drive, leading to the farm. It didn't feel creepy. Under different circumstances, she might even appreciate the country more, living in a place like this had she visited it in its prime.

Her phone buzzed with a new message.

[Tommy: Did I lose your interest? Lol]

She decided not to respond. Eventually, she'd provide an excuse later, but now, she was distracted. Like it or not, this is where life had landed her, and it was time to collect her shit.

She got back in the car and drove up the remainder of the drive. It was surprisingly well kept past the neglected gate and got closer to the antique farmhouse.

Shutting off the ignition, she stepped out and took it all in. There was no one in sight. She walked up to the porch and knocked on the door. No answer.

These country folk ... they're probably out hunting right now.

"Hello?" she yelled out to no one in particular.

She walked around the house; it was in decent shape. If her ex hadn't owned the property, she would have loved it even more. Making her way back to the front, she saw a large van driving up the long road. *The movers were late too.* The truck rumbled up and backed up to the porch steps. Clara crossed her arms, tapping her foot with annoyance. A frail elderly man got out of the cab, followed by three lanky college boys.

He nodded his head to her. "Ma'am."

"Hey." She managed a smile. "I guess we're just waiting on the sheriff?"

"Not unless you plan on giving us a hard time." The old man nodded at her and waved on the motley crew. "These boys will make quick work of it. We'll be out of your hair in no time."

The three college boys reminded her of everything she had left behind in Gandersville: youth and a carefree sex life. The tallest figure moved closer, smiling, reminding her of the picture she'd received from her sexting buddy. He had sandy-blonde hair and a worn-out band shirt. With huge broad shoulders, he wasn't overly bulky but lean and muscular. Her libido kicked into high gear, loving the confidence of his movements and the possibility of other rhythmic activities.

As he came closer, he had a face to match. *He should be on the cover of GQ, not out here in the sticks. Adonis incarnate!*

"What are you boys planning to take from this rundown shithole?" she asked.

The old man snorted. "We got a list from Mr. Worcestershire. We plan on taking just what's there, nothing more, nothing less. Court ordered. If you got a problem with it, you'll have to take it up with the judge."

She was ready to chastise the old man when the hunk's eyes met hers. Sparkling blue eyes memorized her, making her flush with excitement. His gaze roamed her face like a soft caress, and she yearned to have him touch her in all the right places. As he came closer, she could see the strong set of his jaw and the high cheek bones.

She bit her lip. *I wonder how chiseled he is under that shirt and jeans. I'd be more than happy to check for myself.*

"Mrs. Worcestershire?" said a soothing voice.

"Ms. Williams, actually," she amended. It had cost good money to regain her maiden name. "But call me Clara."

A smile spread across his handsome face, revealing a row of perfect white teeth. *Why the hell am I noticing his teeth? What's wrong with me?*

"Thank you for meeting me here...?" Her voice trailed, prying for a name.

"You can call me Trevor," he said. "Just a moment, I'll get the order and we'll begin. I'll still need your signature for this."

As he walked to the van, Clara got the most amazing view of his backside. Long lean legs, no doubt toned thighs. He grabbed a clipboard from the passenger side, nodding to the old man. The men made small talk, but Clara's thoughts were far away.

How can I get a man like that? Sexting and phone sex are a thrill, but to have a chiseled body on top of me, no under me, would be nothing short of amazing. Hearing her ex's name in their conversation brought on flashes of the divorce. She scowled, the tidal wave of emotions drowning her confidence. *I should definitely stick to phone sex. Jumping strangers while reclaiming my ex's portion of the divorce settlement is inappropriate. Right?*

Trevor's form filled the door frame as he walked into the house. Spinning back to her, he leaned against the frame, cocking his head. She shook the thoughts from her mind, mustering an empty smile.

He lifted an eyebrow. "You want to check the list with me? I want to ensure we don't leave anything behind."

Clara struggled to focus on his face, instead of drifting down his frame. "Sure, just let me get my list out of the car."

Ugh, I'm making a fool of myself.

Walking back to her car, she jerked the passenger door open and shuffled through her glove compartment. She had shoved her list from the lawyer there but had forgotten to review it.

The envelope was still sealed. *Well, I have to open it now.*

She tore into it, earning a nice paper cut. *Great.* Unfolding the paper, she looked over the list. Then, she saw at the bottom what clearly was her husband's contribution.

Taking anything other than what's listed will be seen as larceny and Ms. Williams will be prosecuted.

The man knew she was on a warpath and had every right to fear he wouldn't get his way if she had a say.

What an asshole.

She looked at her reflection in the rearview mirror. Clara wasn't unattractive and everything was still in perfect working order. He couldn't satisfy her in bed, unable to keep up with her sex drive. At the end of the marriage, he had turned to her ex-best friend.

Who cares if I make a fool of myself! It's not against the law to flirt my way through this debacle. Not like I ever have to see him again anyway.

She contemplated a moment more, then shrugged out of her button up shirt. With only a white tank top on, she showed just the right amount of cleavage to remain publicly appropriate. Prepped and preened, she grabbed the list and walked inside. The interior of the house was cool and dark. Dust-covered drapes and boxes filled the rooms. It was more of a storage house than a livable home. She heard the men speaking from farther into the house. There was dragging and shuffling. The movers weren't wasting any time.

She caught up with them at the end of a long hallway that opened to a giant country kitchen, where the three young men were pulling some boxes out. Not a single glance came her way. Heat hit her cheeks, she glared at the list and decided it wasn't worth arguing over it. Everything was covered in dust, left here to rot like her.

Exploring the rest of the house was like walking on a country western set. The kitchen was enormous and the stairs creaking like hell under her feet. There were only two bathrooms, the one downstairs broken, and the one upstairs had an ancient clawfoot tub.

By the time she came back downstairs, the movers had emptied everything, leaving behind broken knickknacks and a button-tufted leather loveseat. She had lost sight of the handsome blonde hunk, and the old man approached her, muttering as he read his copy of the list. Clearing his throat, he earned an annoyed look from Clara.

"Ms. Williamson." He narrowed his eyes. "We don't have room for the loveseat."

"Not my problem," she scoffed.

"He's sending a company out to crate and ship it to him." He lifted an eyebrow. "Unless you intend to damage it. We've taken pictures so..."

Clara tilted her head back, staring at the brown popcorn ceiling. "Are you kidding me?" she said in disbelief. "Look, just leave. I won't touch the damn thing."

He nodded, scribbling on the paper and making her sign it as well. She followed him out, but *Trevor* had closed the back of the van and loaded in with the rest of the crew. Clara felt cheated. First her sexting, now Trevor escaping.

I just want to fuck someone.

She watched them leave, frowning. Looking back to the rest of the junk, a devilish idea came to mind.

They never said I couldn't burn his shit.

4

The Fire

Jakob sat in his truck, debating on reasons why Clara had returned. Worse, he'd been using the old ranch as a dumping ground for years. When George Worcestershire and his dad pissed him off, he'd done more than dump carcasses there. He single-handedly ate the bulk of the livestock and drove the rancher's living into the ground. That's what they deserved for the time when the Worcestershires beat him half dead.

They're a shit family, and when Clara still married that asshole...

A shudder rattled him. He could still taste her lips. The hunger for blood was almost insatiable as he covered his mouth. Goosebumps rolled across his skin. For the first time ever, he had a thirst for human blood. Picking up the CB receiver, he prodded Suzie for more answers or to at least pry the last of the gossip from her.

"Why call me and not the fire department?" He held his breath, burying his lust and hunger by pure force of will. "You did say it's a fire."

"Well, George Worcestershire called it in." Suzie sounded smitten with the man. "And he's harmless."

Sour memories boiled up, and Jakob's jaw muscles tensed. What the town didn't know, didn't see, was that Jakob worked on the Worcestershire Ranch as a farmhand. The pay was decent, but he'd wanted out from under George's dad in the worst kind of way. Rumors in town were building after Hercules had been sucked dry. Old superstitions took hold as they'd laid his mother in the ground. Word had gotten out. The Chupacabra was back in Gandersville.

This put him under a lot of pressure. With that, came his temper.

"George called? When did he return to town?" He put the truck in reverse, his curiosity piquing. "And why call me in?"

"Well, he comes and visits his mama in the nursing home once or twice a year." Suzie was settling into the conversation now; he had hit the jackpot. "Anyhow, he had no idea you were sheriff now. Seemed a little taken back by the news."

Jakob smirked, clunking the pickup into drive, retracing his route. "So, did he sell the old place finally?"

"Well, not exactly." After a moment, Suzie whispered over the radio, "You see, Clara lost big time in the divorce. It was ugly as sin, I hear."

Catching a glimpse of gold irises in the rearview, Jakob pushed the aviators up on his nose. "Okay, but what does that have to do with the old Worcestershire Ranch estate?"

"George is being generous. He's giving it to Clara."

Jakob snorted his drink out, choking on the energy drink.

"But she's a mess. Her crazy's showing," Suzie declared. "He's got things he wants out of there before she steps foot in the place."

Jakob could see signs of a fire as he started down a new clay road. "And what does this have to do with me going instead of the fire department?"

"He said that..." she lowered her voice, "crazy bitch," clearing her throat she finished, "set his stuff ablaze in the front yard."

Jakob started to laugh, stopping the truck on the empty road. "As we speak, she's burning her ex-husband's shit in the yard?"

"Oh yes! Terrible, isn't it?" Suzie was sincerely upset by the news.

"Oh, it's terrible all right." He couldn't hide his amusement.

"You better be on your way Sheriff Regadera."

"Almost there. Going as fast as I can, Suzie. Promise." Jakob put the truck in park and leaned back.

"You're such a good sheriff!"

He rolled his eyes, leaning his seat back and tilting his cowboy hat forward. Glancing at his wristwatch, he figured another thirty minutes or so should be enough to do some good damage. His mind wandered, unsettled by last night and even the surge of hunger the cattle had brought. Huffing, he tilted his seat back in place, annoyed.

That was short-lived.

Leaning on the steering wheel, he glared down the road, remembering how many times he had driven this way to work, or snuck in through the patch of trees and underbrush. His skin prickled. As he recalled the past, his last hours with Clara had always been bittersweet. His jaw twitched, remembering how her silky breasts had felt under his calloused hands. Glancing at his hands, he saw he'd lost those callouses years ago.

She used to bitch about how they felt like sandpaper, but it never stopped her from moaning.

Taking in a deep inhale, he could almost smell her perfume again. She was an animal that night of her Bachelorette party. They had shown up at the local bar where he and his bull riding compadres would end their nights. Across the room, he'd locked eyes with her. He had come looking for her, and she had come looking for him.

So blue, like a clear summer day.

He leaned back in his seat and pulled off his sunglasses. Glancing in the side mirror, he snorted at his yellow eyes. A smile came to his face, and he closed his eyes, thinking back to how she'd moaned and clawed at his back. It had been the first time he'd lain with someone who could keep up with his stamina. His eyes had shifted against his will, despite it being a full moon. The way she rocked against him, hungry for him to go deeper. She was all legs, her hair spilled in a curly heap, makeup smearing her beautiful face.

"Fuck me harder..."

Chills rattled him, making his shoulders shudder. He could still hear her haunting words. Looking back, it was as if she were giving him the last taste of her sexual freedom. Jakob inhaled deeply, shifting in his seat.

"Swallow me up, Jakob! I don't ever want to forget tonight..."

The craving for blood hit him like a tidal wave, tantalizing his arousal. His breath caught, and he shook his head, muttering a curse. Something about her drove him crazy back then, even now. The Chupacabra side of him could be sated, feeding on her. Though the idea of taking up the habits of a vampire disgusted him. It wasn't something his kind did out of affection. Plenty of times he'd noticed his father with a bandage on the neck with a smirk on his face.

She had started on top, the girl riding the bull rider.

He covered his mouth, running a tongue over a sharp fang. Now, his memories were returning. He bit her that night. Licked at her neck like a hungry animal and she had reacted with unadulterated passion. Nails ripped open his skin, her voice pleading for more. Jakob shifted, rubbing, shaking free of his memories.

I can't believe just thinking about it makes me this hard.

Groaning, he covered the golden eyes up once more, caving to his curiosity. Pulling the truck onto the road, he crept along. He could see the smoke plume coming closer. All he knew was the fuck of his life was back in town, angry over her divorce, and had left him for his worst enemy. He steeled himself.

I wonder how much she's changed. They've been married for what, ten years? Didn't make it too far. Shit, is that house even holding together enough for anyone to live in?

He turned the bend, pulling past the wrought iron gate. Stopping the truck, he stared at the scene before him. Blinking for a few minutes, he sat staring in disbelief. Flames shot up from the ground, towering over Clara and billowing black, acrid smoke. She threw out her arm, screaming on a cell phone before throwing it across the yard. Spinning on her heel, she locked eyes with him and froze. Her blue eyes coaxed him to tip his sunglasses down as she put her hands on her hips.

The thick lips scowled at him, her gaze measuring, before flicking him the bird. "Tell my ex-husband he can keep this shit pile. I'd rather spend the night in the jailhouse again."

He smirked at the declaration. She hadn't realized who he was yet, and he was glad. *There's no more of that desperate high school girl glow.* There before him, he saw a hungry woman who could kill a man with her libido. Goosebumps rolled over him, the scent of her perfume drifting on the breeze, just as always.

Gucci... Flora, was it?

Turning, she marched away in her tight jeans. Her hips swayed and he licked his lips. Looking to the burning pile, he recognized a few Worcestershire family photo frames, a painting, the old drapes, and... *Is that her wedding dress?*

Flipping a switch on the radio, he blurted over the megaphone, "You can't burn his shit in the yard, Clara."

She froze, staring at the truck in disbelief.

She's every bit as drop dead gorgeous now as she was back then. And those eyes are so hungry for... Christ, I'm so fucked.

5

EVERYTHING'S WET

Clara couldn't move. Those golden eyes, peeking at her over a pair of aviators, were a memory of the past. The last time she'd seen eyes like that, it had belonged to Jakob, a local bull rider who had a reputation for the wildest rides, in the ring and in the bed.

She blinked. *Don't tell me the sheriff is...*

Jakob stepped out of the truck, a receiver in his hand.

Fuck.

He leaned on the open car door and smirked. "Glad you remember me."

Anger and lust burned through her as she remarked, "Glad you remember my name."

His head slumped in defeat. Tossing the receiver in the truck, he slammed the door and headed toward her. The man walked with the graceful stride of some ancient predator that sent a shiver down Clara's spine—a mixture of fear and excitement. A part of her wanted to run, but those golden eyes under the dark lenses held her in place. She never took Jakob as a uniform man but seeing him now, again, took her breath away, rendering her mute.

What is it about those eyes that makes me useless?

He walked past her, breaking her glare. She followed him. He still had a slight limp; no telling if he'd gotten it in a one of the bar fights or bull rides. It reminded her of how he'd stalked across the bar, to *her*, that night at her bachelorette party. She already knew, under that sheriff's uniform, he had a chiseled body that she still ached to touch, just one more time.

I wonder if someone finally tamed the biggest bull in town. Oh? He has no rings on those fingers. He's fair game.

Clara crossed her arms, boosting her girls high enough to reveal some of the red lacy bra underneath. Smiling, she prepared for that moment he would turn and see her. Jakob squatted, turning on the hose bib. He was broader, more seasoned, and something about him made her blood rush. At last, he stood and turned, faltering in his steps. She bit her lips.

"Why are you looking at me like that?" he swallowed and shoved his glasses up. "You look like a hungry cougar ready to strike."

"So, what did you do after that night?" She would play dirty by bringing up the past as long as she got some fun before sundown.

Gripping the kink in the hose tight, he steeled himself. "I thought you'd forgotten something like that."

He feels it too; After all these years, the tension still remains.

"How could a girl forget a night like that?" She shrugged, following him to the fire. "My ex was never that good with his hands anyhow."

Spraying the fire, he grunted at the comment. The fire sizzled, the smoke thickening. Each item fell apart as the stream of water slammed into it. Clara walked closer and Jakob tensed. She grinned at the reaction, seeing an opening to make a move.

I'm about to fuck the sheriff!

Her hands glided across his torso, stopping right above his chiseled abs. The uniform did nothing to hide the herculean body underneath. She nestled herself into his back, the heat of his body tantalizing. He froze, still spraying water on the remains of her fire. Her hands glided up, curious at how far he'd let her go.

Is Jakob still every bit as wild as he was back then? Oh, this beats the sexting and movers hands down. I might get some physical loving after all.

She found the top button and loosened it. He did nothing to stop her as he continued to extinguish the stubborn flames. Another button undone, and his skin warm under her palm as she slid down his chest. She continued to unbutton his uniform, her other hand floating over ripples of muscles. He turned and blasted her with the water hose.

"Christ, do I have to put two fires out!"

Clara's white tank top was practically translucent as she sputtered, "What the hell was that for?"

"I could ask you the same thing!" Jakob dropped the hose, startled. "Stop it."

"No, the hell you didn't." She rung her hair out while glaring at him.

"I..." He stopped as if bewildered by his lack of action.

"Ugh, I needed a shower anyhow." Clara shed the tank top, wringing it out as she marched to the house. "Unless you plan on arresting me, this conversation is over."

"W-wait, you can't just strip naked in broad daylight." He gave chase.

"The hell I can't." She shoved through the front door. "It's my fucking house and property. All but that piece of shit furniture." She motioned at a leather loveseat.

"Clara, what just happened out there, it was..." She started up the stairs, and he grabbed her arm. "Look, I'm not going to lie. I was shocked to hear you were back. And yeah, I didn't forget that night. I couldn't forget that night."

She looked down at his hand, hot against her wrist, and raised an eyebrow. "Being rather physical, Sheriff. What do you plan on doing now that you have me in your grip?"

He tossed his glasses off, those golden eyes jolting her. With a yank, she fell onto him, and they locked lips. Their kiss deepened, increasing their passion. Clara wrapped her arms around his neck, coaxing his tongue into her mouth and began suckling it. The heat of a hand slid over her hip and into the back of her jeans, gripping her ass. She moaned, leaning all her weight into him, but it did nothing to budge him from the bottom of the steps.

Pulling free, she searched his face. "What made you change your mind?"

He smirked. "I could never refuse you when you're wet and ready."

She laughed, changing direction as she peppered his body with kisses. His hands gripped the railing as she untucked his shirt and began unbuttoning. She swore he'd earned a few new scars since the last time she'd explored him. Her fingers grabbed his belt buckle, the fabric tight.

I'm about to fuck the sheriff. How much hotter could this get?

Sitting on a step, she released the pressure, pressing down on his hard-on. He exhaled in relief. With a smirk, she began stroking his long cock. He leaned forward, pressing himself into her rubbing palm. Her body was on fire, throbbing to have him inside her. Memories of that night appeared in the present, and she wanted to have it all over again.

I don't think I ever found a dick bigger than this.

Her lips wrapped around the tip of his cock, twirling the tip as a tease. She unbuttoned her jeans and dove her hand under her panties. Staring up at him with her sky-blue eyes, she thought he glared down like a hungry lion. He rocked his hips, coaxing her to take all of him between her lips. She countered, licking the base to the tip, then continued to suckle. Clara began stroking herself faster, humming on his dick as she grew wet. He moaned, releasing a growl of frustration.

The wooden railing splintered under his grip; the golden eyes glowing.

Clara let him in, the hardened length glided across her tongue. Her fingers dove into her slick pussy, drawing the wetness toward her swollen clit. Circling, she was vigorous and desperate to come from hours of sexual frustration. His breath caught, and he purred as his cock pressed the back of her throat. She tightened her lips around his throbbing erection, rubbing her tongue against the underbelly. Jakob began rocking faster, enjoying the wet heat of her mouth and the power of her suckling.

Good lord. I can't fit the whole thing down my throat. I'm fucked if her tries to deep throat...

The wood creaked and she closed her eyes tight. He grew harder, her lips aching from the increased girth. She was enjoying this, having him at her mercy. This was something new, something they had never tried in the past, after all these years.

Is he going to break the railing?

A moan erupted, his cock pushing deep into her throat. She shook her head, unable to take him any deeper and he released. Throbbing, hot liquid filled her, and she swallowed, silently cursing. He had come like Mt. Everest, fast, hard, and unexpected. Her pussy ached, and she wanted more. Sweat poured from his chiseled chest.

Shit. I just gave the sheriff a free blow job, and I'm left here wet and hung out to dry.

She pulled away, unable to hide her frown as the bitter thoughts consumed her. Swallowing the last of the sweet cum, she wiped her mouth. Too terrified to look up.

You're dreaming again, Clara. This isn't the hungry bull rider from before. Just two adults clinging to one last good time.

6

THE NEED TO FEED

What the hell am I doing?

Jakob panted, assessing his moment of unrestraint lust. His fingers had dug into the wooden rails, and his eyes had yet to revert to their human form. When she placed her lips on his cock, he forced himself to remain still.

At last, he peered down, her look of disappointment rattled him. The Chupacabra side of him could smell it, how close she'd been to coming.

She wiped her mouth, refusing to meet his gaze.

Did I charm her into this? No, she had her hungry paws on me first and I was too afraid to look at her after snaring her from the car even with the glasses on.

He inhaled deeply. "Bend over," he demanded.

"W-what?" She turned and looked at him. His eyes were firmly shut. *I don't want her charmed. I want her ecstasy to be real, not a byproduct of the curse.*

"Turn around. I'm not done." He heard her shuffle.

"Jakob, look you don't..." Peeking, she had done so, unable to meet his gaze.

He reached out and jerked her jeans down off her ass. He sucked on his cheek, marveling at how her curvy hips hadn't changed. Sliding his hands over them, he dove between her thighs, fingers sinking into the throbbing heat. She moaned, leaning back into him, letting him probe her deeper. He licked a fang. His heart raced and the lust rattling through him began to rise.

Despite coming, he hadn't lost his hard-on nor the want to continue to pleasure himself inside her, anywhere she'd allow him to enter. They both moaned as he pressed his cock against her pussy, sliding faster than he had initially aimed to do. *She's so slick. Did she really get this work up sucking my cock? Christ, Clara...*

He grabbed the steps above her, her curves cupping up against him, the heat of their bodies waving into one another. Something about the sweat beading on her skin and the red bra enticed his hunger. Grinding hard and deep, ever faster as she gasped in her rising pleasure. He could feel how she tightened her legs, shaking until her orgasm peaked.

Jakob bit his lip, fighting the urge to taste her blood.

A scream released, her back arching.

Scream louder until...

Jakob saw his clawed hand and panicked. He pulled away, leaving Clara to finish her orgasm on the stairs, alone. He had been to this house plenty of times, so he knew where to dodge into the downstairs bathroom before she noticed his appearance. Locking the door, he glared wildly at himself in the cracked mirror. His golden, slitted eyes contrasted against the rising blue-gray scales speckling his chest.

Was I mid-shift again? And that thirst! Really? Old Bessie didn't do the trick this morning, fuck!

The cold knob snapped off as he turned it. "Shit!"

Knocks pounded on the door. "Jakob? Is everything okay?"

He ignored her, this time turning the hot water knob. "Son of a bitch!" he shouted as scalding water sprayed him from the faucet's base.

"Look. I know I came off aggressive," Clara said, sounding unsure of herself.

Reaching down, he splashed water on his face, praying it would invoke his features to change. He stared at his reflection in the mirror, at the water dripping from his chin. His eyes were fading to brown, scales retreating and normalcy was coming across his entire being. He leaned on the sink basin, getting a closer look at his eyes. It tilted, then cracked, shattering against the floor.

"Dammit!" Rushing, he turned the hot water knob off and it snapped, water spraying everywhere. "Mother fucking..."

He crouched, slowly shutting the water valve closed. Clara was wiggling the knob, banging at the door, and screeching his name. He glared at the old sink and the water flooding the broken tiled floor. *I can't believe they let this house go to tatters.* The thought made his chest swell.

Another wave of beating on the door brought him to the present, to the other mess awaiting him. He stood, inhaling deeply as he swung open the door.

Clara stumbled forward, her feet splashing into the flood. "What the hell happened?"

"About that..." Jakob glanced back at the mirror. *Good, eyes are still normal!* "I broke some shit, but I'll come fix it."

"I..." She took a step back, paling. "Look, I shouldn't have thrown myself on you. This divorce has made me depressed. I thought, if I fucked someone, I'd feel somewhat better about myself."

"Wait, what?" Jakob scrunched his face, confused. "I'm cussing because I broke your shit." *Not because we fucked.*

He started to laugh, then paled when he realized the pure devastation on her face.

"Clara..." he said, his heart skipping a beat. "No! No, no, I wanted that, I seriously was trying to, to..." *Shit! What do I say now? I couldn't admit I was shifting into a fucking Chupacabra?*

"Wait, your eyes." She squinted at him. "They're brown. But weren't they yellow before? Do you wear contacts?"

"YES." The lie left his mouth before he could think it through.

Clara took a minute, assessing her disheveled bathroom. "And the sink broke, how?"

"I had to remove my contacts." His mind raced flailing to grasp onto anything.

"They must've been hurting you when you ran away." She gave him a suspicious glare.

"Killing me."

"Ok, but I don't think..."

The mirror broke loose and scattered across the floor into tiny shards. Jakob cringed, watching the place fall apart around him. Clara shuddered, her skin dimpling. Jakob didn't flinch. Unlike her, he'd heard the moment the glue loosened from the drywall. He stepped out and shut the bathroom door behind him. He felt awkward, towering over her with his uniform laid open and jeans still unbuttoned.

She shivered again, and he wrapped his arms around her reflexively.

"Careful using the upstairs one. It may be in disrepair, too." She nodded her head; her body still damp from the hose earlier. "And I need to return to work. I didn't mean for this to happen, so just forget about it."

"Wait, what?" Clara shoved herself out of his arms, her eyes fiery. "You're just going to fuck me, break my shit, then leave?"

"I said I'd be back to fix it." Jakob now remembered how hot-headed they both could be as the tone in their voices grew stern. "I showed up to extinguish a fire."

"Great job, Jakob," she drawled. "You put my wedding dress out and my pussy."

His brow dropped low as he glared at her. "Now that you're back, stay out of trouble."

"Oh? Is that a threat?" As she crossed her arms, his eyes unwillingly fell to her cleavage.

"I'm leaving." He turned, buttoning his shirt with each stride. "I won't hesitate to put you in the containment cell if you act out, Clara."

"You can't cage me!" she flared, hissing like a feral animal.

The fresh air and sun hit him as he exited the house. He could breathe again, tucking his shirt into place as he glided past the smoldering debris. By the time he made it back to the truck, he paused to look at the front door. Part of him had hoped to see her there, glaring at him. Anything.

But she wasn't. *Good.* The thought was a mixture of pain and relief. *I don't need to rekindle something I didn't have in the first place.*

Swallowing, he got in the truck and started the ignition. He reached into his shirt pocket. Empty. Twisting and turning, he searched the bench seat, then the floorboard, patting the entire place, hoping to find what he needed. *My glasses.*

"Where the hell are my glasses?" he muttered.

"Here." She tapped on the window, startling him. "Lookin' for these?" She held up his aviators, and he rolled the window down.

"Y-yeah. Thanks. I need to put a bell on your neck. Not anyone can sneak up on me like that, you know."

Leaning in, Clara seemed calmer, despite still only wearing a red bra. "We were both releasing some pent-up sexual tension. I get it. Sorry. I was quick to blow up about this being a temporary one-off deal. It's been a shitty day. All and all, it was good to see you again, Jakob." She smirked. "All of you, that is."

He laughed, sliding on the aviators. "I suppose I've had a shitty day too."

She pulled away like a cat who caught the canary.

Let's hope we don't cross paths again. I don't think I could have stopped if it weren't for that untimely shift.

7

THE RODEO

Clara had her hands on her hips, picking herself apart in the mirror. It had been a long time since she wore a getup like this: cowgirl boots, jean skirt, and a bikini top hidden under a tied sleeveless flannel. This was topped only by her seagrass cowgirl hat with a silver and turquoise decorated leather band. She had found it in an abandoned box from her last days in Gandersville. Some part of her still felt defeated, leaving a place only to be dragged back.

"Girl, turn that frown upside down." Brandye nudged her before adjusting her girls in her own bra. "We got some cowboys to herd."

"I don't know, Brandye," Clara sighed, sitting on her friend's bed. "It's been a long time since I wrangled a cowboy."

"Oh c'mon. You know what they say?" She pulled Clara off the bed, and they started out the door to the old pickup.

"What do they say?" Clara climbed in through the creaking passenger door and slammed it shut. "Don't leave me hanging, Brandye-wine."

"Save a horse." She winked, bringing the truck into a roaring rumble. "Ride a cowboy."

They laughed.

The old truck bounced and hummed its way through the small neighborhood before finding its way to the two-lane countryside highway. Clara stared aimlessly at the passing fields and cattle. Unlike the city, it was boring and lacked all the finesse. Worse, she couldn't disappear into the crowds or hide in a café from gawking eyes.

"Clara, you alright girl?" Brandye glanced over at her. "You've been quiet, too quiet. In fact, I'm still salty about you not letting me know you returned to town weeks ago. I had to hear it from Suzie's mouth at the grocery store. Lord, that woman loves to gossip."

"Sorry, I just..." Clara's shoulders slumped, and she caught her exhausted face in the mirror. "I feel old and used up."

"Well, that's why we're headed to the rodeo." She nudged her arm. "Plenty of eye candy and prospects to rustle in the hay. You're a single woman again! Let's find you someone to fuck!"

Clara's face flushed. Her mind still savored the way Jakob had taken her on the stairs, the heat of his hands, the way... *No. Nope. I can't be falling for Jakob. Again. Falling for him is like dropping an anchor in this one-horse town.*

"Why are you blushing?" They were hitting traffic now with the rodeo stadium coming into view. "Don't tell me you hooked up with someone?"

"Maybe." Clara covered her mouth, hiding her smile. "It was just a quick hookup."

"And you're not going to tell me?" Brandye turned the old truck in the direction of where the parking guide had pointed. "Spill the beans, girl!"

"Nope. Last thing I want is for Suzie to tell half the town who I opened my legs for." Clara's brow furrowed as the truck pulled into a spot. "What does Suzie do?"

"She's the dispatcher at the sheriff's station." Brandye shuffled around for her purse. "You okay? You look like you're turning green on me."

Clara grabbed Brandye's purse from under her seat. "She works with ... the sheriff?"

"Yeah." She motioned for Clara to hand it over. "Hard to believe Jakob, the bull rider bad boy, would become the sheriff, right? I heard he was at your place because... wait a damn minute. Don't tell me you and the sheriff... again? Clara, you've got to be kidding me!"

Clara removed the flask of whiskey from Brandye's purse and shoved the green pocketbook toward her. "Not another word."

The liquor burned as she took a swig, wanting but failing to wash Jakob from her mind. Brandye took it back, taking her own gulp before returning it to her bag. The security guard waved them through the bag checker, giving them a wink as he ignored the flask.

They began walking around the staging area with stalls of horses and corrals of bulls and broncos. As far as one could see, Clara's eyes fell on young and seasoned bull riders of all kinds. Luckily, Brandye still had access since she'd gone from a barrel racer to Quarter Horse breeder.

The announcer blared across crackling speakers, "Next up is a real treat, a local favorite."

"Crap, we got here late," Brandye huffed, pulling Clara along to see the unfolding ride. "I swear he calls everyone a local favorite."

"He hasn't been here at Silver Spurs Rodeo for ten years."

Clara paled at the words. "Did he really quit after I left?"

"Who quit what?" Brandye and she found a spot at the railing so they could see the ring unobstructed.

A buzzer went off and a gate banged open. A black, angus bull launched out, a rider in headgear, jeans, long sleeve shirt on top, and a hand on the rope. The massive beast made the ground tremble under Clara's feet. Throwing a hand high, torso shifting to balance as the bull twisted under him with stunning speed, hind legs in the sky.

The rider looked like a jaguar clinging to its prey.

"Jakob," Clara whispered.

The timer flew, the golden eyes glinting under the mask. He lay against the slanted spine before rocking forward. Clara's body flushed with desire as she followed his movements. The bull spun and he started to slip. Again, the bull spun the other way, and Jakob lost his position on the bull's shoulders.

"That's our local sheriff! Ya'll, give him a shout!"

At that, Jakob shook his hand free. The bull rocked forward. Clara's breath caught. Horns were frighteningly close. Jakob's body twisted, dodging as he slid off. Landing on his feet, he ran for the closest gate and scrambled, up and over. He'd always been quick, like a cat landing on his feet. A strange calm came over the bull as if relieved the predator had left.

"Good Lord that man can ride," Brandye declared, pulling away from the gate. "C'mon Clara, let's go find some fun."

Clara followed, her eyes glancing at the fence one last time. He would be pulling off the helmet, sweat soaking his shirt. Jakob would shake off the long-sleeve flannel, grabbing a wifebeater or going bare. She bit her lip. This wasn't why she came, and he wouldn't know she was there like in the past, when they'd sneak off and...

Shaking her head, she cleared her mind of Jakob, instead focusing on the eye candy walking across their path.

Clara smirked. "Hey, cowboys."

It didn't take much to get their full attention. The two cowboys were lean and a little younger. Chaps, spurs, and cowboy hats only added to their sexy broad shoulders and chiseled jaws. Clara flashed a toothy grin, placing a hand on her hip. They returned the motion with their own smiles, relishing their full attention as the blue-eyed hotties took inventory of her body.

"What brings you to the rodeo today?" Clara lifted an eyebrow, the silver and gold belt buckles showing these boys had won at least first or second place at some point.

"Bronco riding. I thought you knew I rode now, Clara," the taller one replied, baffled. "I suppose it's been a while; I was still in the junior bareback division when you ran off and got married."

"Barrett?" Clara paled, glaring at Brandye.

Her friend was gasping for air, tears welling in her eyes as she laughed. "Did you just hit on my little brother?"

Face flushing, Clara bit her tongue. *I'm definitely too old to be hunting for ass in this place. How the hell did that goofy looking kid become so handsome?*

"I thought the bronco riding was still happening?" Brandye straightened herself again.

"Well, one of the bronco's broke a leg. They had to tranquilize the poor thing. They're waiting for the x-ray results to see if he's salvageable for breeding."

"Was the rider okay?" Brandye's fun had spoiled at the news. "The horse didn't roll over them?"

"I'm fine. Sprang an ankle trying to hop off and clear the way." Barret glanced at Clara, then back to his sister. "Are you guys back at it again? Aren't you a little old for that now? Paul will get jealous if..."

"Hush! I'm here for Clara, not me," she shushed.

"And you railed me about not saying anything." Clara crossed her arms. "Paul? Really? The guy from the neighboring ranch?"

"We both love horses?" Brandye shrugged, wincing at the heated glare.

Clara had heard enough. She spun on her heel, marching for the stalls. Not only was it the place to hook up, but a place she had come to resolve her past. This was the part she missed. The ability to go someplace quiet in an instant. Satisfied no one had chased after her, she slowed, she walked down the next lane. Concrete floors and steel I-beams held up the aluminum roofing overhead. Hay and sweet feed was a contrasting scent from the manure and sweat of the ring.

I'm stuck. I can't leave this place for some ungodly reason. All of this just reminds me of everything I failed to escape and... and... Jakob. I went with George to escape here, but I left him here and now...

She stopped, clenching her jaw, fighting her building anxiety. Tears were threatening to fall. Her chest ached. *I hate every part of why I'm here, back in this shitty cowpoke town. Who am I kidding?* Inhaling deep, she held it. She repeated this, calming her nerves. Regaining her composure, she began marching forward, aiming to walk it off. The animals were quiet. Last time she visited, the horses were eager to have their noses petted and checked her for treats. She swiveled her head, curious as to what on earth would cause the behavior.

The stall door swung open. Yellow eyes connected with hers, wide with equal surprise. Jakob rubbed a red line from his chin. Dread filled his face. Chills shook her body.

Is it wrong I feel happy to see him, even in my most vulnerable moments?

8

RUSTLE IN THE HAY

Standing over the horse, Jakob lost his appetite as the body started to grow cold. The poor thing had broken a leg mid-ride. In this industry, it was almost an instant death card. Being around all the livestock had added to the unusual hunger Jakob had been recently fighting. When the owner had pulled him to the side, the veterinarian had said there was no way to fix the leg. At that, they had turned to the local sheriff to put the animal down. The bronco had met him with calm, the jugular pulsing in his gaze. He couldn't say no to a personal favorite meal, and he'd taken his fill, lulling the horse to a peaceful death.

As he stormed out of the stall, he heard a yelp.

"Shit." Jakob's heart clenched, his belly warm with horse blood as he wiped his mouth. "Clara?" He slammed shut the stall behind him, hiding the dinner he had taken for himself. "Dammit, you need a bell or something."

Clara's breasts heaved, the scent of her making him hard. He hadn't imagined he'd ever see her in her hat and boots again. But here she was. And she looked so damn good. His eyes met hers and he could see it, that broken look. It pained him to see it. *Fucking George. She's like a caged, beaten animal now.*

"What are you doing?" Her words switched to defensive as her face flushed.

Jakob smirked. "I was about to ask you the same, Clara."

She puffed out her cheeks, brushing locks of her hair from her shoulder. "Clearing my head."

He raised an eyebrow. "And here I thought you were waiting for a bull rider for some fun."

"Maybe." Clara shrugged. "So, who did you hook up with?"

He frowned. "They asked me to put down the bronco. Vet said he couldn't do anything."

Clara winced. "Sorry, I assumed you… never mind. I've got better things to do than argue with you."

She shook her head and started to walk by him. Lustful wants rattled him. He only took a few long strides to catch her by the arm. She turned with a fiery glare. Her mouth opened to fuss, but he locked lips with her. Gliding his hand across her bare stomach, he slipped under her shirt, groping her breast. She stumbled backward, trapped between him and a stall door.

Her hot fingers worked to claw their way under his wifebeater, riding over his muscled stomach, then travelling to the planes of his back. She moaned as he sucked on her tongue and his free hand started to work her jean skirt up. He placed a knee between her thighs locking her in place. She arched into him, and he pinched her nipple. Another moan and she lashed her tongue out, coaxing his own to enter her mouth.

If she's really up to her old games, then I already know what's waiting under her skirt.

Jakob's hand glided over her bare ass. His smile broke their kiss, and she buried her face in his shoulder. Her hands worked at his belt buckle. His cock throbbed against his jeans; he enjoyed how ravenous he was at her lust. Their heat in their bodies rose with arousal, their desire forgetting all rational thought.

He licked at her ear and goosebumps washed over her skin.

"Dammit, I can't believe I like that," she huffed into him.

At last, his cock was free and in the heat of her soft hands. She stroked him, her thumb firm against the underbelly of his shaft. He moaned as he suckled on her earlobe. Another shiver rattled over her, and he replied with a twist of her nipple. She bit her lip, stifling the urge to shrill in delight. Jakob always loved how she reacted to rough whims.

"Tell me, are you still looking for a bull rider to fuck?" His voice came out, low and husky.

"N-no," she whimpered as he groped her breast tight and rocked his hard dick into her hands. "I found one."

"But you haven't asked me what I want," he teased and kissed her neck.

Circling a thumb on the tip of his cock, she leaned into him, her lips tickling his ear. "You ready to take me for a ride, cowboy?"

His hands abandoned their position. Yanking up on her skirt, he grabbed and lifted her legs up on his hips and slid inside her. She arched, gasping as he ground against her. The stall creaked and shook as he used it to keep her in place. Jakob steadied her with one hand, letting her leg fall as it tippy-toed to meet the height he had risen her to. The other gripped the stall door, clawing into it. He suckled and nibbled at her neck.

I've never felt so hungry for someone before.

She wrapped her arms around his neck, embracing him. A whimper escaped her, and his hunger for her rose. Her nipples hardened under the bikini, and it made his excitement peak. The way her body reacted to his egged him to rock into her faster as her warmth tightened around his cock. She was wet and hot, growing more so with each push and pull. A moan escaped him, his blood rushing.

I haven't messed around in the stalls like this since... Grunting, he pulled away from her. A sobering coldness hit him.

"Why the hell did you stop?" Clara panted, leaning against the stall gate.

Jakob's mind reeled. "I can't do this again. Not with you."

History is repeating itself. Dammit, she's not looking to be with me.

He started to march away, tucking himself into his pants. Clara caught up to him, straightening her skirt. She called his name, but he refused to look back. He could smell her salty tears and it made his chest ache. Ten years ago, it was all about her. He'd wanted to win her, to beat George Worcestershire, but he had convinced himself it had been false love. When she left, his life stopped. He'd given up bull riding, unable to see the ghost of memories of how many times they had snuck off into these very stables.

Shit, I even sold my truck because her scent still lingered inside it. I'm smitten with her, but I'm just a good time for her and I can't bear to do this all over again. Fucking keep it in your pants, JR.

"Dammit, Jakob!" She ran out in front of him, shoving him with her palms. "Don't fucking do this to me! Not now!"

Their eyes locked and he reflexively charmed her. "Fuck!"

Clara stood there, unable to move, waiting with an eerie calm for his command. He searched his pockets and cursed. The sunglasses had been misplaced, yet again. Looking over at her, he didn't want to leave her in a trance like this. Covering his mouth, his tongue licked the point of a fang and hunger washed over him. He was unsatisfied, both in lust and blood.

A shudder shook his shoulders. *I'm a monster. What does it matter if I push my luck?*

"Clara, do you love me?" he swallowed.

"Yes, but..." her voice trailed off, too exhausted to finish.

"But?" he tensed.

"I fucking hate this small town."

He inhaled, turning away to digest the answer. It was a dick move, charming the truth from her, but he had to know. He *wanted* to know. This whole time she had been so hellbent on leaving Gandersville to the point she took the only opening she thought she had. His stomach knotted, the truth ripping through him.

Maybe she knew I'd just root myself here. Fuck, and now I'm the damn sheriff! Just my damn luck.

"Fucking curse," he muttered, leaning on his knees. "Could I really just let it all go for her?"

"Don't." Clara's arms wrapped around him; she had broken free of the charm sooner than expected. "Don't you dare throw your life away for trash like me."

Anger tore his insides. "Never say that again."

"Jakob, I regret not giving up on George. It was a shit deal from the start, and it only sent me back here, back to you and..."

Her words were lost on him. A wave of drowsiness hit Jakob as the word tilted. The adrenaline in his system had died down, allowing the horse blood to hit him at last. Grabbing Clara by the arm, he had to keep it going, stumbling as he went. Pulling her into an empty stall, he began kissing her again. She responded, working his pants back open. Neither of them had wanted the moment to end as it had.

Pulling away, he untied the knot on her shirt. He pulled her bikini top under her breasts and wrapped his lips around a nipple. She had freed his hard cock and frantically pulled her skirt back up to give him access. He slid back into her heat as her back connected with the back wall. He moaned into her breast, and she pulled at his lower back, urging him to stay close as she rocked against him. Her legs shook and the adrenaline started to kick in, the tranquilizer wavering.

Fuck, it will take me forever to come with this in my system. Good thing Clara's known for her voracious libido.

9

SNARED

Clara's body was on fire. The heat of him added to her flames as they ground against each another. Goosebumps rose on her skin as the tip of Jakob's tongue teased her swollen nipple between his lips. She clung to him like life depended on it. He hadn't released her, after all this time, even when she'd abandoned him in that old pick-up ten years ago.

Her breath caught. *He's so rock hard. How the hell is he teetering on the edge like that?*

She ached from the pleasure of being with him. Long, fast, and hard strokes made her body tremble with ecstasy. A purring rattled from his chest, adding to the erotic moment. He abandoned one nipple and moved to the next. She wriggled against the stall wall, making her shoulder blades ache as she failed to fully arch her back.

Sensing her discomfort, Jakob wrapped his arms around her and pulled her away from the wall.

Jakob shed the wifebeater and abandoned his jeans. Clara followed his lead, wiggling out of her skirt, then tossing her boots and cowgirl hat to the side. After watching her untie the bikini top and letting it fall to the ground, he rushed her like a hungry animal. His hands gripped her waist and lifted her with ease. He placed her on a long, wooden saddle stand and her heart fluttered. The horn nudged her back, making her arch. Pulling her legs over each shoulder, he slid her up on the cantle.

He's been wanting to do this to me for a long time and...

His tongue slid across her like hot silk. She hummed as he ran it across her swollen folds a second time. His fingers gripped her thighs, keeping her legs parted as she took in another stroke of his tongue. Her hands frantically fell behind her, steadying herself on the stand. A gasp escaped her as his tongue slid inside her. Biting her lip, she knew the rule was utter silence, adding to the tension and pleasure.

Dammit, I can't move. I'm going to scream at this rate! We'll be caught!

The saddle made it impossible for her to move. He licked upward and found her clit and began to suckle it. Her thighs ached as his fingers kept her from teetering off or closing around him. Her body shivered. In the past, he had been relentless with the way he played with her body. Tonight, he had at last removed every bit of her dominance. His tongue slid across the front of her pussy, and he began trailing kisses across her hip and ribs.

Her breathing staggered; the sensations boiling through her made her ache to have his cock inside her once more. The stubble of his chin tickled as his lips left a trail between her breasts. As he crested over her collarbone, two fingers entered her, and she tightened in response. His tongue licked across her neck and suckled. Stroking between her thighs, her legs couldn't slow him down. Rough and intoxicating. Teeth grazed her neck, adding to her building orgasm.

"Faster," she panted.

He obeyed, biting her neck harder.

"Rougher," she commanded.

And he did. Fangs broke skin as he twisted his wrist, rubbing her in a sweet spot. She peaked, arching her back. His arm slid under her, the other still stroking hard and fast inside her. Suckling at her neck, he growling as she hummed. Clara's eyes rolled back; her thighs wet with her climax. His fangs lightened their hold, and he licked her neck. She was breathless.

"You taste so amazing," he huffed into the crook of her neck. "Was I too rough?"

"More," she panted. "Don't stop. I want more of you."

Her hand found his chest and slid downward. His cock was still rock-hard, and she began stroking him. Meeting his gaze, his eyes were that of a reptile, yellow with slits for pupils. It added to her lust. Something red painted his bottom lip as he weighed her words.

He's a monster and I want him to keep fucking me.

"Clara, I don't know if I can come," he confessed, turning her on the saddle so her feet touched the ground. "Look, I need you to know..."

She melted, kneeling so she could lick his throbbing erection. He lost his words, leaning on the saddle stand as she took him inside her mouth. Her lips ached with the girth of his dick. Rubbing her tongue on the soft shaft, she deep throated him, over and over again. Each time the tip of his dick rode down the back of her throat, he'd throb and moan. She sucked long and hard until her cheeks ached with effort.

Breathless, she took a moment of leave, stroking him with both hands. Looking up, she locked eyes with him. He panted, the fangs in his mouth only adding to her desire to have him eat her alive. She ran her tongue up and down his shaft, suckling on occasion to add to his agony. Sweat glistened on their bodies, the night air cooling and his breath steaming from his lips like a draconic beast.

"Fuck me," she begged. "Fucking come on me or in my ass, but fuck me with this, please."

Again, she ran her tongue against his length. She started suckling on the tip of his penis, her lips sliding to the edge of the cap and back again. Huffing, he looked pained for a moment. Another large puff of steam left him, his yellow eyes bright with hunger.

"Stand up and bend over the saddle."

He shuddered in anticipation as her hands slid up his thighs. She wanted to feel all of him under her hands, riding over his hips, waving over his torso, before cupping his jaw. A deep kiss lingered between them, but his hands stayed firm on the saddle stand. She sucked on his bottom lip, the iron on his tongue strange and alluring. He watched her with hungry eyes, then she bent over.

Clara spread her stance, bending provocatively until her breasts pressed against the saddle. At last, his hands abandoned the stand. Starting at the base of her neck, one hand trailed down her spine like hot wax. The heat of his hand spilled over her ass and fingers dove back inside her. She moaned, leaning into his stroking. He retrieved them, the tip of his dick pressing against her swollen lips. He slid inside, slow and deep.

Christ, his dick is so damn big and hard.

She wiggled, giving him just enough room to glide all the way in, his hips tight against hers. He pulled slow and steady, teasing her as he nearly pulled out, only to dive back in with the same agonizing speed. She squeezed around his cock, wanting him to stay inside her, wanting to ride him and please herself until she couldn't contain the feeling anymore. His hands gripped her hips, continuing to rock, in and out, faster and faster.

She let out a tiny gasp as his balls slapped against her clit, still tender from his sucking.

Jakob towered over her, grinding her with relentless drive. The saddle stand threatened to topple over with each connection. Clara's resolve wavered as yelps escaped her with each erogenous rush. He pushed hard against her, his body laying heavy on top of her now. His tongue slid over her shoulder, and he nuzzled her ear.

"Will you finally give me permission to go all the way this time?"

Exasperated, she tried to glance back at him. He bit her shoulder then licked the spot. This was a side of him she had almost seen in the past, a predator enjoying his meal, slow and ravenous all in a single stride. The tip of his cock pushed against her back door. She leaned into him, forcing the tip to enter further.

"Last time I tried this, you nearly clawed my eyes out," he laughed, daring to press further inside.

"I missed out on something incredible." She pushed against him, forcing him to slide in deeper. "I'm tired of us pulling away before either of us are through. Fuck me like you've always wanted, like I've been needing you to fuck me since that night."

He pressed hard into her, and she yelped, "You're not asking a cowboy to ride you anymore. You're wanting the bull to mount you, own you, make you mine."

She arched her back, rocking against his aching loins, *daring* him by saying, "Then show me the difference."

His hips rocked. "I won't be gentle, Clara."

"Good, I'm tired of being treated like a porcelain doll," her voice shrilled.

"I won't stop, even if you beg me." His hands were like fiery snakes riding over her hips and up the sides of her torso. "You're going to meet your match."

"Fucking prove it."

She tried to stand, but a hand rushed to the back of her neck, pushing her firmly against the saddle.

"Didn't you hear me?" Jakob's voice came out in a low, animal-istic rumble. "You're mine. You want me to let loose, to fuck you how I've wanted since the day we first came back here, in this very stall? Your scent haunted me when you left. Wrecked me, like I'm going to wreck you. I want you to claw at my flesh, cry my name in pleasure, and beg for me to let you go only to come crawling back for more."

"I want that! I want all of that and so much more."
Holy hell, I shook him and I'm about to get the fucking of my life.

10

RIDING THE BULL

Jakob could feel himself slipping deeper into his Chupacabra instincts. The scent of her was haunting and delightful, like a slice of peach rolling across his tongue. The taste of it sweet and savory on the air only added to his wants. He didn't want to drink blood; he simply wanted to mate with her until he exhausted himself. The horse tranquilizers were easing off, Clara's blood invigorating and freeing him from it. He'd never tasted human blood before tonight, but he only wanted hers for the rest of his life. He throbbed in her warmth, a low growl rolling through him, and she tightened.

Jakob tightened his grip on her neck. "You've ruined me," he said as she shuddered with delight.

"Don't stop." She rocked her body against him. "F-faster."

A growl drummed through him, scales surfacing in blue and silvery patches. "Beg me."

"Fuck me faster," she panted, her legs trembling.

"Say my name," his voice hissed in her ear. "Prove that it's me that you want."

The rhythm of his rocking hips against her made her tighten with each push. She couldn't stop the orgasms rising with each motion, keeping her from finding her voice as she gasped. Hearing the choked attempts to scream his name delighted him. Her body was hot, slick under his torso. His free hand slid back across her hip, forcing its way between her wet thighs. She shrieked as his fingers rubbed her pussy, circling her clit with sodden fingertips.

I want to cum, but I want her to beg for it first.

"You done yet?" He pushed hard and deep into her, his fingers sliding inside her. "You know what I want. Say my name."

"J-Ja." Breathless, she still defied him as she rocked her hips. "Jakob! Don't you dare stop."

Impatience rattled him. He released her neck, swooping an arm under her and forcing her to stand as he continued thrusting from behind. Her legs shook, and he denied her the support of the saddle or its stand. His fingers stroked in and out of her, his arm hugging her against him as he groped her breast with the other. Clara squirmed, reaching out for the saddle, only to have him pull her back. Walking backward until the stall door rattled against his back, Jakob stayed where she couldn't reach anything else. He leaned back on the door, tilting her into his own, cuddling her.

"Beg me to finish," he growled.

"N-No."

Nuzzling at her neck, he found the wound where he'd bitten her. Hungry, he licked at it, willing it to bleed once more. With Jakob suckling her neck, goosebumps rolled across her skin like a breeze on a lake's surface. She moaned again, tightening on his fingers.

"I want on top," she fussed. "Let me on top, please."

He ignored her as her hands cupped his own where he stroked her pussy and pushed into her ass. "Beg me to finish."

"Jakob, fucking let me on top." It was her turn to growl. "Jakob, please!"

He released her. She spun. Pushing down on his shoulders, she didn't seem phased by the slitted, yellow eyes, fangs under his lips, or the patches of scales. Her want for him was as feral as his own and he groaned. Sliding to the ground, the stall door banged with their movements. She straddled him.

Biting her lip, she let him slide back into the warm tightness of her backdoor. Locking eyes, he throbbed inside her and she began rocking on his hard cock. Bracing herself with one hand on his shoulder, the other dove between them and she played with herself. She moaned, staring into his eyes with a hunger he had thought only he was capable of feeling. Gripping her hips, he rocked with her, allowing them to push and pull with deeper strides.

"Do you love me?" She narrowed her eyes. "Tell me Jakob."

The question made him throb, nearing his peak. "I fucking love you. Always have."

"Fucking come for me, Jakob." Her body stiffened, an orgasm building in her body. "Please, come for me. I want you to come for me, Jakob!"

Wrapping his arms around her, his lips wrapped around a nipple, sucking long and hard, he ground in and out, fast and hard. A moan erupted from deep at his core and he peaked, hard and stiff inside her. Another moan and he released her breast and tilted his head back. He reached his climax, and she clawed into his shoulders and rocked on him, keeping his orgasm riding out longer than he'd ever know was possible.

When he couldn't take it anymore, he pulled her back to him, kissing her deeply. She stilled, the tension in their bodies fading as they released numbing pleasure from their bodies. She cuddled into him, shivering as the cold air around them crept over, their fires dying. She nuzzled his chest, both of them left breathless and panting.

"Christ, I didn't think you'd ever come," she laughed into him, and he scoffed.

"I almost thought you'd fuck me into eternity."

Her face heated against his chest. "Thank you."

Inhaling deeply, he leaned his head against hers and asked, "For what?"

"For loving me, despite it all."

"I could say the same."

Pulling away, she cupped his jaw and searched his eyes. "What are you?"

Scales had started to recede, but he couldn't deny this. Not anymore. "You wouldn't believe me if I told you."

"I don't fucking care." She kissed his lips, hard. "All I know is that you know how to fuck a girl and fuck her right."

Jakob laughed. "Sometimes I wonder which of us is the bigger monster in this small town."

Without warning, she stood and started picking up her clothes. He stared at her, confused. Clara wiggled into her skirt, circled once, found her bikini top, and tossed him his pants. Jakob's heart skipped a beat, the past drowning him with what would come next. Stumbling to his feet, he started to pull his legs into his pants, watching her.

"Why rush to leave?" He couldn't hide the panic in his voice.

She put her cowgirl hat on. "I can't let them find me here with you," she said, picking straw from her hair.

"Why not?" He glared at her, lost in his anger.

"Are you fucking kidding me?" She slipped on a boot and tossed him his wifebeater. "If this small town learned the town whore fucked the sheriff, both of us will have hell to pay."

"Clara, I won't keep this a secret."

Slamming on her other boot, she was on her feet, across the stall with a nail poking into his chest. "I left this shit ten years ago. If you let it slip, it'll make the front-page news. And..."

"And what?" His chest heaved as he bowed over her. "So what if the town knows?"

Her face reddened. "You don't get it."

She shoved past him, her voice cracking.

There it is. She can't hide and she hates herself. Seeing and hearing it from the gossipers eats her alive. "Do you even care about how I feel?"

She stopped at the stable door, refusing to turn and look at him. "You better not leave town this time."

Shoving the door open, she murmured, "My wings are already clipped."

Jakob's heart pounded with anxiety. After all of that, the confessions of love and seeing a glimpse of his true nature, she still chose to run. He leaned against the saddle stand, lost. She had done this that faithful night of her bachelorette party. Every time he made any ground with her, she ran. He didn't understand it, the fear of loving someone for real. Her love for George Worcestershire was like a royal wedding, but their affair had been kept secret.

What happened? Did I do or say something to make you act this way?

A hushed whisper and crackle of his radio brought him back to who he was, who she hated: the small-town sheriff.

"You there, Sheriff Regadera?" Suzie's voice sputtered across the silence.

Reluctant, he walked over and answered, "Yeah. What is it?"

"We need someone to come fill in the nightshift," Suzie demanded.

"What happened to old Bill?" He leaned on the table, shooting a dirty glare at his uniform shirt. "It's his turn; I'm at the rodeo."

"I told him that, but he's got crutches, Jakob," she whined. "It's Friday night and you know that someone's going to have to go sort things out at 8 Seconds."

He hung his head in defeat. "Give me time to shower. I'm a mess, Mrs. Suzie."

"Just make it out there before the first fight breaks out."

He dropped the radio and began pacing the stall like a caged tiger. Flashes of the last several minutes still rolled through his body. Swallowing, he looked back to the tack table. He had left everything there before his ride. It was bad enough he had bittersweet memories of Clara in this small space, but her scent was everywhere, on *him*. Anger coursed through him, and he kicked the saddle stand across the stall. Every fiber in his body seethed with hurt and self-hatred.

Fuck. I'm back to where I started ten years ago. I don't know who I hate more: Clara or myself.

11

8 SECONDS

Clara sat silently in the passenger seat. Brandye glared over. All attempts to weasel an answer had failed. She made it clear it was time to go and go now. Without further prying, they'd loaded up and left, the rodeo lit brightly in the darkness of the countryside and the roar of locals cheering on the riders.

Clara spotted another stray piece of hay in her hair and pulled it out.

"Are we going to talk about what the hell happened to you?" Brandye lifted an eyebrow, twisting her lips. "Bite marks, hay... really, Clara?"

"Nope." Clara shot her a cautionary look. "I got what I came for and now I want to go home."

"Oh no we don't." Brandye turned, placing distance between Clara and her rundown shit-shack.

"Brandye-wine," she huffed. "Take me home. Please."

"Don't tell me you don't need a drink." Her eyebrows raised high.

Clara forced a smirk. "Yeah. I need a few drinks."

Leaning back into the seat, she stared up at the roof. Her body was still hot and buzzing as the phantom touch of Jakob's hands on her body made her shudder. She would have continued if they hadn't exhausted themselves. Closing her eyes tight, she shoved him from her mind. Echoes of the past sent a tidal wave of regret, the weight of it smashing down on her. Years ago, she had convinced herself she'd be settling for Jakob, but instead, she had settled with...

"Shit." She leaned forward, pained by the realization. "Have you ever looked back and wondered why the hell you thought something was a good idea?"

"Oh yeah." Brandye pulled into the parking lot, the truck squeaking to a stop. "And I just make an excuse. Then it's time for a glass of wine or an old fashioned to remind me I will do better next time."

"What if you fucked over your next time?" Clara climbed out and followed Brandye to the line at the door of the club. "Like royally fucked up the only second chance you had?"

Brandye narrowed her eyes, weighing each word. "You better hope you're just meant to cross paths and be together then."

"ID's?" The bouncer maintained a neutral expression as he scanned their licenses into the machine. "Hands."

They held up their fists, a blue stamp saying, *8 Seconds Bar & Dance Hall,* were smudged across them. Inside, the smell of stale cigarette smoke still lingered in the building, despite changing over to non-smoking ages ago. Neon signs from ales and beers glowed above the bartender stations throughout the dark warehouse. In the back, line dancers were mid-swing in a cult classic, *Boot Scootin' Boogie,* as Brandye dragged her through the crowd.

Leaning on the bar, she managed to grab a seat and wait for her drink. She didn't care what Brandye ordered; she just wanted to get hammered. A flash of Jakob's fingers gripping her hips crossed her mind, and she turned to the bartender to escape it. He slid an old fashioned to her, and she started chugging. All she wanted was to drown, to forget she'd let her guard down, that *he'd* let his guard down. Nothing in her life had felt more real than those moments in the stall, and she had abandoned it.

I'm a monster. He loves me and I can't accept it. What the fuck is wrong with me?

Brandye turned to face her and blinked. The glass emptied and clunking on the bar top, she tilted her head at Clara. Ignoring her friend's cautionary glare, she waved the bartender back. An old fashioned wasn't strong enough to forget the lustful vibrations still shaking her core.

"Two Sambucas," Clara announced. *Need to get shitfaced. I don't want to remember our time together. It'll only keep hurting.*

"That's some hard shit. You don't have to get me a shot." Brandye sipped on her own old fashioned.

"They're both for me." *Faster, stronger, drunker, longer... Ha! Daft Punk has nothing on me!*

"What the hell happened?" Brandye choked on her drink, adding, "And who the hell did you hook up with?"

Clara took the first Sambuca in a single gulp. *Jakob. I can't resist him, I want him, he's... no fuck this. I need to get over him just like I got over Asshole fucking my so-called friend Sharon. Fuck you, Sharon.*

"Don't tell me." Putting her drink down, Brandye leaned in and whispered, "Did you go back there and fuck Jakob? Are you kidding me?"

Clara gave her a side glance, but the arriving second shot came and was gone. *If she weren't my real friend, I'd throw my drink across the bar. Jakob, of course with Jakob. You know I loved him. You caught us that night at my bachelorette party and never said a damn thing. You even asked if I wanted out of the wedding. You knew. And you were right. I fucking love him.*

"Clara!" Brandye rubbed her temples. "Are you out of your mind? If the town gets wind, fuck, if Geor..."

"Don't you dare mention that asshole's name." She spun, leaning back on the bar top, her body still warm from the alcohol. "I just need to find someone else to ride. After that, I'll be fine. Fuck Jakob. Fuck this town. Fuck... Trevor?"

Her eyes caught a familiar face. A grin crept across her face. She had her target. Standing, she wobbled as if hit by a rogue wave. Straightening, she took a minute to adjust her girls and fluff her hair. Hay flakes fell and she marched off, ready to take down her prey. He was chatting it up with some fellow fraternity boys as she closed the gap. She slid a hand up his bicep and shoulder, and he spun and paled.

"Miss Williams?" His momentary panic didn't faze her.

"Call me, Clara," she cooed, batting her eyes up at him. "Didn't think I'd run into you here of all places, Trevor."

He swallowed, releasing a nervous laugh. "Yeah, actually, I'm here with some friends."

She glanced at the other boys and winked. "Hi, friends."

"Look, Clara? I'm actually here with..."

Her scalp lit on fire as she stumbled backward, her hat falling to the floor as she was dragged. "What the fuck!"

"No bitch touches my man like that," she heard a female screech.

Gritting her teeth, she managed to spin herself into a more controlling pose, her hair obscuring her view. Seeing the cheap Wal-Mart flip flops as the cool outside air hit her skin, Clara unraveled. Reaching out, she grabbed a fistful of shirt and yanked the girl forward. Her grip faltered on Clara's hair, and she stood tall, drunk and fuming. Like the crack of a whip, Clara's palm connected with a makeup caked cheek. The College brat wide-eyed, ears ringing.

"Don't fucking touch me." Clara stood, unshaking.

The girl cupped her face, snarling as her hair loosened from its bun. "You bitch!"

She came at Clara, and her other hand snapped against the other cheek. "Try me."

Tears welled up and Clara smirked. The girl had challenged Gandersville's most notorious cat-fight champion. Nails were next and if the cops took too long, clothes would be ripped, and hair pulled out. The college girl recovered and tackled Clara, knocking the wind from her. But Clara didn't back down. Her claws were out, already scraping across the girl's back.

She retreated, flicking Clara the bird.

Clara hissed, a warning for her to back down.

Hands on hips, she stood proud in her drunken haze. Blue and red lights illuminated the back of the building like a disco ball. The siren had been silenced, announcing their arrival. She turned, too damn tried to run like the college girl. Chin high she watched as the truck came to a stop.

"Clara." Jakob's voice came the megaphone, bringing her a wave of nausea. "What did I say about starting trouble?"

He stepped out of the driver's side, his uniform in disarray. He hadn't bothered to button it. His mouth held a deep scowl, his eyes hidden under his sunglasses. She wasn't sure what he was waiting for. And she was too fucking drunk to run away. *Fuck it.*

Throwing out her arms, she inhaled deeply. "Come on. Arrest me." She raised her chin, too prideful to back down. "I'll let you cage me this time. You're welcome."

Snorting, he marched across the span and pulled her arms behind her. She closed her eyes; the cold steel handcuffs a harsh contrast to the heat of his hands. Biting her lip, she waited for the questions or fight she had put into motion, but it never came. She had abandoned him in the stalls, running from the idea of having a meaningful relationship.

"How much did you drink?" His voice dropped to a muttered rumble.

"Not enough."

Shaking his head, he helped her into the passenger side. "I'm taking you back to the station."

"I know." She refused to look at his face.

Getting into the driver's side, he flipped the lights off. "Is it so terrible to think we could…"

Jakob's words failed, and he ignored her the whole way back. Clara hated herself, hated that even now, neither of them could deny their mutual attraction.

Am I cursed? Are we both cursed?

12

JAILHOUSE

Clara's silence only added to Jakob's agony. There were many things he wanted to ask, but he knew she would never tell him. Glancing over, he saw that she had dozed off. Her head was cocked back and snoring. Sighing, he reached over and coaxed her until her head was in his lap. At least, she would be more comfortable. She nuzzled against his thigh, the smell of Sambuca and whiskey rising to his nostrils. He reached down to pull her hair from her face but stopped.

Last time I saw her this smashed, she'd been celebrating her bachelorette party.

"You didn't want to go, did you?" he muttered, heaving another sigh.

They had arrived at the station to find the building and parking lot completely empty. Pulling into the reserved spot by the door, he shut the truck off. He leaned on his steering wheel and looked back down to her. Her eyes were open, the blue visible in the dim glowing streetlamps. She searched his face, and he twisted his lips, waiting to see what venom she'd spew. *Here it comes. That folding of the brow, the parting of frowning lips.*

"How the hell can you see anything at night?" She rolled up, yawning, and stretching.

"Wait, what?" He stared at her back, licking his lips as he imagined her bent over a saddle. The idea sent a shiver through him. "I got us here wearing them, didn't I? What does it matter?"

Jakob steeled himself, ignoring the sudden rise of lust. He walked around and helped her out. She didn't say anything, stumbling as he guided her through the station. Pausing at the desk, he checked her skirt pockets. She laughed and muttered a slurred something under her breath, too difficult to decipher. Emptying the keys and her cellphone onto the desk, he led her into the containment cell. He let her sit before closing the sliding barred door. Sitting at his desk, he began writing his report.

Bing! He paused and glanced at her phone but returned to writing. A quick glance at the screen showed the text that popped up.

[BrandyeWine: Call me if you need a ride from the jailhouse again. Love you!]

None of my business.

He cleared his throat and tossed his sunglasses aside. Again, he started reviewing the reports and cursed old Billy for his shit writing and Suzie for overexplaining. Powering through, he took solace in the fact that he managed a small town and not a big city. A shiver rattled his shoulders. The report of the horse had been reported over the radio, and Suzie had jotted down the details. Jakob's eyes danced across the paper, reading the cursive as he covered his mouth. Glancing over, he saw that Clara had laid down on the bench and he hoped she'd fallen back to sleep.

A feral dog tore into the Hawthorne's bronco. She was in her stall for a broken leg. Poor Barret almost got rolled on by the horse when it happened. Anyhow, they called Doc Samson, but he had left...

Bing! Jakob skipped a line at the sound.

...he had left because Little Jenny's dog was having puppies. They got the X-rays and there's no saving a horse with a break in that many pieces, shattered like a broken vase. Well, we were trying to reach Jakob when...

Bing! Stopping, he looked over at Clara's phone, the texts still visible in preview mode.

[Tommy: Hey Sexy]

[Tommy: You ready for some fun tonight?]

He snorted, ignoring it, and continued to read.

...a hold of Jakob when crazy old Mr. Baker said the Chupacabra got to it first. There's no such thing; the boys think a coyote came in there and spooked before anyone found out.

"Well, Mr. Baker isn't as crazy as you think, Suzie." Jakob signed the paper and slid it away.

Bing!

[Tommy: Tell me what you're wearing? I'm betting it's those lacy black panties I love so much.]

Jokes on you buddy. She ain't got anything on under her skirt tonight.

Jakob twisted his lips, glaring at the screen. Drumming his fingers, he looked at Clara, then returned to her phone.

Who the fuck is Tommy?

Bing!

[Tommy: How about this: I'll show you mine if you show me yours?]

Narrowing his eyes, he grabbed the cell phone. He slid his finger across the screen, unlocking it, prompting a passcode. Raising an eyebrow, he smirked. Without fail, it was her birthday, and it took him promptly to the texts between Clara and Tommy. He began scrolling up, the sexting marathon unveiled. Heat flushed his face, sexy teaser pics and racy words sending him into a wave of lust and jealousy.

Inhaling deeply, he glanced over his shoulder, making sure she hadn't caught him. His thumbs flew over the keys as he typed.

[Clara: Not tonight. I'm busy.]

[Tommy: Busy? Don't make me beg ;)]

Jakob scoffed.

[Clara: I have better things to do.]

[Tommy: Better and bigger than this <DICK PIC>]

Jakob's jealousy flared. Rage consumed him, ceasing all rational thought. He unbuckled his belt and unzipped his pants, freeing his hardened length, which throbbed from Clara's provocative photos.

Click!

[Clara: Definitely bigger and better <DICK PIC WITH MIDDLE FINGER>]

"What the hell are you doing with my phone?" Clara's voice startled him, and he dropped her phone to the floor. "Jakob, give it back."

"Look, Clara, it kept ringing and..." He spun, standing.

"Were you fucking taking dick pics on my phone?" She blinked, glaring at his raging hard on, a smile filing her face. Shrugging, she laughed. "Granted, I wouldn't mind adding yours to the collection."

Spinning around, he tucked himself away. Grabbing the phone off the floor, he turned it off and tossed it on the desk. Jakob leaned against the tabletop, his emotions raging in his self-hatred. He waited for her to rail him further, crack the small-town sheriff jab or something else to remind him she couldn't accept him. Nothing. He looked over his shoulder, watching her as she turned away and marched back. Her boot slipped, her body still drunk and slow, and her head connected with the corner of the bench.

Jakob opened the cell door and flew to her side. She sat up, hissing as a rivulet of blood slid down her forehead. Something inside him shifted. He pulled her head to him and ran his tongue across the sweet aromatic liquid. The blood hot and thick on his tongue, he kissed the swollen knot forming, sucking on the wound for a moment. She sat still, calm even. Alcohol tinged in the flavor, riding down his throat as he swallowed, and Jakob jerked back.

"Clara..."

"Your eyes." She glared at him in awe. "Those golden eyes. I love them." He stood, reaching for his sunglasses, but she grabbed his arm, stopping him. "Don't leave."

He closed his eyes, feeling hopeless. "Clara, I can't risk charming you."

She laughed, gripping his shirt to steady herself. "You charmed me a long time ago. I have a feeling it doesn't last ten years."

He smirked. "I'm not that good."

"Stay here." Her hands relaxed, sliding to his jeans and unzipped them.

"Don't," he whispered, grabbing her hands, afraid to open his eyes. "We can't. Not here."

"You can't waste a hard-on like that." She pouted, shoving his hands off, letting her hot fingers wrap around his shaft. "Let me have some fun first."

"You're drunk." His heart raced, his resolve crumbling with each beat.

"And you just took a dick pic on my phone." She circled her tongue on the tip. "And that deserves a punishment."

"Well, I don't think Tommy liked that idea quite like you." He breathed, the wave of arousal drowning him. A flash of the picture with her fingers in her pussy made him moan. "Clara, stop. We can't do this."

She paused. "Open your eyes and make me stop."

He opened one golden eye and looked down at her. Licking his lips, he shut it and exhaled, long and slow. Nothing about this had anything but raw want driving it into the next ridiculous moment. Reaching one hand out, he found a bar to balance on. His shoulders relaxed in defeat. He wanted this as much as she did, and the idea that she'd rather suck on his cock than sext with Tommy gave Jakob satisfaction.

"That's what I thought."

Her wet, silken tongue connected with the top of his hard cock. Sliding him between her lips, she leaned into him and let his dick ride until he hit the back of her throat. She wiggled her head, letting him go a little deeper, tighter. As slowly as she'd taken his length in, she pulled out with the pop of her lips. Again, her tongue circled the head and repeated the agonizing deep dive into the wet heat of her mouth.

Jakob leaned into her, wanting to linger longer. The suckling made him moan as another pop of lips left him cold. Clara started trailing kisses from the tip to the base of his shaft. Fingertips kept his throbbing erection firm against her lips. Hints of her tongue and the occasional sucking of the tender underbelly made him weak in the knees. Something about the way she made love to his cock made him hungry to fuck her, just to end the teasing banter.

Her hands gripped his ass cheeks. Once more, he slid between her tight lips, to the silken road to the back of her throat. Another moan escaped him, and she began pushing and pulling. Shifting his stance, she followed. He braced himself against the bars of the containment cell.

His eyes cracked open, staring down at her as they locked stares. The pop of her lips on the tip of his dick made him grunt and shudder, again.

"Was wondering when you'd join the party," she smirked, running her tongue along his shaft. "I want to see your face when you come, Jakob."

He ran his tongue over his fangs and teeth. "Careful, or you'll make me nibble you again."

"Is that a promise?" she smirked.

Hell, yes.

13

TIME TO GO

Clara loved that look in his eyes, a mixture of admiration and desire, simple and raw. Jakob wanted *her*. And only *her*. That heavy-lidded glare said it all, and more, and it made her wet, knowing what he would do to her body. She made love to his throbbing cock, kissing the soft flesh deeply, passionately. Her mind wandered, questioning her own agenda and the events of the last few weeks.

I can handle settling down in this town as long as I have him.

Daring the golden eyes to watch her, she took him back into her mouth. Her cheeks ached with the effort, his moaning driving her to release one ass cheek and dive her hand between her thighs. The blow job had made her wet, throbbing to have him enter her once more. Her fingers inside her pussy, she moaned on his cock, and it throbbed in response. At last, his greed surfaced.

Thick fingers tangled and gripped the hair on her head. He thrust in and out of her mouth, the effort making her break from their stare. Her other hand fell away from him, joining the other under her skirt. Jakob was on the verge of coming, his dick hard as a rock as he rode across her tongue. Another moan as she circled her clit, her body still sensitive from earlier in the day. His grip tightened. The tip diving deep into the back of her throat. Both of them moaned as they peaked, her thighs wet as she swallowed the hot liquid.

Jakob pulled out slowly, a string of her saliva lingering between her lips and the tip of his dick. They locked eyes. Each of them panting still flushed from their orgasms.

BUZZ!

"Fuck!" Jakob squatted, shielding himself behind Clara, keeping his distance from the front door.

"W-what the hell is that sound?" Clara wiped her lips.

"Someone's coming through the front door." Jakob patted his shirt pockets. "Shit. Where did they go?"

Clara watched his rising panic, and without thinking, she cupped his jaw and kissed him. Her tongue dipped between his lips, rubbing against a fang before pulling away. She searched his face, the blue-grey scales were gone, and his eyes had returned to brown. He blinked at her, and it excited her knowing she could bring out and put away the beast of the Chupacabra with such ease.

"There," she whispered. "Your eyes are brown, and the scales have disappeared."

"T-thank you." He brushed her hair from her forehead, a bruise already forming. "You need to be home. That's gonna hurt in the morning."

"Oh, Jakob!" Suzie screeched. "Is that Clara Wor-Williams?"

"Hey, Suzie," Clara drawled.

Jakob stood, calm and reserved. "She slipped and hit her head."

Clara smirked; glad Suzie couldn't see her face. *Slipped on his dick and gave him head. Ha!*

"Oh dear." She entered the cell, erasing Clara's smirk. "Are you alright?"

"I'll live. I wouldn't be here if I hadn't started trouble at the bar. It's my fault really."

"Aren't you too old to be up to your old habits, young lady?" Suzie seemed as if time hadn't passed. The silver-haired woman in cat eyeglasses put her hands on her hip. "Jakob, you take her home. I'll lock up."

"Why are you here?" Jakob looked at the clock on the far wall. "And at almost three in the morning?"

"I forgot my pocketbook and just couldn't sleep thinking about it." She spun on her heel and grabbed a purse out of the front desk's largest drawer. "I advise you just to take the poor thing home. She's had it rough."

Clara blinked, stunned to hear her Ex's number one fan's pity.

"I just got wind what really happened in the city between you two." She sighed, her brow furrowing. "A real damn shame, but I hope you find someone worth keeping. Maybe Jakob might be a good option."

Clara's face heated. "Thank ... you?"

"Mrs. Suzie that's rather..." Jakob's face turned red and his eyes shot off to the side as if caught doing something. "You shouldn't assume..."

"Oh, come on, Jakob." She cackled, hands still on her hips. "You two have been giving each other puppy dog eyes since high school. I'm shocked I didn't catch you bending her over your desk just now."

Another wave of heat hit Clara's face. *Has it always been that obvious to the whole town? Why hadn't anyone said anything sooner? Why not pry and twist things like they always do with every aspect of my life? Had she missed something? Exactly how long has the damn town known about me and Jakob fucking on the side?*

Panic filled her face.

"Don't you look so shocked," Suzie laughed again. "Even a small town has its secrets, darlin' and we all secretly knew about you two.

Damn shame you didn't end up together. Pride is a terrible thing, but at least you're home where you belong."

Do I belong here? She looked at Jakob's pursed lips, his eyes flickering a hint of gold. She jumped to her feet. *What on earth has him shifting again?*

"Thank you, Suzie." Clara sidled to block Jakob from Suzie's prying eyes. "I didn't think... why didn't anyone say something?"

"About what?" Suzie pulled out her keys from her coat pocket. "You two sneaking off together?"

"Yeah." Clara knew if she turned the questions on the old woman, she'd rush off. "Normally shit around here is front page news."

"Honey, you've got much to learn." She shuffled for the exit, her back to them now. "No one comes between love and lust. People kill for money, for power ... and love. You don't mess with that hornets' nest."

With that, she disappeared, and Clara spun to face Jakob. His face was pale and gaunt. His eyes shifted to gold and he searched the air. Lips tight, he had that panic building in his face once more.

"It doesn't matter if they know," Clara shrugged, leaning against the bars.

"I don't care that they know about us, but..." He inhaled deep, steadying his nerves. "I can't shake the feeling they just might know about this." He motioned to his eyes. Clara bit her lip. "And why the hell has no one confronted me about it? They have to know, right?"

"Shit." *This whole time I didn't realize he had far more at risk staying here than I will ever fathom.* "Take me home," Clara said, redirecting the conversation. "We can talk on the way there."

He grabbed her hand and led her out of the cell, gathering their things at his desk. His jaw was set tight, eyes still glazed with the wave of thoughts drowning him. She followed, silent and measuring his every expression and movement. Suzie winked at them as he led her out, again a tight hand gripping hers. She was the only thing keeping him from losing it. Like always, he helped her into the passenger side, walked around, and sat. He froze.

"Can you drive?" Clara realized the weight of his situation crashing down on him.

He looked at her at last, his voice a mumble. "Did you hear how my mother died?"

Clara bit her lip, remembering the rumors. "She was shot ... for trespassing."

His eyes shifted to gold. "Yeah, but what I thought no one knew..."

"What really happened? Wasn't she a maid for the Worcestershire Estate?" Clara's chest swelled, the dots connecting, and she shared his building anxiety. "That fight between you and George in high school... don't..." A wave of nausea hit her. She leaned forward and covered her mouth. The untapped anger, the hurt in his face that she would be engaged and marrying. Tears welled up.

"He shot her. Caught her eating one of the old cows." He covered his face and took in an unsteady breath. "He fucking shot her. And left her out there. Not once apologized, not once gave a flying fuck. His dad saw it all, and they dragged me to the barn to *beat the beast out of me.*"

Another wave of emotions rolled through her, rattling her to her core. "The limp. Your limp is from..."

"You weren't the only one aiming to leave town, Clara." At last, he wrangled in his panic, starting the truck, and leaving the station far behind. "It was either the football scholarship or hoping I could join the PBR and compete regionally in bull riding. George knew that. I had confided in him. I though he was my friend."

Clara frowned, looking out the window, unable to face Jakob as she took it all in. *Yeah, he's really good at taking your dreams and choking you with them.*

"He broke the fucking bat over my shin." Anger rose in his voice. "And when he cornered me at the rodeo and rubbed it in my face, you were planning to elope and celebrating your bachelorette party…"

Clara's eyes widened, that night coming back. "You didn't do your last ride. That's why you were there before the rest." She turned to him, but he wouldn't meet her eyes as they turned down the last road toward the Worcestershire estate. "You didn't quit bull riding. You got suspended. And with your leg, football got fucked."

He pulled the truck to the door, shutting off the engine to look at her. "Sorry. I can't be the one to sweep you off your feet and take you away from here."

Clara glared around the property, thinking back to their youth, to the days she'd catch him shirtless, repairing the barn or sneaking off to fuck in the tool shed. Memories of his mother were blurry, fleeting. She didn't speak much English, but she had been kind, spoiling guests with homemade sweets and cold iced tea.

"Do you hate this place?"

"No," he whispered. "A lot of pride went into this heap. Mom loved it. And now someone I care about lives here."

She turned to him. He cupped her jaw and kissed her deeply and passionately. They pulled away, slow, still gazing at one another but with a new sense of self.

"I made a horrible mistake," Clara muttered.

"You wanted out."

"You were hurting, and I was too narcissistic to…" His lips pressed against hers, silencing her.

"You mind if I crash here? I've got an issue to take care of, to get out of my system."

He was getting out of the truck, and she scrambled to meet him by the headlights, resting her hands on his chest. "Where are you going?"

"It's a new moon." He shuddered, then his eyes began to glow. "It's the one night I can't control my shifting or running through the pastures."

She kissed him and his eyes calmed. "Stay with me, just a little longer. Until I fall asleep."

14

The Couch

Jakob couldn't say no to her, to that face. She pushed on his chest, and he allowed her to spin him around and prod him up the porch steps and through the door. The living room was bare besides the few boxes in a corner and a leather Victorian loveseat in the center of the room. Clara shut the door and slid the lock in place. He spun to face her, an eyebrow lifting high. She began to shed her clothes and he tilted his head.

"Clara, are you still drunk?"

Wiggling out of the skirt and pulling off her boots, she scoffed. "We both know I'm not belligerent and my buzz died the moment you arrested me."

"I'm serious. It's a new moon and control is..." She stalked across the space. "Clara, this is a bad idea. Even my parents limited..."

She shushed him, tugging off his uniform shirt and pulled up on his wifebeater. "You have to get naked to change, right, Mr. Chupacabra?"

He laughed, looking away in disbelief. "Yeah, but not like this. I don't usually need assistance from a hot, naked chick to make that part happen."

"Well tonight you do." She tugged on his wifebeater again and he caved, taking it off. "There, now let me help with this too."

Her skillful fingers worked until his pants fell away.

His face heated, agonizing over the new moon and his need to feed had hit a new level, including his sex drive. As a child, his father would get a hotel room for three days during the new moon. He always shrugged and frowned at Jakob, saying, *that's a dangerous night for me. Your mother could kill a man with stamina like that.*

"Aren't you exhausted?" Her hands were hot across his torso as she shoved him backward. "You've had quite the day. I mean, you and I, we've been at each other twice and…"

Another hard push and the back of his knees hit the loveseat. He sat. With his golden eyes, he didn't need lights to see her in the dark, to see her pink erect nipples and the goosebumps rippling across her body in a flurry of excitement. He throbbed, his desire to have her again made his blood boil. Her thighs slid across his lap, her hand stroking his erection as she leaned forward. The heat of her breath poured over him as her breasts pressed against his chest. He throbbed harder into her palm and her fingers tightened on his shaft in reply.

"If you're already tired, then let me handle it from here."

Her lips were hot on his ears as she sucked on his earlobe. The kissing trailed down to his neck, and he inhaled deeply, humming in pleasure. His fingers gripped the top of the back rest, leaning his head to encourage her to keep going. The heat of her body atop him sent his senses into overdrive. Scent and touch had become electrifying, adding to his building frenzy. Rocking his hips, he pressed his cock against the heat of her stroking hand.

The smell of her made him purr, taking it in and holding it. Heart racing, the tickling of her hair added to the way her thumb circled the tip of his dick. She shuffled, pushing his cock under the wet heat of her pussy, and sat slowly. He slid inside, her body tightening in greeting. She let out a moan, and he reached to kiss her neck, the urge to nibble and drink rattling his core.

"Not yet." Her voice was sultry as she shoved him back in place. "I'm in charge."

She bit his neck, nibbling. "Ouch. What was that for?"

"I thought that's what you're into now." Brushing her hair to one shoulder, she pointed at the fang marks.

Jakob licked his lips. "Careful. You do make me hungry."

Collapsing back into him, she nibbled his neck once more. He shifted, pushing his pelvis up to ride deeper inside her. Her teeth abandoned their play, moaning into his neck. Clara ground against him, arching back with her hands pressing down on his chest. Blue eyes glared down at him, holding him prisoner. Hot and tight, his cock throbbed inside her wet heat while her body rocked atop him, her breast swaying.

Each tilt of her hips made him grip the couch tighter. The wood creaked and cracked under the pressure. Claws popped through the leather. Jakob's body came alive, but he willed himself to indulge the swaying goddess on his lap. Fangs ached, a want for blood creeping forward. His eyes shifted to the bite mark and the flavor still fresh on his mind made him growl with want.

Clara's hand lifted, gripping his throat, demanding he meet her eyes. "Not yet."

She shifted and her pussy tightened on him. His breath caught, her pace changing, more aggressive. Fingers tightened on his throat, and he clawed into the leather. The growling grew in his chest. Her other hand trailed like searing wax trickling down his torso. He throbbed inside her, and she clamped tight, gasping. His eyes went to chase her hand to her pussy, and she leaned in, choking him. Wild and enthralled, his golden stare returned to the blue eyes. Her body gripping his cock tight, rubbing, and stroking his entire length.

"I want you to watch me come."

Jakob licked his lips, her body tensing, lifting and grinding down on him ever faster as she moaned. Her breath quickened. He could smell the rise of a coming orgasm. His claws slicing through the leather, balling into a fist on the shreds, fighting his want to feed on her, to overpower her.

"Are you hungry?"

His body tensed under her, and she smirked, slowing her rocking. A cold wake hit his neck where she had kept him at bay. Every muscle twitched in his body, fighting the desire to lunge forward, to sink his fangs into her so he may have another sampling of the sweet red nectar within her. Clara leaned back, her hands bracing against his knees. He took in her body, the plump breasts, the way her waist dipped just enough to break away into curvy hips. Her body throbbed around his dick, reminding him she had brought them to the edge of coming only to abandon it with reckless desire.

"Touch me," she commanded.

He released the leather tatters, his clawed hands gentle as they gripped her hips. Sliding her forward, he realigned with her, his cock diving deep again. She moaned and rocked slowly. Jakob licked a fang as his hands wandered up her body to grip her breasts. She tightened, and he responded by pinching her nipples. Her breath caught, and he twisted them, earning him a shriek. Again, her body throbbed around his dick, and it excited him to feel her react to him at every level. His hands snaked over her ribs and wrapped the arch in her back.

Caving to his hunger, he opened his jaws wide, fangs flashing. Clara rocked forward, her nails digging into his lower jaw, slamming him back. A growl escaped his lips, vibrating through her.

Her lips hovered above his, eyes searching as he hissed. "I didn't say you could eat," she warned.

His jaw ached from the hold. A shudder of rising arousal rolled through him. "I'm starving," he protested.

Grinding against him, her other hand slid between them. Fingers pressed against the base of his shaft, slick with her honey, curious to feel how he slid in and out of her. He gripped her ass cheeks, thrusting angry and hard against her. Her lips pressed firm onto his, breasts hot on his skin. Powerful strokes made her hum into his mouth, their tongues rubbing and diving, lapping out for one another. She caught his between her teeth and earned another growl from him. Her fingers between them tightened, demanding he keep going.

Pulling away, she leaned back, her grip on his jaw falling away. She went back to rocking on him, her nipples bouncing from the efforts of his pounding. Little yelps escaped her, his cock hard and engorged. Her eyebrows lifted high.

"Don't you dare come. I didn't say you could, Jakob."

Grunting, he slowed, agonized to fill her, to have her take it into her body and cry out into the night.

"Am I allowed to do anything?" he whined, his voice deepened, frustrated.

She smirked, sitting still, and pushing his hands from her. "You may taste me."

Biting her lip, she raised an eyebrow. Her heartbeat fluttered at her own words. She tensed, rising to her feet, leaving his throbbing erection to the cold air. The shine showed her dripping thighs; her body elated to have him inside her. Jakob licked his lips, his eyes lingering on her pussy.

Why does it smell like peaches? And I just feel... thirsty for them, for her, for the honey her body is pouring forth for me and only me.

15
SWEET RELEASE

Clara's body shook in anticipation. Jakob looked monstrous and ravenous. Yet, she had kept him in place, and he had allowed her to take charge, folding to her every whim and desire. On any day, he could overpower her, his animalistic instinct filling with the undying need to fuck and feed. His end game would be to taste her blood, but only if she allowed it. It scared her, and yet, she couldn't deny how much how much she wanted to feel his fangs on her neck, piercing her skin.

He stood, rising slowly as he towered over her. Her heart skipped a beat, her chest aching. A silken tongue licked the wound there, laying a tender kiss. She closed her eyes, letting his hands travel down her cheeks, stroking her hair. Another stroke of his tongue, wet against the fang marks and again, a tender kiss. Enthralled with his touch, she did nothing, standing still so he may *taste her* as promised.

The suckling kisses flowed downward, leaving a burning trail over her collarbone, between her breasts, and through the center

189

of her torso. Then hovered above her bellybutton. The heat of his kisses, his breath made her swollen pussy ache, and she could feel herself growing wet once more. The anticipation. Then his hands glided down her hips, cupping her ass cheeks as Jakob shouldered between her thighs, kneeling before her, taking one leg over.

"Swallow me up, Jakob." And there it was. The echo of their past he had longed to hear, goading him.

He glared at her with those slitted golden eyes. She balanced herself, a hand on his free shoulder. A wave of yearning filled her, her other hand gripping her breast. His lips pressed into her folds, capturing her clit and her leg buckled in response, but he wrapped his arms around, anchoring his meal from moving. He twisted, letting the cold of the leather loveseat add to the sensory overload unfolding between her thighs. And she screamed and screamed, and it only made him suck harder, longer, intertwining their passion.

Both of her hands clawed on the top of his head, fighting the sensations to push and pull him into her pussy. A numbing pleasure wracked her body. Each leg laid over a heavily muscled shoulder. They shook with the orgasm exploding from her. Another cry into the night did nothing to quell how deeply he drank from her. His tongue rolled across and flicked her jewel and she arched.

Failing to let her catch her breath, Jakob's tongue slid inside her; her eyes rolled back, legs shuddering as she pulled his face into her. A purr rolled from him, adding to the unfolding orgasm. His lips wrapped around her clit and his fingers slipped inside, thrusting to keep her at the peak of pleasure. A primal scream filled the room as she squeezed around them, ecstasy electrifying her body, her mind lost to passion.

Jakob abandoned his suckling.

He kissed and licked her inner thigh. His stroking fingers aggressively riding a sweet spot that took her breath away. His fangs popped through her skin. Her hands reached to brace herself on the couch as he ate her offering. With each gulp and suck on her inner thigh, she throbbed against his stroking fingers. He released his bite and licked the wound he'd inflicted.

Clara gasped for air, overwhelmed, as he abandoned her quivering legs and stood. He towered over her, his presence dominating.

"Fuck me," she commanded.

His hands rode up her thighs while his hard cock slid inside her wet pussy. They moaned as he braced himself on the loveseat. She arched into him, her ass cheeks barely teetering on the edge only kept in place by the fast-paced pounding. He grew harder with each knock of their hips, his purring transitioning to moaning. Leather ripped and shredded where he clung to the couch. Her hands were lost, fluttering, and searching where to hold onto him. They pulled on his arms, his waist, and his back and repeated the desperation of keeping him in and on top of her.

"Come on top of me!"

Another moan escaped him. He pulled out, rubbing his throbbing cock. She arched, giving him the full canvas of flesh to paint. Hot cum squirted across her stomach and breasts. She rubbed it across her skin, smitten by his need to follow her every whim despite looking so monstrous.

"Again. I want to watch you come again."

A growl was his answer, and his hardened length returned inside her. She orgasmed, yet again, peaking as her body shook in a wave of exhilaration. Through heavy, lidded eyes, she stared into his golden glare. All he saw, all he felt, all he wanted was her. He would devour her in more than one way, and she wanted it, gave herself up to it. Another moan and grunt came from him. Again, he abandoned her body and ejaculated across the canvas. She hummed, arching to greet the hot liquid once more. He knelt, fangs pressing through the wound they had created moments before. He drank from her and to her surprise, she peaked again. Her breath caught and she lunged forward. His fingers pressed inside her, and she wailed from the orgasmic sensation. Her fingers clawed his back and shoulder, her body shuddering with pleasure.

At last, he released, rocking back to sit on the floor and releasing her to melt into the couch. Both panted, their skin glistening in the low light of the rising sun. He stared at her in disbelief, and she grinned, a shudder rolling through her.

"You okay?" He leaned back on his arms, the couch in tatters from his claws. "Sorry, I ruined the couch."

She laughed, swallowing. "It's not mine."

He laughed. "Aren't you going to be in a heap of trouble over that?"

She smirked. "He said I couldn't steal or destroy it. Not my fault he kept it in a broken home and a wild animal tore it to hell."

Jakob collapsed onto his back. She pulled herself from the couch. Before he could protest, she straddled him, capturing his still hard erection back into the warmth of her pussy. She rocked on him, playing with herself. His body ached. He had spent the whole time doing everything in his power not to shift, not to become the Chupacabra. He had clawed into the couch, sucked her blood to take the edge off, and Clara had taken care of the lustful whims. Even when his mind hit a point of scattered thoughts, she had taken charge, rode him like a rider on a bull with one hand on his neck.

He tilted back, enjoying the building waves he knew would soon tighten, encircling him as she peaked. Again, her fingers wiggled between where they connected, wanting to feel him move in and out of her. He reached up, gripping her breasts and she moaned. Her pace sped up, more aggressively as the throbbing inside her escalated. She arched, leaned into his hands as he twisted her nipples. Her eyes cracked open, meeting his stare. He licked his lips.

"You could kill a man with a libido like that," he muttered, marveling over her unapologetic enjoyment of his body.

She grinned, on the edge of an orgasm. "But you're no man."

CUDDLING WITH CHUPACABRA
SWEET RELEASE

His hands fell away, pulling her down to him, his breath hot on her neck. "You're right."

Wrapping his arms around her, squeezing her firm, he thrust hard and fast. She screamed, wiggling like an animal in his grasp. He could feel the wet rush soaking them both as she came hard and unforgiving. Another shriek, and he kept going, making her ride out her hardest orgasm, torturing her until her voice finally broke. He rolled her over, hovering over her as she throbbed. Pressing his lips onto her, he ground slowly until he too began to moan. Once more, he left her pussy, rubbing his hard cock and painted her body. She panted, goosebumps drifting across her skin.

He lay beside her, catching his breath. "I can't."

Swallowing, she laughed. "Me neither. How the hell did you rebound like that?"

"That's a three-day advantage I get once a month," he snorted. "I could ask you how the hell you came that much and wanted more."

"Getting off on your cock only makes me want to go, again and again."

He looked at her. "I think that's the best compliment I've ever gotten."

She laughed and rolled up to her feet. "I need a shower."

"Shit." Jakob covered his face. "I need to fix your bathroom!"

Clara nudged his leg. "Upstairs works fine. I'll get the water going, takes a whole five minutes for the hot water to start anyhow. You going to join me?"

Jakob inhaled deeply, "Yeah, I'll be up once I catch my breath."

She laughed at the remark. He watched as her body sashayed up the stairs. Looking back to the destroyed antique loveseat, he grinned. One last *fuck you* to the asshole who had taken everything from him. He had it all back. Clara and the property. He didn't care if it had been his at some point, only that he could restore the rotting estate back to its former glory, to honor the stories his mother told of their ancestors and the Chupacabra.

Bing! He blinked, looking up at the cracked popcorn ceiling, brown with water stains. Rolling to his side, he reached for his pants and slid them over. Diving into the pockets, he found two cell phones. First was Clara's.

[MotherFuckingDick: You can keep the couch.]

Jakob furrowed his brow, glancing at the tattered thing and laughed. He then grabbed his own to see voicemails from his father. Sighing, he stood on his feet and climbed the stairs as he listened. His dad sounded panicked, unsettled, and rushed as he spoke.

"Jakob, you need to be careful. I just got off the phone with a Doc Samson. He apparently knew your mother, was her doctor of sorts and... look, he's a local vet in your town. Go see him. It's too dangerous to talk about over the phone. He can help. He said if you don't settle down soon, you won't be able to shift back. JR, be careful."

The message ended. Jakob could hear the shower going. The sound of the curtain sliding and the creaking of a body stepping into a clawfoot tub, letting him know Clara had started to wash herself. He pulled up Doc Samson's cell phone number. He aimed to call, and thought better of it, afraid Clara would overhear. He texted the old man:

[Jakob: Hey, my old man said you could help me out with my condition.]

"Jakob, the water is hot," Clara called out in a sing-song voice.

He smirked and announced, "The Mother Fucking Dick said you can keep the couch."

His phone buzzed. "Why would he change his mind?"

"Hell, if I know. Be in there in just a minute. Need to charge my phone." He walked away from the bathroom door, following her scent into the room she had been staying in.

[Doc Samson: Please tell me Clara is with you.]

Jakob scratched his chest, weighing the question.

[Jakob: Yeah. Why does that matter?]

[Doc Samson: You'll need someone to keep you human.]

[Jakob: What the fuck does that mean??!!]

[Doc Samson: It's either you get stuck in a shift, or you fuck the beast out of you, son. If you're hungry, come see me. I have anything you could want. Free buffet.]

Jakob hung his head in defeat.

[Jakob: Does this whole damn town know?]

There was a delay before...

[Doc Samson: We've always known ;)]

16

Epilogue

George Worcestershire paled. To spite Clara, he had installed a hidden camera, but he never imagined it would return to haunt him. When Suzie had revealed Jakob Regadera had become town sheriff, he had changed his mind on making an unannounced visit. Instead, he had sent Sharon, not realizing she'd have the gall to brag about their sexual relationship while he was still married.

In short, the town gossiper ate her alive and sent her back to him.

Bile burned in his throat as he glared at the video playing on the screen. Physical proof that Jakob was indeed a monster. Swallowing, he hit rewind and pushed play. Glowing eyes, shiny patches of scales. As Jakob fucked his ex-wife, George pushed pause. He never got that face from her, never allowed her to be the dominant one in the bedroom in the ten years they were married.

He pushed play, watching as fangs flashed, then paused it again.

CUDDLING WITH CHUPACABRA
EPILOGUE

"Did you know this whole time he was a monster, Clara?" he muttered, judging her calm expression, a hand reaching for Jakob's throat.

Again, he pushed play, fast forwarding as Jakob shredded the couch and Clara knelt before him. Panic rattled through him. He exited the video. With a drag and drop, it was in the virtual trash can. Right clicking, he hovered over the *empty trash can* command.

"What good is this to me?" Lost in his anger, his face turned red. "I caught the damn Chupacabra on tape..." He bit his lip, blood trickling down. "I caught my wife cuddling with Chupacabra after fucking him on my damn couch."

With a click, the file ceased to exist.

The End

Naked WITH THE
NEW JERSEY
DEVIL

HONEY CUMMINGS
URBAN LEGEND EROTICA COLLECTION

TABLE OF CONTENTS

DEDICATION

To Kim & Deidre

Your real life stories of Jersey & Philly were quite the inspiration! Stay awesome and keep writing ladies!

XOXO
Honey Cummings

1
TAKE ME TO CHURCH

Abigail Montgomery inhaled deeply as she pushed through the church doors. *Why am I so nervous?* Her pastel-toned floral sundress floated behind her as she strode down the center aisleway. The pews were bare, the church a silent tomb. *Not like I'm getting married today.* Her mulatto complexion was a warm contrast to the flowery colors backed in white on the thin fabric. *This is a little lower cut than normal, but it's not like I'm here for Sunday service.*

She'd taken the day off work, hoping to sneak her fiancé, Pastor Bradley O'Malley, lunch. Lately, they were so busy with her long days dealing with a mid-year review and him seeming to be more active with church activities during the weekdays, and sometimes evenings. At times, she couldn't shake the feeling that it all started the night they were going to have sex; something he had started and stopped before making her promise to *save it for our wedding night. I want our first time to be special.* Abigail grimaced. *It's not like either of us are virgins. Maybe he feels he should as a pastor? I should respect that.*

The place was empty as she paused in the center of the main aisle. Her plump lips frowned, her tight curls framing her face as her mahogany brown eyes glance at her phone. *Did I read his text wrong?*

[Abigail: Hey, what are your plans for lunch?]

[BJ: Sorry, Abby. Busy mentoring a congressional member.]

Weird. When did he become a mentor?

Scanning the room, she caught sight of Bradley's Bible, laid open on the podium. Wandering around the pulpit, she closed the cover on the organ keys out of habit. She had enjoyed playing it, learning the songs. *I miss this, but after playing at mom's funeral...* Furrowing her brow, her thoughts redirected, shielding her from her own emotions. It all seemed odd.

He goes nowhere without that book. Even got mad when I touched it once. Where could he be?

The sound of muffled voices brought her attention to the open hallway, to the offices located behind the worship room, in the back half of the building. If he was mentoring at this time, then he must be using his office for private discussion.

Don't they schedule these things in tandem with another Pastor in case someone walks in? It must have been...

Goosebumps rolled over her. The muffled voices turned into moans. Not of pain, but something she knew too well. Abigail tilted her head, her mind racing with speculation. *Is, is someone having sex in the church?* Her heart fluttered; her mouth parched as she bit her lip. She was even with his office door; it was wide open and empty. Halting, she questioned what she should do next. *Is the deacon taking booty calls now?* Forcing her body to continue, the sounds were louder, more erotic. Some part of her felt excited, from imagining the act or perhaps the idea of catching a couple in a lude act in the holiest of places.

It's coming from the private baptism room. Somebody is having a hell of a time. I mean, I used to have some fun at the club like this, but they're in the damn church doing this.

Pressing her palm flat on the door, it cracked open. *How careless, they didn't close it all the way or even bother to lock it.* She pushed slowly and held her breath. *Don't squeak, I just want a peak.* At last, she could see a reflection from a glass case full of keepsakes and novelty items. None of that came into focus as she could see a man's bare backside. Two legs spread wide on either side of him; the woman laid across the receiving table. Abigail licked her lips, swallowing as their grinding came into view.

Who is that? Do I know them? I mean, I think I know most of the congregation.

The legs encircled the man's waist, arms reaching up to him. As the woman arched and her face came into few, Abigail's eyes widened. *Tammy the organ player? That old hag? Really? Who in the hell would go out with her? She has a laugh like Fran Drescher from The Nanny.* Her shoulders shuddered, but... *Still, what a wild sex life she has. I can't say I haven't fantasized about Pastor Bradley and me...* Tammy's moaning interrupted her thoughts.

Abigail leaned too much on the door and it banged against something. She squatted and covered her ears with her hands. *What the hell am I doing?* Removing them, she shot back to the reflection. She could see the rest of him, the muscled ass cheeks and thighs, the pants that had slid to his ankles. *He's got a nice ass! I'm impressed. Though I think he could be working her...*

The man stopped, aiming to turn but Tammy grabbed his shoulder. "Did you hear that?"

"Don't stop. Please, fuck me harder." She begged, panting as she tilted her hips against him.

"Tammy." She forced the man's face back to her. "If we..."

She pushed against him, her knees rising higher as they hugged his ribs. "Take me to church, Pastor."

A PASTOR! But which one? Abigail watched the reflection, wondering how long they would continue. *I just want to watch a little longer, see a little more of this pastor who would...*

Her blood ran cold. *It can't be.* A wristwatch glinted in the reflection, and she stood in alarm. Pushing through the door, making a ruckus as chairs toppled over, she laid her eyes directly on the fucking couple, no longer caring about satisfying sexual curiosity. "B-Bradley?"

He swiveled his head around, locking his blue eyes with hers.

Abigail's stomach twisted. *Mentoring someone my ass! And with... with TAMMY THE ORGAN PLAYER! What happened to all those nights telling me you wanted to 'wait' and 'do this right' and, and... fucking five years! FIVE YEARS TOGETHER!*

"Abigail?" His voice shrieked. "I... I can explain."

"With Tammy?" Her thoughts were colliding, a constant firework display of sporadic disbelief and pain. "And wouldn't even so much as touch me after groping me two weeks ago? Why even give me..."

Gritting her teeth, she yanked the engagement ring off. With all her might, she gave it a hard-over hand chuck. *At last, that time in little league might pay off for something.* The ring launched with great speed, pinging with a sharp sound off the metal cross above the interlocked couple. Ricocheting with greater speed, it conked off of Pastor Bradley, falling to the floor and rolling right down the drain. *Good! It belongs there!*

"Shit!" He grabbed his face, stumbling away too fast and Tammy landed on her ass on the floor with a great shriek. "My deposit!" He spun and dove for the drain, but his pants intervened. "Shit!" Like any tree, he fell.

"HOW COULD YOU!" Hot tears slid down Abigail's face. "AND WITH THE ORGAN PLAYER! REALLY?" *Who would've thought? An older woman? Is that what he's into? FUCK THIS!*

"Hey!" Tammy tried standing but slammed her head on the table she had previously been on. "Dammit, you promised to give me that ring."

"Do you even have a lick of decency?" Abigail's pain shifted into anger. "You red-headed harlot! And you!" She turned on Pastor Bradley, her now ex-fiancé. "Son of a Jezebel! You promised her our ring? The ring you bought me and swore..." She lost the thought, disbelief and heartbreak taking the lead. "What will the congregation think?"

"Don't you dare!" Pastor Bradley rolled to look up at her. "It's your word against mine and Tammy's. The odds are against you if you want to stay in this church."

Abigail gaped. Shaking her head, she wandered out of the room, aimless as she leaned on the hall walls. *Did I hear him right? This unholy son of a bitch is threatening to turn the entire church against me. Can he? Could he? Oh, I'll have to pray on this... What the hell do I do now?*

2

CALL ME DEVIL

Dylan Johnson dried his hair with a hotel towel. Lean, athletic build in a solid six-foot package. His hair black, and eyes just as dark. The tanned skin showed he had frequented the beach plenty of times this year when he didn't haunt the local casinos. He brushed his teeth, fanged like any carnivore-loving fiend. Winking at himself, he rinsed his mouth and strode out into the main room. Tattoos painted his torso, front and back. Layers of black dahlias made a dark background for a devilishly red oni mask on his back, while angels prayed from his upper arms, and tigers crawled across his pecs.

Not a bad start to my Friday.

"Please Dylan. One more time." A naked, tattooed beauty lay tangled in his bed sheets. Her black lipstick and mascara smudged. "I know we just do this to pass the time, but you're a devil in the bed, Dylan."

He snorted, lifting an eyebrow. "That's why they call me Dylan "the Devil" Johnson."

She scoffed, sitting up to stretch her lithe body. "Stop being so smug. It's unbecoming of you."

"Are you refusing to leave unless we go again? I have work to finish. Besides, you need to go home and rest before your night shift later." Dylan twisted his lips, unamused with her delay tactics. "Well?"

Seriously, go home. There's a reason I maintain my privacy. There's no way I'll bring you to my actual room.

She crawled across the bed on all fours, growling, attempting to be sexy. "I'll gobble you up one more time, Dylan. Like a tiger to its prey."

"More like a rabid raccoon," he muttered, just low enough for only him to hear.

She paused. "What did you say?"

"Nothing." He tugged at the towel around his waist, letting it pool around his feet before rushing at her. "Just shut up and fuck me." *If she won't leave, I'll make her want to leave.*

"Yes sir—" He pressed his lips against hers as he climbed onto the bed.

Overpowering her, she rolled back and hugged his neck. The heat of her legs slid across his ribs, and he deepened the kiss. At last, she was on her back, giving him access to rub his hard cock against her lower stomach. Goosebumps washed over her, and she moaned into his mouth. They broke away and he leaned back, letting his hands trail over her shoulders, collarbone, the tender spot between her subtle breasts, until he reached her pussy.

He smirked at her. "Already wet?" he asked, rubbing the opening.

"I was already masturbating while you showered." Biting her lip, she batted her eyes.

She should know better unless she wants me to have the advantage.

"Is that so?" His thumb circled her swollen clit, until she howled, arching her back. "Why yes, you were. I don't know if that's fair." Her knees dug into his muscled ribs as he continued to circle her clit, firmer and faster with each pass. "If I'd known, I could have gotten started while in the shower... I think I ought to punish you."

She gasped. "Not that."

"Oh yea, *that.*" *If you thought I would take it easy after refusing to let me leave without a fuss...*

"W-wait, I could..." She struggled to speak through the waves of pleasure as his slid his other fingers into her wet pussy. "D-Dylan, I... I'll do it."

"Hmm?" He slowed, his dark eyes locking with hers. "You promise what?"

She smirked, failing to stop his hands. "I p-p-promise to swallow."

He stopped, arching a brow. "Funny. If I remember, you told me last week, last night, and I'm pretty sure this morning, that swallowing wasn't your style."

Finally! I'm getting something out of this.

"I did, but I don't think my body can take another round of you pleasuring my pussy, to the level of last night." He let her retreat, his eyes locking on her lips, making his cock throb. "Was it that horrendous?"

"Oh no, it ruined me. Just thinking of you makes me horny." She was back on her hands and knees, the heat of her breath rolling across the tip of his dick. "I just want to return the favor, by taking charge instead."

You lack the same caliber, but I don't know a guy who'd refuse a blow job.

"Are you really going to swallow?" Dylan raised a brow, caressing his knuckles across her spine, flowing down between the hills of her shoulder blades. "I won't play nice if that's the case."

"I'm betting on that."

The heat of her lips flowed over his long, hard shaft. He moaned as her soft, wet tongue wiggled against the underbelly of his dick. His knuckles met the nape of her neck and like a vicious animal, the wrist turned, and he gripped her hair, shoving her further onto his cock. The tip pressed against her throat. His hips rocked, sliding out until the edge of his cap smacked her lips before thrusting forward again.

Her hands crawled across his body, caressing the side and back of his thighs until she squeezed his ass cheeks. He pushed into her deeply once more, and she held him, sucking long, hard, and threatening to swallow his cock whole. Moaning, he closed his eyes, enjoying the heat and tightness of it all.

She did warn she would gobble me up.

The alarm on his watch started to beep. He didn't stop grinding, in and out of her mouth, as he shut it off. *Time to get to work.*

Gripping her hair once more, he let himself relax, soaking in every detail. The way her hard nipples grazed his legs, the hint of nails as she clung to him, even the way the tip of his cock pushed down into— He started moaning more, pressing himself harder into her throat. *Time to swallow, Raccoon Girl.* He glared down, her tongue wiggling, sucking as he started to come. The waves of her mouth and throat tightened around him as she swallowed again and again. Panting, he pulled out. She wiped her lips, the lipstick smudging in a new direction.

Blinking, he looked down to his dick and cursed. "Great, now my dick has a black eye." Rolling away, he shifted into the business-minded casino owner, returning to the bathroom to clean himself up. "Feel free to use this room to wash up before leaving. I'll delay the maid till this afternoon."

She lay on her belly, watching him. "See, I kept my promise."

He laughed. "Yes, you did. You want a cookie or something?"

"Just wish I could spend a Friday or Saturday night with you. The real you, like a proper girlfriend for a change." She frowned. "I suppose I get you on a whim for weekday fun. Are you sure you don't want a relationship?"

He marched back into the room, dressing in a suit and tie. "I'm no one's man."

"Is that so?" She rolled onto her back, stretching her arms out. "What if one of those angels tattooed on your arms spoiled that thought?"

"Then she'd better be worth it," he muttered, buttoning his shirt, then crouching to put on his socks. "By surviving a night of hellfire."

"And I haven't?" She rolled to face him, but he didn't meet her gaze.

"Didn't you just beg to swallow, then attempt a second time?"

She opened her mouth but was at a loss for words.

He chuckled, rising to his feet, and marching to the bathroom. He took a moment to knot his tie and spun back to her. Leaning against the bathroom door frame, he knew he had hurt her pride. "You think you're a tiger, love." His smirk faded. "But you're only a pussy cat—in heat."

"And you're a man whore."

He chuckled. "Never said I wasn't. And besides," grabbing his smartphone off the dresser, "You're a bartender who likes fucking the owner for bragging rights. What makes you better than me?"

The look on her face and her darting eyes told him he was right.

"So, let's not make this more complicated, by making it anything more than one last hoorah." He started for the door, then paused. "It's over, Alexi."

Scoffing, she laughed. "I'll bet my right boob it's not. Not unless you find someone to love or someone willing to keep up with your never-ending libido."

Opening the hotel door, he winked. "Maybe I'll find someone who can do both. Wish me luck."

"Go to hell, Dylan," she barked, cackling.

The door shut loudly in the hallway, and he leaned into the opposite wall. Sighing, he looked at the time. *8:45 AM. Shit, I should've left two hours ago. Why can't that witch of a bartender take no for an answer. Besides, I need to stop drinking so much, or I would've avoided this whole relationship-bullshit drama again.*

His phone buzzed and he answered it. "Yea, yea. I know. I'm late." Rubbing his forehead, he started for the elevator. "Why'd you let me drink so much last night?"

"Where are you?" another male voice asked.

"Upstairs," he drawled.

Laughter erupted. "I knew it! You hooked up with the hot bartender!"

"To be fair, Satch, we hook up often so it's not something to celebrate." He pressed the elevator button and waited. "Are the Morozov's arrangements for their family Gala organized?"

"Yea, boss. It's paid up and the vendors are on schedule. You headed down here to review their work?" He could hear Satch typing on a keyboard. "Or do you want Haley to do it?"

"I'll do it." The elevator opened and he walked in, glad it was empty.

"Do you want either of us to assist?"

"You. I don't want a female around right now." He looked at his reflection, devil horns surfacing in the reflection, but he managed to suppress them, through sheer willpower. "I'm having issues with my shifting today it seems."

"What the hell's going on?" Satch blurted. "You're like the third person this month."

He licked a fang. "Who else? Another devil?"

"My buddy Bif, and a rumor from Gandersville about a Chupacabra."

Dylan paused. "Isn't that where George Worcestershire tried to sell me that ranch?"

"Yea, but he's not a shifter."

"No shit," Dylan scoffed, scanning his keycard, then pressing a button to the top floor. "Is there something in the water?"

"I drank it and nothing's wrong with me." Satch laughed. "We both got laid last night so I can't give you the same advice I told Bif this morning."

"What was that?" Dylan made as face as instant regret hit him.

"Go fuck somebody."

"Sex doesn't solve everything, Satch."

And this is why I can't depend on you. Even when I'm way over my head.

3

CAN'T HELP FALLING IN LOVE

Abigail's tears wouldn't stop. And she couldn't decide if she cried from a broken heart? Or the pure rage building in her core?

She sat in a back pew, head bowed, praying for relief. There was a lot of foot traffic, but she didn't let that bother her. She wasn't afraid of exposing her puffy red eyes. Normally, Saturdays were a ghost town in the main worship room. Bradley was home, where they lived together, and she couldn't stand the idea of having to see him. Worse, if she went to her family's house, she'd have to endure her brother and the constant pressure of telling him the truth. And she didn't want him in jail for strangling a pastor. Though she had considered this.

Ugh, I keep forgetting they have a deal with the casino in Atlantic City. They meet and load up this morning, but I wanted to be out of the house before Bradley woke up. Of all days to come cry in a pew...

"A-abigail?"

She shot upright at the female voice's owner, alarmed. *No! Why is it someone I know who always sees me at my worst?*

"DeeDee!" In a desperate rush, she wiped her face. "I didn't know you went to the Casino on Saturdays."

"Well, why not? But honestly, I just volunteer to chaperone folks." She slid in and hugged Abigail. "Why are you in a dark corner, crying?"

Busted.

Abigail's gaze landed on the organ. "No. I don't think I can. Just know that Pastor Bradley and I are no longer..." She swallowed, fighting the building tidal wave of tears. "...no longer together."

She refused to look at her friend. Afraid she could see the truth written in her eyes. Still, she couldn't help but wonder: what story he'd tell his colleagues and the congregation tomorrow morning?

Will I even be here? Do I want to attend Sunday service? At least I could...

DeeDee leaned into her vision. "You got plans today?"

"Not anymore," she replied bitterly. *Maybe, never again.*

"Perfect." She grabbed her hand and tugged her out of the church.

"W-wait, DeeDee." They made it through the front doors, the sunlight stinging her eyes. "Where are you taking me?"

"To Atlantic City." She pointed at the bus where a church group and strangers climbed on board. "Come with me, have some fun."

"I..." She looked at herself; Baggy sweatpants and oversized shirts were her only go-to attire since walking in on Pastor Bradley and Tammy. "I can't go like this."

I feel like a mobile couch potato who forgot her chips at home!

"Of course, you can." Bracing a hand on the bus door to keep it from closing, Abigail listened as Deidre continued her mischievous plan. "Sweats are great for a long bus ride. We'll go shopping once we're there."

She's going to shove me on this bus!

Abigail's face heated, the heel of DeeDee's hands shoved into her back. "With what money!"

I only have a small purse, a phone, and my license! Is she mad?

"My money if I have to." She put her elbow into the small of Abigail's back, earning a yelp. "I'm buying. So, walk up those steps and grab us a seat, would ya?"

DeeDee! You won't give up and I am too tired to...

Back aching, Abigail folded. She let go and went fumbling forward with DeeDee toppling onto her. The bus driver looked down his steps at them, completely baffled by their actions. Righting themselves, they laughed and gave him a nod as they climbed on board. The two of them ignored the glares from the other passengers.

"You're so embarrassing," Abigail hissed, smirking as they sat in the first open side.

"I know, but I got a laugh and smile from you. That's all that matters." DeeDee beamed, elbowing her in the ribs as she chuckled. "You'll see. This is a lot of fun."

The bus door slammed shut, the air brake hissing as it released. Then the vehicle surged forward. Abigail's stomach knotted, her smile starting to fade. She was surrounded by unfamiliar faces, minus her friend's. *At least if I embarrass myself, none of them will tattle to the pastor.* As she took them all in, her brow furrowed, and she looked back at DeeDee.

"Do any of these people even go to our church?" she whispered.

She shrugged. "Nope. I only see them on Saturday bus rides."

"Uh, but I thought you had to be a member to buy a ticket?" Abigail sunk into her seat, fiddling with the pendant on her necklace.

At least I can wear this again. It might bring me some luck.

"They never said you had to attend to be considered a church member." DeeDee watched with intrigue as Abigail rolled the sunstone between her fingers. "What is that?"

"Oh, this?" She let it dangle, the edges of the gemstone translucent while the center burst red like a droplet of blood caught in crystal. "Just an old family heirloom."

"It's gorgeous. I've never seen you wear it before."

"Well, Bradley..." She choked and forced the words out. "My ex didn't like me wearing it. Said it was creepy. It didn't help that my great granny called it the Devil's Stone. Not exactly appropriate for a pastor's wife... to... never mind. That doesn't matter anymore."

If I ever see Tammy again, I swear...

DeeDee snorted. "Something tells me I'll need you really drunk to learn the full story."

"I might not tell you even if I get shitfaced." Abigail dropped the necklace and shifted her gaze to the bus window.

"Well, time for rollcall and see who's coming back and who's staying." DeeDee paused and spun back. "In fact, do you want to stay?"

Abigail shrugged, refusing to meet her gaze. Tears wavered on the edge of her eyelids.

Maybe I should stay. Besides, I'm so pissed at him. I just know I wouldn't be able to keep my mouth shut the moment he looked over at me, Tammy, or even the damn organ itself. My mother played on that organ before that harlot defiled it and my fiancé. Now I look at it and all I see is those two fucking, all over again.

It wasn't long before the exhaustion from crying and the white noise of a three-hour drive had lulled her to sleep. Only waking as the heat of DeeDee's hand shook her shoulder, her thoughts still stinging in her chest. *Did I blink away the trip, I just got on the bus, didn't I?*

DeeDee pointed to Abigail's chin, giving her a sympathetic expression. Alarmed, she wiped the line of drool from her face. *I didn't sleep at all last night. Of all the places to completely pass out.* Abigail vacated the bus, standing before the entrance to the *Saint's Hotel and Casino.* With a rumble, the bus rode away, revealing a grandiose fountain, large and obscuring whatever view from the other side of the massive pool.

She spun back to the doors, heart racing, and a smile forming on her lips. *Why not forget about it all; live my life like I used to when I did pub crawls and club hops. I'm a free woman and I'm officially on the rebound! First, let's get out of these sweats and into something cute.*

"You said you were buying?" She lifted an eyebrow at DeeDee.

Grinning, she hooked her arm in Abigail's and led her into the lobby. "Yes, ma'am. And I know exactly what you need."

They traversed the crowds, bypassing the casino entrance to a row of novelty shops. Before she could catch the name on the sign, DeeDee had her in a small room, crowded with tuxedos, suits, and cocktail dresses.

DeeDee weaved them through the towers of hangers, before settling on a long skirted black velvet cocktail dress. "Now give me a chance," she announced, thrusting the dress into Abigail's hands. "I know you normally wear brighter colors, but this is better suited at mourning the death of your engagement."

I'm too plump to pull that dress off. Even if I love the gold embroidery and ribbons that lace-up the back.

Abigail snorted. "Black cocktail dress. What ball am I attending?" She returned it to the rack and grabbed a softer, pink-colored dress, a design she felt more comfortable wearing. "I don't want to give the wrong impression of others assuming I have money. If I'm dancing and drinking, I want to feel at home. Be myself … again."

"Aww, live a little." DeeDee pouted, slumping her shoulders in defeat. "Fine. I'll get you that one if you at least wear those cute sandals with it."

"Do they have size 9?" Abigail cringed, feeling like she had hobbit feet.

"Sure do!" interjected the sales associate. She eyed Abigail and declared her assumption. "Aww, first night out after having the baby."

The woman paled under Abigail's stare, but DeeDee chimed in, coming between them. "Bad breakup. You know how it is, the bigger and baggier the clothes, the better."

Did she just mistake me for freshly pregnant? Looking down, Abigail puffed out her cheeks. *Yeah, ok. This outfit isn't flattering and makes me look ten times fatter.*

"Oh." Her voice came out weak and she said, "Sorry, with the sweats on... look, I can give you an additional fifteen percent off your entire purchase. If you need anything at all, just ask. And happy hunting tonight, ladies!"

Looking at the shoes and pink dress, Abigail sucked on the inside of her cheek. "Fine. If it gets me out of these sweats and everyone thinking I'm a new mom, it's worth the discount."

I think I'm going to hit the slots first! And maybe, if I'm feeling frisky, find myself a one-night stand!

It didn't take long to dress and with DeeDee's help, her hair was woven into a simple updo.

DeeDee handed her some chips and the two headed for the casino floor. The neon lights gave the place a mixture of other-worldly meets adult arcade vibe. Combined with the *cha-ching*'s of slots and shouts from the Blackjack table, it added fuel to her rising adrenaline rush. The first slot machine she met, she placed a chip in, pulled the lever and... *CLUNK-CLUNK-CLUNK... a complete bust.*

"Abby, don't stop after one try." DeeDee nudged her. "Second chances for the win, right?"

Another chip in the slot. The cranking of the lever and the rollers spun, blurring the images written on them. Again, they stopped, one after another. And again, bust. Abigail's temper rose and she repeated this until she'd burnt through every chip. NOTHING.

I can't win at love, life, or luck. This is shitty. Gripping the charm, she scoffed at it. *Some lucky charm you make.*

"I need a drink." DeeDee furrowed her brow and walked toward a dark corner near blue neon accents, and images of flames and clouds. "DeeDee, I think I'm cursed."

"Oh, c'mon. You can't really believe that?" They grabbed a pair of empty stools and waited for the bartender to finish with her current customers. "Exactly, what happened between you and Bradley?"

And there it is. Abigail scowled, ignoring the question. *I've got to avoid answering at all costs.*

The bartender spun around, the girl tattooed, tall, and skinny, unlike herself. Abigail was curvy and petite, but she didn't feel pretty lately. Bradley had stopped complimenting her weeks ago. Her confidence had left her long ago, being with someone for five years does that to a person.

I bet she could catch any guy in this joint. What I wouldn't give for a body like that. I wouldn't have to try to find a man, they'd line up out the door.

DeeDee leaned into Abigail's ear and said, "Is it me or does her smoky eyeshadow look a little heavy?"

A smirk lifted the corner of her mouth. "She looks like a raccoon," she muttered low, so the approaching bartender couldn't overhear.

Ok, I suppose with makeup like that, she'd come off as one-night stand material. Maybe I should go edgy too?

"Welcome to Purgatory, our special tonight is two for one Dead End Margaritas and Second Life Cocktails."

"Give me both," Abigail blurted without hesitation. *I've hit a dead end and need a second life really bad.*

"Those guys are staring at us." DeeDee elbowed Abigail and she grimaced. "What kind of response is that?"

"They're too handsome for like a plain girl like me." The first drink slid to her, and she started gulping it down. *If I'm going to have any chance at a rebound, I'll have to settle with a less dangerous, smaller fry. Those look like the sort of men with deep pockets and...*

"I think they're interested Abigail." DeeDee smirked, raising her brow high. "The one pointed over here. There's no one else at the bar but us."

"Yea right." The bartender returned, pushing the other drink toward her. "How much do we owe you?"

Poor DeeDee, she's blown a lot of money on me. I don't know how much these damn drinks cost.

The bartender looked Abigail over before nodding her head toward the handsome men still staring at them. "Dylan's buying all your drinks tonight. You might just get lucky and find yourself sleeping with the Devil tonight. I'm jealous. He's never bought me a drink."

Abigail choked on her margarita, locking eyes with the man who raised a drink in acknowledgment. Her eyes widened as she gripped her pendant. His friend covered his face in sheer embarrassment. *Oh, I feel you, buddy. Your friend is a bit much for me, drunk or sober. Duly noted: The Devil just bought my drinks and wants to sleep with me. Time to enjoy free drinks but avoid that man in the pin-striped suit at all costs. What ridiculous odds I have when it comes to bad luck.*

4

DEVIL'S PLAYGROUND

Dylan pulled on his overcoat, glad to leave his top floor office. As he pushed through his office door, Satch leaned on the counter talking to his secretary, Yvette. Arching one eyebrow, he listened a moment before clearing his throat, bringing them to attention. The Morozov family had invested in the casino and hotel from the beginning, so it was the least he could do when he hired their youngest daughter.

"You two play a dangerous game," he chuckled. "None of my business. Are you joining me tonight, Satch?"

"I don't understand why you play the roulette table every night, just to prove your luck." Satch winked at Yvette, then followed Dylan down the hallway. "You don't even take the chips. It's a waste."

"If you missed the memo, I'm the COO for the whole place. Why do I need to take my own money?" Snorting, he waited for the elevator doors to close. "Seriously, flirting and dating a Morozov girl is dangerous. They'll kill you over it. In fact, I'm convinced they started the Russian mafia when they migrated north from the Himalayan Mountains. You don't fuck with Yetis."

"Do I look scared?" Satch made a suave face.

"No." Dylan straightened his tie in the reflection of the metal doors. Then made eye contact with Satch. "You look like an idiot."

"You're cruel to your PA's, Boss Man."

"That's what you think." The doors opened to a cacophony of music and slot machines. "I never grow tired of this."

"Hey, hey!" Satch elbowed him, nodding at two women near the slots. "That's a regular, but the girl in the sundress, she's new. Whatcha think?"

"And what makes you think I'm looking for new prospects?" He then locked eyes with the roulette table tenant, and they frowned noticing his smirk. "I've got luck to play with."

Satch stepped into his view, unamused. "No, really dude. Tell me what you see. It's killing me. I can't peg your type, and I'm curious. You're settling for less than what you deserve. I've never seen you be with a girl beyond a quickie then you're out."

Shit, has he figured me out so easily? Damn it, I hired him for his insightful talent, but this is backfiring in unexpected ways.

Dylan scowled. "I can say the same. Does Yvette know you're flirting with every vagina at the bar last night."

"Far as I know, she's using me to get back at her Daddy or Big Bro for whatever reason." He rolled his eyes. "Humor me tonight."

I was thinking the same thing... so he's just an opportunist.

Huffing, Dylan spun back to the girls at the slots, observing as the temper flared on the new girl. *Bust after bust. I need to check the odds on that machine, shit.* The regular he recognized as one of the church volunteers from Philadelphia. He was terrible with names, but his assistants kept track of the details.

His glare shifted back to the other girl, and he blinked. She wore a scowl, not a face he preferred his customers to have when they came here to unwind for the weekend. She was a natural beauty, a rare sight in a casino where most tended to overdress in cocktail dresses and pressed suits. Her minimalistic makeup and pink sundress were a warm contrast to her cool brown skin. The curves of her body were inviting.

If she's sassy, fiery, or even the slightest bit bossy... He spun back to the roulette table, marching toward it with dread weighing down on him. *Everything about her is my type. But I'm not in the place to settle down with someone. Commitment is the last thing I want, and that's the kind of girl you date long term, hell, even put a ring on. My life is managing this place and having the flexibility to sleep with any stranger I want. I love my life! I think I do? Who the hell am I kidding? I'm fucking lonely...*

"Hey!" Satch caught up, baffled. "You didn't tell me."

"I'm not shallow like you Satch. Everyone woman is beautiful in their own way. So yes, she's pretty if that's what you wondered."

"Ok. Mr. Philosophical. You got a point." He snatched two cocktails from a passing tray. "But would you take her upstairs if *she* offered?"

"I don't sleep with women like that."

"Like what?" Glowered Satch, denying Dylan's reach for one of the drinks.

"The kind you take back home to mom and marry." He claimed his drink and emptied it, then abandoned it on a side table with another cluster of empty glasses. "What kind of monster do you take me for? I'm not interested in breaking hearts."

"I'm betting hers is already broken and she's on the rebound. Do her a favor by having her sleeping with someone of your reputation." Satch sipped his drink, knowing full-well Dylan was fighting the tide of temptation.

Rebound. That doesn't make this ok to take advantage.

"Is that so?" When they reached the roulette table, he pulled a stack of chips from his inner coat pocket, placing them on red nineteen.

"Again," added the dealer.

Where's he going with this?

Dylan winked at him, leaning back to watch the other suitors place bets. "If you're implying that I need to be her rebound, forget it."

"Oh, so we are continuing this discussion, are we?" Satch finished his drink, a dangerous glint in his eye.

"What are the chances you pegged her? So what if she's on the rebound? Or a girl's night out? Maybe her cat died?" Dylan snorted, and the roulette wheel spun to life. "You're assuming too much."

Satch leaned back into the table, watching the commotion on the floor. "Nope. I'm telling you. The look in her eyes ... she's on a rebound. Maybe undecided on how far she's willing to go. She's a long way from Philly and a first timer to the casino. I bet her friend dragged her here against her will."

There it is. That thing he does where he picks apart the target on a particular topic as if he knows it by pure instinct. Intuition of a Sasquatch, I suppose. This isn't a board meeting, so it's him, being him.

A smirk formed on Dylan's face. "You got proof?"

"Oh yea." The roulette wheel slowed, the ball teasing along a set of numbers. "That dress is from our shop. And she lost hard at the slots, now heading for Purgatory. She wants to get shit faced first, but I doubt she has the money. That's why her friend has that concerned look. In fact, the downstairs sales associate was in tears because she called a girl fat or preggers or something; I bet it was these two. I had to clear a discount she offered them."

"We sell that dress?" The ball landed in black twenty. He leaned in, wide-eyed. "I lost."

My luck never fails me unless...

"You lost," echoed the dealer, his eyes widened. "That's a first. Again?"

Dylan frowned. "No, it seems my luck has a new game in mind."

Satch, this is your fault. You knew it before I did. Fuck. Sasquatch intuition is a beast.

Silent and stoic, Dylan left the roulette table and headed for the bar, his focus recalling the woman's beauty and sadness. *Yes. A broken look of desperation, of wanting to forget. The bar's a horrible idea. What's her friend thinking? Or was this her idea?*

He wound through the bustling casino with practiced skill, Satch following. They entered the dark bar like two predators, the blue neon casting ambiguous shadows. Satch aimed for the empty seats near the girls who were now talking to the bartender, but Dylan dragged him to the opposite end. He forced him to sit, and he joined him.

The bartender turned and cracked a wide smile.

Shit, I forgot Racoon Girl was working tonight.

Satch waved her over. "Hey! Put her drinks on Dylan's tab. Tell her he's buying."

She turned to Dylan, and he shrugged. "Sure, why not."

"Ok, and here's some dirty martinis. The new waitress couldn't handle a full load." She slid them over but didn't let go of Dylan's drink. "If she doesn't pan out, you know my number."

With that, she left, and Dylan covered his face. "How do I get myself into these situations?"

"The Devil's luck." Satch waved at the girls, excited like a teenage boy. "Sounds like you and Alexi had fun last night... or was that this morning? Both, hey-hey!"

"Stop it. And sit down. You look like an amateur wingman in that pin-striped suit." Dylan laughed into his hand. "In fact, I wouldn't be shocked if she avoids you—no us, after buying her drinks. If she's smart enough, she'll ghost us both when she sees an opening."

"Well, you're the one that should hook up with her. Yvette's getting jealous lately." At last, Satch settled into his seat. "Are you?"

"Am I what?" drawled Dylan, nursing his drink as he stole a glance at the curly haired beauty. *Dammit, she caught me staring.*

"Interested in a bet?"

Dylan raised an eyebrow at Satch's words. "What kind of bet?"

"That she won't hook up with you."

Dylan shook his head, baffled. "But you insisted I hook up with her. What gives?"

"Right. I was aiming to get you interested into someone new, but..." He snorted. "Look. See how fast she's downing those drinks? You'll be lucky if she says two coherent words to you. I think I underestimated how broken-hearted she is and like you said, that's not your strong suit."

"Not my strong suit." Dylan echoed. "What makes you say that?"

Satch met Dylan's glare with smug expression. "You're too much of a hard-ass to be able to handle a girl that fragile."

Dylan set his drink down and watched the two girls talk. Their conversation turned serious, and her friend frowned, hugging her. Whatever happened, she'd finally told her friend the truth. Her eyes wandered to Satch, her brow lowering as she sucked her drink through a straw. Her friend said something and motioned their way. She shook her hands and locked eyes with him. Chills rolled over him, something electrifying and triggering that Devil's Luck high the roulette table had denied him.

I can't remember the last time I felt this excited about meeting a girl's gaze. So that's where my luck went. I mean, it's just for tonight, right? What do I have to lose?

"Fine. I accept your bet. What do you want if you win?" Dylan shifted, unamused at Satch's toothy grin.

"Alexi's number."

He laughed. "Ha. Deal. And now, we wait."

"Wait? For what?" Satch sipped his drink. "For her to be alone? How old school are you playing this?"

He gave a stern glance to Satch. "I'm waiting for my annoying PA to leave so I can actually make a move. You've already botched the approach."

Satch choked on his drink. "Fine." He cleared his throat. "If you really think you can succeed without your best wingman, then go, Boss Man."

With that, Satch walked away. Messing with his phone.

[Satch: I want to know every detail in the morning. You owe me that much!]

[Dylan: Don't you have to go get your buddy Bif out of trouble?]

[Satch: He's a big guy. I doubt mister redneck bigfoot needs my help.]

Dylan finally relaxed. He watched the two women, then checked his watch. *The church bus would load in the next hour.* Alexi circled back, continuing to fuel him and the broken-heart girl with drinks.

"Do you want her name?" she teased.

He glimpsed at the girl as she played with the straw on her margarita. "You trying to help me get laid with someone other than you, Alexi? I don't know how I feel about that."

"Abigail. Or was it, Abby?" She bit her dark lipstick.

"I imagine both." He sucked on his cheek. "So, tell me, what makes you so invested in my interest."

She smirked. "If anyone here tonight qualified as angel status, you may have found it, Mr. Devil."

"Oh?" Again, they locked eyes and Abby shot her eyes downward, brow furrowing. "I suppose telling her she has nice shoes; let's fuck would work as well as it did on you."

Alexi cackled, grabbing up a rag and starting to wipe down the bar top. "You got my number."

"I do, and if this goes in the right direction, Satch will also have your number." He hid his smirk behind the martini glass as he sipped it.

"Don't you dare." Dread filled her face.

Time dragged by and this time when Dylan glanced back to the girl, she was alone.

Her friend gone.

Finally. I got to give it to Satch; he knew I'd wait. He peered at his watch and paled. *When the hell did it hit closing time? Shit! Her bus left already!* Panic washed over him. Looking back to her she was … gone. He jerked to his feet, glancing around the bar. *Where the hell did she go? Shit, she ghosted! She couldn't have gone far.*

"You ok, Dylan?" The bartender started grabbing the empty martini glasses. "If you're looking for the girl, she muttered something about church?"

"Dammit, my luck is failing me tonight." He bolted from his seat.

"Don't give that sasquatch my number!" Alexi crossed her arms.

Since when did I have bad luck and bad timing? What the hell is wrong with me tonight?

5

LUCKY

*T*he man in the pin-striped suit left early, but his friend still lingered.

Abigail ordered another round of margaritas and narrowed her eyes at him. He had dark hair and sharp features. This was the kind of man she'd seen in cologne advertisements in a doctor's lobby, wondering whether they truly existed. *Yes, they do.* She laughed, sucking on the straw, humming to herself.

Any girl would feel like a queen sleeping with a guy like that. But hot guys are jerks. Yet... Shit. I need dick.

DeeDee shook her shoulder. "Abby, it's time to go."

"I'm staying," she slurred. "Go on without me." *I haven't found dick yet, but I can't tell you that!*

DeeDee sighed. "Abigail, I can't wait for you," she said, turning away. "Call me if you need a ride home. I'll pick you up or I'll get you a Guber."

"Home is a shit show." She shoved the empty glass away and slid the other drink to her. "I live with him, DeeDee. He told me to save it for marriage, but he gave himself to Tammy instead. You know who that bitch reminds me of? Meredith. From *The Office*. What. The. Fuck. I'm no virgin and neither was he..."

Besides, I can't hunt for a rebound with you still here. You're every bit as daring, if not more. I can't do this with a witness. Go! Leave! This is a risk I'm willing to take if it means forgetting that whole scene in the Baptism room!

"It's ok. You can stay with me when you decide to come home to Philly. I have a couch that will do." Deidre gave her a hug. "Are you sure you want to stay here all night? Alone?"

Abigail sighed. "Yeah. This is my last drink. I'm buzzed but not belligerent. Though I wish I were and could stop the heartache from swelling in my chest. I just need a break from Philly for a while. Come back for me tomorrow if I haven't called."

"Ok. But here, just in case." She slipped a twenty-dollar bill into Abigail's purse. "Remember, the buffet is free. So are the mimosas. Take it easy, girlie." With that, she left.

The bartender came over. "Hey, sweetheart," she said. "I closed your tab; we're closing for the night, but the casino runs all night. Breakfast starts at seven if you're in for the long haul."

"Aww." She pouted, abandoning her last margarita before slurring, "But I'm not drunk enough to forget the organ-player-*fucking* pastor."

The bartender laughed. "I don't know what happened but promise to share your story with me sometime."

Sighing, Abigail pulled away and stumbled into the buzz of bodies on the casino floor. Her head swam as thoughts collided from shouts and dings of the slots. The glow of signs featuring saints, angels, and devils seemed to charge at her.

What the hell am I doing? Am I really going this far? No, no...

She searched the room, anxiety tightening her chest. *I need fresh air. No, I need to go home. Is the bus still here? Hell. I'm not that one-night stand kind of girl anymore.*

At last, she caught sight of the lobby. She'd come through it, to reach the casino, that much she remembered. Shoving through scores of people, she began singing to herself, focusing on the lyrics to calm herself. With the fog of alcohol, she couldn't tell if she lipped them or sang them out loud. A few double takes and looks from people made it clear she sang it aloud and her choice of music slammed several patrons with nostalgic smirks.

I don't care if they can hear me. Keep singing, keep your mind off the situation.

The doors opened and she faced the fountain, glowing and shifting colors against the stark black night. She mumbled to herself; the singing continuing as she stared in awe. Inhaling deeply for a moment, she closed her eyes. It was quiet and the song kept playing in her mind, stopping the thoughts, and letting her anxiety fall away.

Her phone buzzed: a text message. Several actually.

[DeeDee: We had to leave, love. Please stay safe and call me when you're ready to return to Philly. XOXO DeeDee]

SHIT! The bus! It's too late to change my mind. I'm stuck. Calling her now would make her feel bad. What was I thinking? I can't do this, I can't go home, and I can't even go to church.

She started to cry. Digging in her tiny purse, she cursed under her breath. All she had was her identification and her phone... *oh, and twenty bucks.* Her tears felt heavy, but she kept on singing *Lucky*, hoping Britney Spears would save her from this emotional breakdown.

Her phone started ringing; the screen read: *Bradley.*

Panic jolted her. She threw her phone hard and fast. *Get out of my life already!*

The bellhop blinked and whistled. "I've never seen anyone throw that good. And it's the first time someone's hit the fountain from the front door."

Panic shifted into rage. *How the hell am I getting home! I haven't remembered a phone number since before cell phones were affordable!* She tossed her purse, pissed at overthrowing the phone into the fountain.

Splash!

Gasping, she covered her mouth and stumbled backward. *Damn little league! No-no-no-no! What did I just do!* She clung to the song once more, aiming to calm herself.

A hand tapped her shoulder and she spun, singing the main chorus.

The handsome stranger furrowed his brow. "Lonely heart? Are you singing?"

Tears fell, and she lost her voice, her singing falling apart. *The other man from the bar found me. Dammit. Do I have to sleep with someone to get out of this?*

"Calm down." He examined the fountain a minute before his gaze returned to her. "D-did you just throw your stuff in my fountain?"

"Y-yes," she wailed. "I'm sorry, I'm drunk." *Just go all in, Abby. Play the rebound card like you did at the clubs in college.*

"I see." He gave her a pitiful expression. "You're quite the mess; we can't have that. You should be enjoying yourself. I imagine you came here to escape..."

"He fucked the organ player." His eyes widened, and she covered her mouth. *Why the hell did I say that!*

"Ok. Not sure if I've ever seen a sexy organ player, but maybe he did you a favor?" The man waved the bellhop over. "Timmy, add a note to the maintenance log. Tell them to bring me a box of any contents found in the fountain by tomorrow morning."

Oh shit. Is this guy the manager? How embarrassing! I can't handle much more of this...

"To your room directly?" His eyes shifted to Abigail, covering her face. "She's got an arm, Boss. She tossed her phone from there."

"And her purse. Yes, she should have pitched for a Major League Baseball team. Perhaps, the Yankees wouldn't have lost their last game."

"Right?"

Abigail glared at them, unamused as she wiped the running mascara and tears from her face.

"Does she need an escort to her room?" added the bellhop.

"I don't hav—" Dylan hugged her into him, muffling her in the warmth of his chest. *Wait, do I know this man? Why is he hugging me? Oh my, he smells nice. Cologne magazine looks and smell! He's the complete package!*

"Don't worry." He rubbed her back, and she wiggled in his embrace. "I got her. She's pretty upset."

The bellhop strode through the automatic doors, and Dylan released her. Her crying had ceased, but her eyes shifted into anger. Temper rising, she searched for words, but the haze of alcohol stilled her. Flashes from the bar made her realize—*he waited all night to get me alone.*

She shoved him back, her feet clumsy, missing the curb.

"SHIT!" Yelping, she tensed as she fell backward.

His arms wrapped around her. She froze as he pressed her into his chest, against his soft cotton shirt and pricey cologne. And the way his arms shielded her, so strong and gentle, she couldn't help but lean into him.

He sighed.

I give up.

"I don't know who you are, but something tells me you're in quite the predicament." She nodded against him. "Were you supposed to be on that bus back to Philly?" Another shake of her head as she confessed in silent defeat. "All right. Now, if you're calm, I'd like to have your name in exchange for mine."

Sniffling, she pulled out of his arms. "Abigail Montgomery."

"May I call you Abby?" She met his eyes; the dark pools were mesmerizing, and the horns peeking from his forehead seemed so *realistic*. "I'm Dylan Johnson, the COO for the Saint's Hotel and Casino."

"Dylan, The Devil," she mumbled, echoing the bartender's words as she lifted her fingers to touch a horn.

His eyes widened, cupping her hand, and slid across her fingers until he reached the horn. Dylan searched the air and spun around. There, he narrowed his eyes at his reflection on the glass walls and swallowed. Reaching for Abigail's hand, he held it tight, leading her back into the bustling casino. Before she could gauge where he was leading her, they were in an elevator.

He scanned a card and it ascended.

Where is he taking me?

Curious, she watched him peer into the metal doors, flicking a finger at a horn. "Shit. What the hell triggered this to appear again?"

"The bartender." Her tongue let loose, still aimed to spite her efforts in following her plan to play the rebound card. She cursed the margaritas. "She said if I was lucky, I'd get to sleep with the devil himself. She was talking about you, wasn't she?"

I get it. This is on par. I'm next on your menu. That's ok, I need a place to stay the night, I did say I needed dick, and this counts as an epic rebound, right? And maybe...

He palmed his face, turning to her. "Look, about that..."

The elevator doors opened, and she marched out with a new sense of resolve. "Let's get this over with. I suppose I've got nothing else to lose. Not like I'm a virgin or anything."

"Abby." He caught up to her, and she paused.

This isn't a hotel room. Holy cow.

The entire floor was like walking into a mansion. In one corner, a mini gym overlooked the beach, the leather couches were arranged before a large screen television, even a kitchen that could hold the entire staff from her local Applebee's, and a hallway hinted there would be far more to see.

"I can get you a room, it's on me." He snorted as the elevator closed behind them. "And no, there's no need to offer me anything. I don't trade sexual favors for free lodging. I might be loose, but I'm not a douchebag." He walked past her, aiming for the hallway. "Make yourself at home."

He disappeared down the corridor, the rise of her anxiety prompting her to follow. "Wait!" *He can't leave me here alone in this, this monstrous penthouse!*

Dylan turned to meet her panicked face. "Yes? You want a room?"

"I..." Swallowing, her face flushed. *I can't believe I'm about to say this. And to a complete stranger, but the idea of it.* "I don't want to be alone."

A smile bloomed on his face. "Then follow me to the master bedroom. You can have my bed tonight. Without me in it, of course." He motioned for her to take the lead. "Last door. The rest is an office I use when I don't want to go downstairs or as a backup security room for monitoring the casino. Sorry. There's no spare bedroom in this place."

"It's fine. Just my luck, not your fault." Passing through the open door, she slowed and spun.

The bed was massive, matching the chest and elegant dresser filling the walls and the leather loveseat opposite the headboard. Turning back to Dylan, he tossed his coat and shirt to the floor. Her breath caught. He was stacked, and the array of tattoos gave her an excuse to admire his muscles and broad build. Oriental dragons and koi sleeved his arms and wrists. He turned his back to her, and she gasped once more. A devilish face met her gaze.

He froze, realizing what she saw, then chuckled. "It doesn't bite." He smirked, enjoying her curiosity. "Want to touch it?"

"It's terrifying and beautiful." Abigail stepped closer, admiring the red and yellow oni mask that stretched his entire backside. Her fingers traced the mask's tears, while her eyes tracked the hints of a serpentine dragon. "Did it hurt?"

"Less than a broken heart." They locked eyes for a moment, but he walked into the bathroom, then leaned into the vanity.

What's that look for? "The horns, they match," she added, intrigued by the emotions he sparked deep inside her.

They locked gazes through the mirror. "The horns... I suppose I should explain them, but it's not what you would expect. I consider myself a modern version of the New Jersey Devil. A shifter, but it doesn't normally happen unless I wanted to ... impress you."

I don't know what the hell he's talking about, but...

"The tattoo. Does that represent you?" He tilted his head as if unsure how to reply. "It's sad, like your eyes."

Dylan's head slumped in defeat. "Yea, it's how I perceive myself. A devil with no hope."

Is it wrong, wanting to hug him? Feel those arms around me one more time?

She walked into the bathroom, lost in the size of his shower. "Oh my..." Kicking off the sandals, she began removing her sundress. "Now, I want a shower."

Damn this unfiltered sense of self. Why can't I be this confident all the time? Or is it clear he has no intention of taking advantage, that I feel this way? And is it wrong to secretly hope he would?

6

BE YOUR MAN

Dylan watched Abigail through the vanity mirror like a predator lurking in the grass. He bit his lip, his canines a little bigger than before, his horns continuing to grow. If he ever felt like the devil, it was in this moment. The girl hadn't planned on hooking up with him, but still, the cute cherry print cotton panties and matching bra tickled his fancy.

She reached behind her back and fumbled to unhook her bra.

"You do realize I'm still in here, right?" From this angle, Dylan couldn't see her face, but the contours of her soft, curvy body stirred his arousal, fueling his dark desires. "Or are you so drunk you don't care?"

Dammit, is she trying to seduce me or put me in the friend zone?

"You're not my first one-night stand," she blurted, finally unlatching the bra, and sliding it off her arms. "I used to live that wild life of clubbing and hooking up in the bathroom or back alley."

He laughed, catching a glimpse of side boob and an erect nipple before her arm obscured the view. "And here I thought you were a church woman."

"I am. Or was. Well … until I caught him cheating." She paused, her thumbs hooking the top of her panties. "I can't go back. Not when I can run into Tammy. I need to find another church?"

She couldn't have been… what are the chances? I wonder…

He waited as she paused from shedding her last stitch of clothes, hungry to see all of her. "I've got to ask. Why the hell sent you to my casino, to lose yourself to margaritas for an entire night?"

She glanced over her shoulder, locking eyes with his reflection. "Would you believe me if I said I was once engaged to a pastor?"

Dylan lifted his brow. "You're very pretty. So that isn't a far stretch."

"Not pretty enough." She fussed and slid her panties off.

When was the last time I got a chance to sleep with a girl like her? Shit, was it the last actual relationship? She's the kind of girl you take back to mom all right, even if she's drunk and unfiltered. No, that's not true. This whole time she's been distraught but she's not slurring.

"So what happened? I take it the engagement is null and void." He leaned into the vanity, watching as she bent down, stepping out of her panties. "For a girl comfortable in her birthday suit, why would he leave you?"

"That's the alcohol." She didn't turn around, her face hidden once more as she stood, holding her arms.

Good thing she's not looking this way, I'm getting hard just taking her body in with my eyes.

"Says the girl who once hooked up in back alleys and has the pitching arm fit for the Boston Red Sox."

That march of confidence, but her eyes and words just don't match it. There's a story behind that pretty face, and she has my full attention. I want to know more. What about her makes my body want to shift, though?

She stepped into the large shower, standing before a cluster of showerheads and knobs. "Well, apparently Tammy was prettier."

"Ah, so that's what happened." He wrenched his lips, watching as she twisted knobs, failing to turn on the shower. "How did you find out?"

At least she's willing to answer my questions. What an ass though. Really? The organ player? Over this gorgeous, sassy, mulatto girl? Did he lose his nerve to get married?

Dylan's eyes took her in; the curves of her hips and ass made his erection throb.

Sorry, Raccoon Girl, it seems I prefer my girls plump and saucy. I'm in so much trouble with someone like Abby. Dammit, but will a pastor's ex-fiancée allow me near her with fangs and horns fit for the devil himself. At this rate, my wings and tail will burst out too. And that hasn't happened since college when I got wasted at the Bridgewater Triangle.

She put her hands on her hips, and Dylan bit his lip again. "I walked in on them, fucking in the baptism room."

"Ouch." He stepped from the vanity and walked up behind her. *Would she let me... could we...?*

"How does this fucking fancy shower even work?"

Temptation won out. He slipped his arms through the triangular gaps bracketing Abby. Elbows clamped down, only pushing his muscular arms against her hips as they slid forward and pulled on the center knob. Water sputtered over them, and she yelped. He didn't flinch as the first burst of cold soon warmed. Bracing his palms on the gray and white marble tiles, he started kissing her neck, then her shoulder, inhaling her sweet perfume. She arched into him. Head tilting her wet body against his torso, their bodies hot and wet. His hard cock pushed against her, rubbing against the top of her hip with nothing but a thin layer of fabric between them.

"I want the big one," she breathed.

Pausing, he blinked as his brow furrowed. "What?"

"That shower head up there," she pointed, "if we're gonna fuck in the shower, I want the big one."

Shit, she's drunker than I thought. I can't go through with this.

Puffing out his cheeks, Dylan obliged. He pulled the top knob, and a warm waterfall rained over them. She laughed, a smile gracing her face at last, making her eyes sparkle. He caught his breath and pulled away, leaving her alone in the shower. Abandoning his drenched pants on the floor beside her own clothes, he attempted to dry his hair with a towel, cursing as the fabric snagged on the horns.

"Wait." Her voice made him pause, his back still turned to her. "I thought we were about to have awesome shower sex."

He scoffed. "I can't tell if you're too drunk to regret this later or not. So, forget it. Enjoy the shower."

Agitated, he walked out of the bathroom and began pacing. A few times, he eyed the leather chair, wondering if he'd have time to jack off. His erection throbbed as his mind shifted the thought, imagining himself sitting there, watching her masturbate on the bed with...

"Son of a bitch." He covered his face. "This is your fault Satch. What a fucking mess."

He went to the bedroom door. The sound of something crashing in the bathroom made him pause. Then a whimper made him charge for the open bathroom door. Inhaling deep, a moan from her made him panic, and he forced himself to return there.

Inside the shower, Abigail was sitting on the marble bench, her head and back pressed up against the glass as steam filled the room.

"Hey, you ok?" he asked, stopping on the step down. She didn't respond. "Are you getting sick on me?"

Her shoulders slumped, and she frowned. His eyes flowed from her shoulder, down a slender arm until they reached where her fingers touched her pussy. *You've got to be fucking kidding me, what kind of luck...* Dylan swallowed, paling as a revelation came to him.

The Devil's luck. Abigail looked away, uncaring and miserable as she attempted to continue playing with herself.

"Uh, are you seriously masturbating while I watch?" His cock throbbed. *If she only knew how much I'm into that.*

"Why not?" A coy smirk curved her lips. "It's not every day a hot guy kisses me with an erection."

He crossed his arms. *Definitely not drunk.* "You want help?"

"I thought you weren't that kind of guy?" she drawled.

"If you want my cock, you need to prove your skill set."

She arched an eyebrow. "Kinky. What are you proposing?"

Dylan smirked, licking a fang. "So, what's got you so flustered where you needed a release?"

Abigail looked away, ashamed as she confessed, "I can't get wet."

"Oh?" He marched into the shower, towering over her, arms still crossed. "I can help with that."

She turned her eyes to him; the hunger and lust made him ache. "Are you seriously wearing your pants in the shower?"

"Why not? We're not fucking, are we?" *Now I see it. A short temper and stubbornness. I want to tame her, something about her wild but broken. She wants a rebound, but is too scared to go all-in. Good thing I'm a gambler. And I'm going to go all-in on this bet.*

She glared at the tent between his pants, as if weighing her options. "And how are you ever going to satisfy me without that."

"Is that a challenge?"

A sparkle in his eyes made her grin. "Yes." She pulled her hands away, bracing herself as she leaned back, spreading her legs wide. "I want to see your method of..."

Dylan knelt and ran a tongue from her knee, up her inner thigh. Her breath caught. Her skin was soft and wet under the heat of his hands as they rolled over her hips, upward until they cupped her breasts. His lips wrapped and sucked on one nipple, then moved to the other. Stolen glances made it clear he had her full attention as she moaned, arching so his lips had their fill of her breast.

Releasing her nipple, he pushed his luck further, becoming more intimate. His lips met hers, and he kissed her. She deepened the kiss, the tips of their tongues dancing against each other. At last, he licked into hers, a full-bodied rubbing of tongues as she moaned once more. Her hot fingers glided across his shoulders, before snaking into his hair. Her knees rose higher, her hips daring to rub against his hard cock still imprisoned in his pants.

Her hands slid down his torso, exposing her truest desires.

He pulled away, brushing his thumb over a cheek, down her neck and through the center of her body. She gasped, goosebumps rolling across the valleys of her body as his fingers glided down her slick pussy, rubbing between the swollen folds.

"I fixed your plumbing issue," he announced, smirking.

"Do I get to see what's behind the curtain?" She teased. "Or you still hoping I come first?"

"Something tells me you're used to dealing with guys into tits and ass." He gave her a toothy grin. "But tonight, you just met a man who's all about the pussy."

You have no idea how much I will enjoy making you come, again and again, before I bother to finish myself off.

7
BEDROOM HYMNS

*T*he Devil is about to rock my world.

Dylan's touch made her melt. Abigail's body trembled, and she cursed herself for ruining the chance to have sex with him when he started the shower. His dark eyes had her ensnared, his horns fueling her wanton desires. His fingers glided over her slick pussy, daring to enter her before retreating to her clit. She squealed with the way he rolled over her bean, making her body jolt and tingle.

Why can't it feel this amazing when I touch myself? Is this why they call it the devil's doorbell!

She leaned forward, her rising orgasm tensing her pussy. Her knees pressed into his shoulders, her hands trying to pull him from her.

He slowed, tilting his head at her. "You're close, why stop me?"

"I... I can't." She panted, her embarrassment killing her mood. "When I come, I..."

His brow lowered, and her eyes darted away. "Why the sudden sense of bashfulness?"

Dylan's fingers abandoned her clit, in favor of rubbing the slick opening. "Look, when I come, I..." Her words caught again as his fingers slid inside. She gasped, tightening on his fingers. "D-d-don't, it's just..."

"Just what?" His head bowed, the heat of his breath making her pussy ache with anticipation. "What's your dirty little secret, Angel Abby?"

The devil is about to eat me alive, and I can't even confess about what happens when I come. Come on, just blurt it out!

With a twist of his wrist, his fingers rubbed against a sweet spot, and she panicked. "Dylan don't! I'll squirt!"

He froze, and she looked away, avoiding his face. She squeezed her eyes tight, waiting for him to pull away like so many others had before. Looking back, she had told Bradley about it a week or two ago. His face had twisted into disgust, one she imagined Dylan wearing now. Her body shook with anger and frustration. Cursing it all, cursing the world for giving her such a horrendous flaw.

Of all the things my body does, why that?

Dylan moved closer, his lips tickling her ear as his breath brushed her neck and shoulder like hot wax. "Good. We're in the shower, and I'm feeling lucky. I'm pretty good with slots, so..."

The heat of his lips kissed down her neck, over her collarbone, only stopping to suckle a nipple. His fingers started to rub, stroking in and out, as her legs shook. She arched into the cold glass wall, a stark comparison to the heat of Dylan's body. He released her nipple, leaning back to admire her as their eyes met.

"Relax," he demanded. "I want to see you come, don't hold back."

She bit her lip, eyes tight. *Dammit, I'm just getting more tense.*

"Open your eyes." The command had a dark tone, and it rattled her to meet his gaze. "Good girl. Now, open your legs wider." She followed the provocative instruction, her heart racing. "Now, again. Relax. Lean back, moan and scream if that's what it takes to keep yourself from locking up. I want you to enjoy every touch, every stroke."

He leaned down, never breaking their gaze as he ran his tongue across her clit, slow and hot. Her breath caught, pressing herself against the glass wall as she gripped the edge of the marble bench. A sparkle glinted in his eye, his eyes falling to her wet pussy. She moaned as the heat of his lips wrapped around her bean. He kissed it with passion, making love to it. She tightened on the slow, stroking fingers, tilting her hips.

Closing her eyes, she slowed her breath, enjoying the sensations he gave her. It took everything she had to keep her thighs apart for him. She let go of the bench moaning as she began rocking into him, making him stroke deeper. With each tilt, he'd reward her with another long sucking of her swollen jewel. Her hands wandered down to his head. Fingers brushed against his horns, and she looked down at him with heavy-lidded eyes. Pulling his fingers from her, his hands gripped her inner thighs and pushed her open. Her fingers caressed the horns, and they locked eyes once more.

He's enjoying this, and I want more. I want to come for him.

She gripped his horns, long and devilish. His tongue dove between the folds, his goatee tickling the swollen flesh, making her arch. The hungry slurping and sucking made her pull him into her, the idea he would eat her like dessert added to her arousal. His tongue licked upward, back to her clit flicking and licking it faster. She yelped, abandoning her hold on his head to brace against the bench. His fingers thrust inside her, hard and fast, rubbing the sweet spot from before. Her voice was lost to moaning and screaming, her legs jittering from the rising climax.

Her body tensed. The heat wrapped tight on thrusting fingers. A rush of fluid released. Dylan leaned back his fingers, rubbing harder, increasing the orgasm. His eyes were focused on her pussy, focused on making her come, longer and harder.

A visceral howl escaped her, the last of her reservations broken. Another gush and she could feel it spray like an unkempt water hose.

Dylan's grin only grew.

Oh... holy hell... I've never cum so hard in all...

"Don't stop." He shifted his wrist and another rise and gush hit her. "That's a good girl, keeping cumming for me."

She leaned forward, her body tensing in new ways. The release, freeing and invigorating. His lips met hers, kissing her deeply. Her arms wrapped around his neck, the shower still running and steaming around them. Breaking the kiss, he nibbled her ear, his fingers still stroking her, never slowing, or missing the rhythm that kept her edging on another orgasm.

"I want you." His voice was raw and gruff. "I want to feel you come on my dick."

"Fuck me." She breathed. "Fucking take me to hell and back again. But dammit, fuck me like you mean it."

"As you wish." He bit her ear lobe and goosebumps rattled her body.

His fingers left her as he teased her with his lips, sucking on her ear before kissing her neck. The sound of his pants unzipping made her shudder. She wanted him inside her, wanted to hear him moan, to feel him throb within her. With a thump, his soaked pants hit the shower floor, heavy and wet. Inhaling, she tensed as the bare skin of his hips slid up her wet thighs, the tip of his hard cock pushing against her opening. He halted. Leaning back, his lips left her neck. She stared up, startled by the hesitation, but as their eyes met, he entered her.

Slowly, his thick hard cock filled her until their hips pressed against each other. Those dark eyes peering down at her, his hands bracketing her sides as they hooked her knees. Her legs rose higher on his torso, allowing him to press deeper, knees hung on muscled arms. Abigail's body slid on the marble as he shuffled and redirected their position. The glass had disappeared behind her as he laid her gently on the bench. Grinding against her slowly, she moaned, arching. He lowered atop her, her breasts pressing against his chest.

"You promise to be a good girl?" He huffed, his cock sliding out. "Promise you'll come for me one more time?" Shoving forward, she shrieked with delight.

"Y-yes."

"Promise me Abigail." He rocked his hips with skill, his cock riding in and out of her, teasing her pussy. "Promise you'll not hold back."

"I p-p-promise."

Again, his lips locked with hers. He rocked in and out of her, slow to retrieve, hard and fast to enter her. His hands gripped her ass, tilting her up and she moaned into his mouth. He began to moan with her, she could feel him throbbing inside her, growing harder as his own orgasm neared its peak. The stiffness sent her over the edge. Arching, he captured a nipple between his lips, teasing it with his teeth. She gushed, the heat of her squirting trickling down her ass cheeks. He abandoned her breast. Moaning as he pulled out and rubbed himself. He came across her belly, but she could care less. The orgasm she'd gained was reward enough as she drowned in it.

They both panted as he stumbled back until he leaned his back on the shower wall. "Dammit."

"What's wrong?" she panicked, sitting up.

He had his face covered; horns now vanished. "You're amazing. And I'm in so much trouble."

What's that supposed to mean?

Peeking over his hand, his eyes flowed over her once more and she shuddered. "You feel that too, huh?"

Inhaling deep, Abigail gauged the entire scene. "That raw want. Like I was..." She searched for the word.

"Lucky."

"Y-yea. Something similar. I guess I could say that, but I normally have bad luck." She stood and stepped into the stream of water, shocked it hadn't gone cold. "Yes, lucky definitely describes it."

"We call it the Devil's Luck." He ran his hand over his hair, a smirk on his face. "But I have to be honest, I normally get that high when gambling on something. This is the first time it's been ... sexual."

"Ok... you're talking like this is some sort of paranormal miracle." She lathered her body in his body soap, wondering if she should just buy it for herself when this moment of luck ended. "I may go to church, but I don't necessarily believe in free miracles."

He scoffed. "It wouldn't be so alarming if it weren't for the fact, I recognize the sensation of the power. Like magnets, drawn together. I don't normally enjoy... never mind."

She gave him a cautionary glare. "Never mind what?"

"I'll tell you later if you decide to stick around." He closed the gap between them, reaching for the soap over her shoulder. "And Abigail?"

"Y-yes." Her heart fluttered at the man who'd rocked her world minutes before... so close, *too close, too soon.*

"Don't you ever hold back in bed with me, either."

Is he threatening me?

"You make that sound like we're continuing this in the bedroom."

A soapy finger slid between her thighs, making her lean into him. "If we're as lucky as I think, we will continue this in more than the bedroom."

He pulled away, rinsing off and leaving her alone in the shower. She could breathe again, her mind racing. A shiver rolled through her. The way he touched her, his erotic words haunting and making her body heat by stepping close to her. She'd be lying to think she didn't want one more time with him.

Satisfied, she grabbed a towel and dried herself off. Catching a glance of herself in the mirror, she paused, then smiled. *I've never been with someone who made me feel like a goddess before.*

Wrapping the towel around herself, she wandered into the bedroom and paused.

He was on the bed, naked, waiting for her. "I've decided I'll just share my bed." He gave a devilish smirk, and she couldn't resist smiling. "Can you live with that?"

Shrugging, she sashayed along the bed's edge, the covers thoughtfully pulled back for her. "It's your bed."

"I sleep naked," he warned, nodding at the dresser behind her. "But if you don't, you can borrow my clothes."

"You know..." Abigail let her towel fall to the floor, and she slid into the covers. "I think I might give this a try."

"Oh?" He slid into the covers with her, curving his body around her. "So, do you like being naked with the New Jersey Devil?"

She snaked his arm around her, wanting to be held. "Yea, I like this."

This is how I always imagined feeling—safe and warm, in the arms I could trust.

8

HALO

Dylan slid his arm out from under Abigail, twisting so he hovered over her. Her face was calmer as she slept, a stark difference from the emotions she'd displayed the night before. Smirking, he broke his admiration and moved through the bedroom like a phantom. He left her in a tangle of sheets.

She's so damn beautiful.

Grabbing some items from his dresser, he grabbed his phone and made a call, closing the bedroom door and marched down the hall. The other line rang several times until a familiar voice answered, his excitement unmistakable.

Let's just get this conversation over and done with.

"So," Satch cooed. "How did last night go?"

"None of your business." Dylan scoffed, walking into his kitchen. "What time is the gala?"

"Right!" The sound of a chair squeaking was followed by keys clacking, filling the dead air before he answered, "It's starting at five tonight. Looks like the florist just showed up and stored some of the centerpieces in the spare fridge. That was a good call you made to reorganize the kitchen. The ice sculpture seems to be on the way. Chef Bordeaux says he will have full staff, and a few showing up for stand-by. Did you want to oversee the last of the setup today?"

"Actually, no. I'll let you and Sireena handle that this time. Were you able to convince her to sing for the entertainment? If not, see who else can fill it. In fact, just handle it. I have other shit to do today." Opening the fridge, he grabbed the orange juice, then shut the door. "Can I get an exclusive shopping spree in that shop downstairs? ASAP."

"Which shop?" Satch's chair squeaked again, halting the typing. "You do know there's three of them, right?"

Grabbing a glass from the cupboard, Dylan sighed. "Since when did we have three stores?"

"I'm pretty sure *you* signed off on the paperwork." Satch chuckled, then whispered, "It's for that girl, Abigail?"

Dylan choked on his orange juice. *Damn him...*

"You want to reserve the dress shop, don't you? You're trying to buy your way into her panties." Satch cackled as the choking increased. "Let me guess, you plan on bringing her to the gala tonight? Boy, I wish I could've seen her reject you."

At least, he thinks he won the bet. Let's keep it that way.

Dylan glanced up, meeting Abigail's gaze as she rounded the hallway, using his finger to signal her to remain quiet. "You're right, she wasn't impressed by me at all." She paused, twisting her lips. "Look, I'll text you as soon as you confirm that the store is ready. I want her to be able to shop without intrusion."

Abigail tilted her head and pointed to herself.

Huh, that necklace... Dylan winked, taking down the last sip of his orange juice. *That. Necklace. That. Stone. I know it.*

"Giving her the princess treatment?" Satch quipped, tapping again on the keyboard.

An old story, about never being able to face love again. That's the Devil's Stone. It couldn't be the same one as when I...

"More like giving a princess what she deserves."

Damn family curses and fate. Being a shifter can be annoying. To think, humans get dragged in like the rest of us.

Abigail marched across the living room, dragging the sheet behind her. "Look, I don't need people buying..."

"Got to go, Satch." Panicking, Dylan hung up on him.

Glaring at her, he bit his bottom lip. *They always said, when the time's right, the stone would return to the Devil who earned it. I just didn't know it came with baggage. Granted, sexy baggage that tastes like sweet peach pie.* Memories from last night, the excitement and orgasmic waves haunted him.

"Dylan." She tugged up the sheet, nothing between them except the island countertop. "Look, you don't have to buy me anything. Last night, I was... well, I..."

"You?" Dylan poured himself another glass, lifting an eyebrow. "Last night, yes? Go on..."

"I..." Abigail's eyes fell. "I need to return to Philly. Thank you for letting me crash here, but I need to go home."

"Oh?" He grabbed a second glass and began filling it. "I'll take you there, but you'll have to wait until after I take care of business with my boss tonight. Technically, I should've worked this morning, but I've made arrangements to care for my guest instead."

"R-right. I wouldn't want to be an inconvenience, but you don't have to entertain me. I can just sit here and wait for you. Or in the downstairs bar?"

"That'd be boring for you and me." He chucked the empty jug into the trash. "Besides, I didn't want to show up stag to this event. The boss's daughters are rather ... thirsty."

Abigail searched the air, gathering her thoughts. "Wait, last night, you said you were the chief ... manager?"

"Close." He rounded the counter, as her eyes averted his naked body for the ceiling. "Chief Operating Officer. Part owner, in fact. Tonight, the CEO is having a Gala. I don't intend to stay long, so you'll make the perfect excuse to ditch early. Trust me, I will owe you a favor. Hope you don't ... mind..." He approached, offering her the other glass, leaning into her stare. "You can stare. It won't stop me from staring at you when you drop that sheet."

Abigail blushed.

I guess mulatto girls can turn red after all! How cute!

He spun on his heels, returning to the counter as he gulped down his glass. A smile stretched across his face. Stealing a glance over his shoulder, he caught her gaze. Goosebumps crawled across his skin, the heat of his arousal making him shudder.

"But in all fairness, it's only right if you decide what to wear tonight." He abandoned the glass on the counter. "Sadly, I don't keep spare clothes for women around, but you can borrow my sweatpants and hoodie." Abigail choked on the orange juice as he breezed past her. "I'm pretty sure you don't want to wear the same dress today. Anyhow, it's all still wet from my pants. So, you have any spare clothes to wear downstairs?"

"C-crap!" Panicking, she shuffled in the sheet and chased after him. "Dylan, that is your name, right?"

He paused, allowing her to lead the way. "Yes, Abby?"

There was a pause before she huffed out her frustration. "How can you be so casual about this?"

Dylan cracked a smile. "Can't a man walk around his own apartment naked?"

"Not that." Tugging up the sheet to keep herself covered, she relented, "Me. How can you be so calm about me?!"

He laughed, and her blush deepened. "Last night, I may have brought you to my room, but you didn't have anywhere else to go. If I recall right, you offered to sleep with me in the elevator, I offered to get you a hotel room, then in the shower you asked for my help and how could I say no? It took everything I had to gently turn you down during the shower bit, but…"

"You're right. I did offer." She rolled her eyes before locking with his playful stare. "But…?"

I wonder if she knows. "It's almost like fate brought you here."

She stiffened. "What's that supposed to mean?"

"That necklace." He stepped forward, rolling the stone amulet in his fingers. "You know what this is called, don't you?"

The stone was like a hot coal, but he ignored the searing heat. Its magic vibrated through him, his joints feeling the tinge of electricity, exciting his body. Devil horns, fangs, and even a pointy tail appeared as his body reacted to the direct contact. His dark irises shifted to blood red as they looked at her at last.

"The Devil's Stone," she whispered in awe.

"Do you know the story behind it?" He dropped it, and the shift ended, his eyes dark and devilish features returned to normal.

Her eyes searched his; confusion written on her face. "It's a family heirloom. A lover's gift before he died in the mines."

And there's the explanation. That mine was cursed and turned every man who entered into a devil shifter and every male offspring thereafter. In her case, it's been passed down in the family like a lucky charm, but have they been free of the curse? How are they avoiding the whiplash unless someone put their luck into the stone… could it be?

He shook his head. "It's beautiful, but let's find you a dress for the gala. Ready to go downstairs?" he asked, changing topics.

Perhaps my Devil's Luck is the real deal. Granted it was my father who was cursed, unwilling to get rid of the last stone until his son found it. Unlike him, I was the first to be born a devil.

Dylan walked ahead of Abby, glaring at his fingers, as if they still touched the stone. *A lover's gift. How strange. Just maybe his Devil's luck granted him a wish. Since they closed that mine, there's been no more devils made. Many have shifted and lost their minds, others hunted or killed at birth out of fear and mass hysteria. Honestly,*

I don't want to be the only Jersey Devil in existence... It's the worst kind of loneliness.

9

THE DEVIL WEARS A SUIT AND TIE

Abigail did her best to ignore the stares and whispers. Dylan's hoodie swamped her, and she was thankful for the pull string around the waist. He unlocked the store, and she shoved past him. Another chuckle rattled out of him. She stopped, her fingers fumbling the hem of the hoodie as she looked over the dresses once more.

Without customers or the sales associate, the store was silent, and the casino muted.

"Buy anything and everything you want. It's on me." He grabbed a pair of thongs. "That includes underwear for now and later."

"Stop it!" she hissed, tugging the lingerie from his fingers. "You're so embarrassing."

"Me? Embarrassing?" he asked, shocked and amused by this revelation. "I don't find myself embarrassing at all."

"Of course not." She looked at the thongs a moment before tossing them back in the pile.

"Aw, I thought those would look good on you." Pouting, she turned away, hiding her face in the hood. "Seriously, Abby. Don't just buy stuff for today or tonight. Anything you want. You have no idea how big of a favor this is, being my guest at the Gala."

"So you keep telling me," she drawled, heading for the clearance bin, riffling through the selection once more. "Just, let me see if there's anything I consider acceptable."

It kills me. Why is a man this rich and good-looking wanting to pamper me like this? I don't deserve it. I'm only here because I got wasted, searching for a rebound, and missed my bus in the process, while avoiding going home to... She paused, the black cocktail dress from yesterday was in her hand. *I suppose I should heed the initial advice and just enjoy myself. Mourn the loss of my engagement, not that fucking scumbag Bradley.*

Circling back to the lingerie section, she paid no heed to his curious eyes. "That was in clearance?"

She ignored him, looking for her size in bras. *Dammit, his pants soaked everything I came here with. It was so damn awkward, walking through that crowd, knowing how naked I was under this.*

She smacked a mischievous hand from her ass. "Stop it. Not here," she grumbled, pulling a bra free, then turning to the underwear section.

Dylan frowned. "You said the same thing on the elevator. No fun."

"To be honest, I didn't think you'd pick a dress like that one. Doesn't seem your style."

"It's not," she confessed, heading for the fitting room before he could see her grab the thongs he'd picked out. "Taking a friend's advice to let loose and have some fun. I should've done this yesterday. I'm not wasting my second chance."

"Good advice, and I like where this is going." He leaned against the wall, just outside the door, his voice soothing her nerves.

"Only thing you like about it is a second chance to..." She snapped her jaw closed as she wiggled out of his hoodie and sweatpants. *What am I saying! That I plan on fucking him again? Why can't I just keep my mouth shut!*

"Second chances are my specialty," he chuckled.

Again, she focused on the task at hand. *There's always something sexy about sliding on a lacy black thong and matching bra.* A smile came to her face. She peeked at herself in the mirror before sighing. Grabbing the cocktail dress up, she slipped it on. It flowed off her hips like velvety waterfalls of fabric. Adjusting her breasts into the top, she paused, catching something shiny. A golden embroidery bordered the halter top and chased down the back center. Here she hummed to herself, a small train exploding in a grand firework design where the two-sides met as one.

It's prettier than I realized.

Reaching behind herself as she attempted to tie up the back. Her arms and wrists ached from the effort as she cursed her inflexible body. Another growl of frustration exploded and a knock at the door startled her. Her heart pounded against her chest making it ache.

Shit, how'd I forget he was circling just outside the door?

"You need help with lacing up the back?" he cooed.

He was hoping for this moment.

She cracked the door ajar. "No funny business."

"You act like I haven't seen what's under that." He lifted his eyebrows, and she let him in. "Sorry, you make it easy to get a rise out of you. Consider it a compliment from me, I don't indulge in flirting like this often."

Abigail stiffened, catching the sincere expression on his face as the heat of his fingers laced the back of the dress. "You call that flirting?"

As his fingers worked up the pattern of cross-stitched ribbon, he caught her stare in the reflection. "It's working to get a grin out of you on occasion, isn't it? That flushed look is quite sexy after all." He tightened the top and vanished out of the room, door closing.

Abigail stood there, staring at where he should've been, should have stayed and it felt ... empty. *Painfully empty and cold without him there.* Snapping out of it, she swirled before the mirror, running her hands down her sides. The dress was stunning. It may not have caught her eye but seeing it on her frame, she understood why DeeDee had suggested it. She filled it in all the right places. Satisfied, she tugged the ribbon knot free and wiggled out.

This will be the dress for tonight but until then... She looked at his hoodie and sweatpants and laughed. *Second time this weekend I've had to shop here in sweats.*

"Hey, Dylan. Did you mean it when you said I can buy more than one?" she shouted through the door. "And am I allowed to wear the merchandise out the door?"

"Yes, to both. We'll leave a list, or you can settle up and add it on my tab later."

Abigail flinched; he sounded *sad?* "In that case, to be fair..."

"Fair?"

Yes, sad. "Pick out something for me. Something you like."

"You sure about that? You didn't seem to care for my choice in panties." He laughed and she smiled as she placed the dress back on its hanger and worked the wrinkles out.

"Go pick something." There was silence.

The minutes ticked by; a chill rattling over her. She reached for the knob and stopped. *I'm in my underwear! Where the hell did he go?* Turning to the dress, she shook her head. *That's for tonight.* Grabbing the hoodie, she pulled it back on and tugged it down. It was every bit as long as the sundress she wore yesterday, and she laughed as she ventured out of the fitting room.

"Dylan?" The store lay silent, empty from where she stood.

I have to confess something to myself. Her heart pounded in her ears, her blood rushing. *Every part of me wants to stay here with him. It's not the money. It's not that he's so damn handsome, and dammit he looks good in a suit and tie but...* She tip-toed, circling around the racks of clothes wondering where he could be. *There's something devilish about him that just makes me want him more and more with each passing minute. The idea we might part ways tonight makes me want to...* Her eyes began to water.

"Where are you?"

Again, silence and she swallowed. Someone knocked on the shop door and she hid behind a nearby rack. They moved on and she could breathe again. *I'm being ridiculous. He had to do something for work.* The aching in her chest only added to the weight of her depression. Staring at her feet, she marched right back into the fitting room, slamming the door.

"That's exactly what I was hoping you'd be wearing."

Her head jerked up. He'd snuck into the fitting room in her distraction. She couldn't contain the smile. Rushing her, his lips locked with hers, the kiss hungry and passionate. Her tongue dove into the warmth of his mouth and her body heated with the memories of what it had done, had tasted of her last night.

His hands glided up her thighs and under his hoodie. The throb of want rattled through her and his shoulders shuddered as she let herself be pinned against the door. It rattled under their fast and desperate movements. His fingers looped into the thong and his grin broke their kiss.

"I thought you didn't like these."

"They weren't for me." He started to slide them slowly and teasingly off her, his lips leaving a burning trail down her leg. "And they were supposed to be a surprise for later."

"Oh I'm surprised." She lifted one foot then the other.

A tongue chased the trail back up the inside of her leg and she gasped. He shouldered the leg as he crested over her knee and up her thigh, never slowing to reach the prize swollen and wet. *I've never gotten so hot and bothered in my life from a look, a kiss, or a...* A squeal erupted from her, his lips wrapping around her clit. He sucked long and hard, his tongue circling slowly and purposefully. *He's been thinking about this all day.*

A hand rolled up the center of her torso and her breathe caught in her throat. She tensed, an orgasm coming on quick if he kept instigating her body in this way. *Should I stop him? What about...* He changed tactics as his fingers slid under the bra, groping her breast. The suckling had ended, and his tongue lapped up everything her pussy offered. She moaned, giving way to the waves of pleasure rolling through her. Her leg shook under the pressure, and she was failing to brace herself against the door.

Don't let this end... I don't want him to stop... I don't want to leave him.

10

DEVILS DON'T FLY

Dylan pulled away, his cock hard from teetering her on the edge of a monstrous orgasm. He let her leg slide off as she hummed against the door. He shed his clothes, fast and eager. Searching a pocket, he found a condom and she laughed. Shrugging he rolled it onto his throbbing erection. She started to pull off his hoodie and he rushed her once more. Lips hot against his own as he kissed her deeply. Her breast heaved against him; he pinned her hard against the door.

After a blind search, he found her wrists and pinned them up above her head. Compared to him, she seemed small and delicate. A single hand could pin her crisscrossed arms and her kiss pressing back told him she would let him. His thigh slipped between her own, wet from her building arousal. Breaking the kiss, he licked and nibbled at her ear. Her body shook, her pussy grinding against his leg as she whimpered.

"The moment you walked out of my room wearing this, I've wanted to fuck you." Breathless, she moaned as he kissed her neck. "Don't you dare take it off."

His leg shifted, opening her to receive him. He slid in slowly, soaking in her heavy-lidded look. Licking a fang, he realized the stone glowed from under the fabric, and it egged him to keep going. His free hand slid down to grip her ass, pushing further inside her before slowly grinding against her. They both moaned enjoying the slow, deep thrusting.

She lifted her leg up on his hip and he began thrusting harder and faster. The way her body shook in anticipation of the inevitable orgasm only added to his own. To know he could bring her to the edge, so close that she grew wet with each stroke of his cock inside her.

"You promise you won't hold back, right?" he huffed, goosebumps rattling him.

"I promise." She huffed, shifting into him, making him throb inside her.

"Tell me, my dear Abby, my beloved Angel..." He suckled her ear, inhaling her intoxicating scent. "Tell me what you desire?"

"I want..." He started kissing down her neck, enjoying how easily each touch disrupted her words. "Want... D..."

"I can't hear you." His voice gruff as his hand slid down between their bodies. "Speak up."

"Desire..." She gasped for air. "I des..."

His fingers found her clit. The touch making her pussy tighten on his cock and he moaned in her ears. He nuzzled around to her other ear. Licking up her neck, kissing and suckling as he wore a devilish grin. Fanged and wild, he enjoyed the game of cat and mouse he played with her pleasure and her voice.

"Dylan." His name fell with provocative want, and he throbbed once more.

Pulling from the nest of her hair, he leaned back catching her gaze. "Yes?"

She laughed, his grip on her arms letting go. Abigail cupped his jaw, and he soaked up her smile. *It's so beautiful. And to think, it's only meant for me. Who could be so blind to give you up? I guess the only heart breaking when you leave will be my own.* He heaved a sigh, searching her face. *Would you stay if I asked you to? Would you stay even after confessing what I am?*

"You asked for what I desired." She gave him a peculiar look.

"And I would give you the world if I could." He furrowed his brow. "So what do you desire most?"

"You, silly. I desire ... Dylan."

His smile fell away, *did I just have a seizure?* It wasn't the answer he had expected. Not in this moment of sexual play.

She pressed her lips against his and he fumbled backward. They crossed the tiny span of the fitting room until his back locked with the cold mirror. *She can't want me. She shouldn't want me ... even though it's what I wanted; it just makes this so much worse.* Her lips abandoned their play and the hot silk of them started down his neck, over his collarbone. The trail was slow and agonizing, like a ribbon brushing against his skin, teasing as it fell to the place that throbbed with want.

Should we even be going this far if I intend to make this more? If she wants more than this weekend of lust, if she feels like I do and wants to see where we can go from here...

Her fingers grabbed his hard cock, yanking the condom off. Moaning, he closed his eyes, bracing his arms on the sides of the tiny room. The urge to rush her, to press his dick between those fleshy petals tantalizing. A hot blanket of her breath made him groan and throb once more. Her lips at last kissed along his length. First one side, then the other and back again. He bit his lip as her tongue circled the tip.

I've never felt so alive with someone. Is this what it means to start falling for someone. If that happens, it'll only mean … danger. Yes, she'll be in danger with me and with this otherworld I live in. It's not frowned upon for shifters and humans to be together, but I'm involved with so many predators…

At last, he peered down at her, licking his lips. She ran her tongue, firmly from base to tip on the underbelly of his cock and he moaned again. Her eyes looked at him, and she paused. She stroked his length before a look of contemplation passed on her face.

I might just lose control of that part of me I hate so much. The part I haven't been able to keep secret since she stepped foot in this place.

"I know you keep saying this is who you are, but…" She motioned to her forehead, and he realized the horns had crept forward yet again. "Is that make up or another illusion?"

"Dammit." He eyed the mirror behind him; they were large and every bit of eight inches long.

"How does that even happen? I mean, they look so real. When did you slip them back on?" She licked the tip of his dick, teasing him. "Don't make me tease you until you confess. It's a little sexy so…"

"That's just mean," he huffed. *Son of a bitch. I can't do this. Not to her. Not when she deserves better. She deserves the truth.* Dylan pulled her away and she looked up in confusion from the hard shift from sex to serious discussion time. "Look, Abigail, I'm a shifter. Touch them. They're the real deal and if I lose control, it will only get … *uglier*. Horns, tail, wings as black as night: these are who I am."

"You're a shifter? Like in those romance novels?" She gave a nervous laugh before sputtering, "You're joking, right?" Her smile faltered. "Please tell me you're joking, Dylan?"

Dammit, if I want her to stay, I need her to understand what it means to be with me.

"Yea, well, those are based on more fact than you think. Half the time the authors are shifters themselves." Dylan averted his eyes from her as he sank to the floor. *What a buzz-kill this is going to be.*

"I'm not completely human. We still don't understand it all ourselves, but there's a level of magic involved. Curses and blessings have all been blamed. Legends and mythology, hell even history has left clues. Look, I'm wild about you. I can't keep this from happening around you," he pointed to the horns, "and I can't keep ignoring it and neither can you, though I appreciate the way you've handled it so far."

Abigail broke away, adding space between them as the weight of the situation hit her. "Last night I told myself it was the alcohol. Even this morning I thought maybe, maybe a dream and I wasn't quite awake all the way or ... it can't be."

"We both know you weren't that drunk. Denial is normal." He refused her gaze, accepting the inevitable end. *I don't want to see that kind of hurt in those eyes. Rather break it now, it only gets messier the longer I keep this to myself.* "So, before I dare take this any further... I needed you to know. To see what I am. Just, feel free to hate me but don't go blasting it to the press." He swallowed, the anxiety of it all tight in his chest as he covered his face. *I've spent my entire life avoiding this moment. It's only happened once before, and it ruined me. What the hell was I thinking. I knew I'd fall for her the moment I saw her at the slots. Fuck!* "Forget everything. Let's take you back to Philly. I'm sorry I strung you along-"

"STOP!" Her shriek jolted him.

Pulling his hand down his face, he dared to look her way, but she buried her face in the sleeves of his hoodie. "Look, the deal holds. Pick what you want, and I'll take you home. You don't worry about the gala it's..."

"Just ... let me enjoy this a little longer." At first, he wasn't sure what he heard. "Let me stay with you a little longer. Don't make me go back there."

He blinked, the tears glazing her eyes. "I didn't mean to hurt you. I didn't want to make you cry."

"These aren't from you." She sniffled, her voice shaking. "This is for what waits for me in Philly."

A profound look hit his face. "Why did you run away?"

She laughed, "Like I said, he fucked the organ player. My ex-fiancé is the pastor, and he fucking cheated on me." Burying her face back into the sleeves of his hoodie, she forced the words out. "The man threatened to turn the whole congregation on me for catching them, and here you are rewarding me for weaseling my way to your bed. I thought it fitting I was dragged to a casino and in the bed of the Devil. At first it just seemed like a lucid dream, even a drunken dream. You've been nothing but kind and you fucking make me feel like a person again. Like I matter."

"You do matter." He crawled closer and forced her hands down. "In the flitting time we've been together you have caught me off guard on more than one occasion. You're funny and brave when you want to be. At times outspoken, but I hate seeing you hurt and hiding away within yourself. I want to see more of these glimpses, more of that smile ... that you give me and me alone." He thumbed her bottom lip, his eyes lingering on them before wiping a tear from her cheek. "Fuck the asshole who made you doubt who you are."

"I feel like I'm using you." She shook her head. "I'm a horrible person. I deserve every bit of this."

Her words made his heart sink. *And here I thought I was ... using her, getting what I deserved by letting her go.* "So what. You used me for your rebound. Sleeping with the devil seems like a great way to get back at a cheating pastor but..."

She rushed forward, arms wrapping around him, her voice desperate as it vibrated into him. "I'm falling for you. I don't want to leave, and I don't know what's right or wrong anymore. I don't know if it's good luck or bad luck that brought me to you."

You're not alone, my Angel. I'm starting to wonder too.

11

MY CHURCH

"**O**k, Angel." Abigail was forced to her feet and the sweatpants shoved in her hands. "I'll loan you some of my Devil's Luck in that case."

Can he even do that? Is this a shifter thing? Even after confessing I'm using him, then...

"You're not mad at me?" She looked at him, bewildered as he shuffled on his pants.

"As long as you're not upset that I'm a shifter, I think we can call this even." He winked at her, and she began to put the pants on. "Let's get you what you need, a proper shower, and I'll pay the salon to do your hair and makeup. I want you to be the sexiest thing walking into that gala tonight, if you're up for the task."

If I'm being honest, I don't quite understand what being a shifter means. What I do understand is he's the biggest playboy bachelor with deep pockets in Jersey and... Abigail's self-esteem wavered again. "It's still a pig, even if you put make up on it."

He backed her against the door again, whispering in her ear. "Call me shallow, but I only fuck pretty women."

Arousal washed over her, he refused to let her shove him away. "You can't mean that."

"Why else would I be in this fitting room with you and not out on the casino floor on the prowl, Abby." Her heart jolted at the statement. "Come on. Let me show you what you can have if you want it bad enough."

She laughed. "Are you tempting me?"

"Maybe." He pulled away, his eyes glowing red as the horns receded.

Abigail left it at that. She had aired her confession, but Dylan seemed unphased by it. *Motivated at the thought of it.* As she gathered the dress and lingerie, he encouraged her to grab a few more things just as the sales associate from before came through the door. She smirked, seeing her with him and when Dylan looked away gestured her kudos. Apparently, this was the ultimate prize for anyone on the rebound, but it didn't stop the guilt knotting in her stomach.

Returning to the penthouse suite, the silence and stolen glances continued. Their discussion in the midst of lust and shame inside that tiny fitting room had built an invisible wall between them. Room service came and went, dropping off finger foods. He had gone ahead of her to shower and when she noticed he was done; he had disappeared into his office. Biting her lip, she went about her own business, the apartment unbearably silent and lonesome.

Is this how he normally spends his day in this place? It seems like a miserable existence. Sobering in fact, compared to downstairs.

Wiggling on the sexy black lace lingerie, she avoided the mirror. She couldn't afford to lose what little confidence she had left. *I'm going to a big business gala for the first time, but can I even pull this off?* Sliding the dress on, she flustered. *Dammit, I can't tie up the back on my own.*

"Here." His voice startled her as the heat of fingers tickled against her back. "After I get you tied up, Angel, we'll head downstairs for some pampering for you. Have you ever had someone professionally do your make up before?"

"N-no." She glimpsed at the mirror, at his stern face. "Is everything ok?"

"Yea." When the last knot was tied, he leaned into her ear. "As long as you stay with me tonight. Just one more night."

He thinks I am to leave immediately. Did I want to leave tonight? Do I ever want to leave? What do I want?

"But you can tell me no." He broke away, and she grabbed his arm. "Yes?"

"I... would love to stay tonight too." The beating of her heart thumped in her chest like a racing horse. "Please let me stay."

He laughed, the features of his face softened, and the smile returned. "Of course."

There's nothing he hadn't handled. As soon as she passed into the salon, a flock of attendants rushed her into a chair and began their work. She would have asked them a million questions, but every time she opened her mouth, they fussed for her to stay still. Make up meant to follow instructions and give the reigns of her own face and lips to the harpy who painted her face with makeup brands she'd never seen in her local grocery store. Her hair on the other hand, was at the mercy of a gentleman who doused her in compliments of how well-kept it was and thanking her for braving to go all natural.

The minutes dragged; she lost track of the time and surely a good hour or more had passed by the time the two attendants pulled away from her. They had her stand now, no mirror in sight as they adjusted how the dress fit her, going as far as redoing the lacing in the back. Having a woman do it instead of Dylan made her face heat. Granted, she couldn't deny how the dress hugged her more comfortably after the tugging and shifting of fabric.

"Now let's have a look. Tell us what you think." The makeup artist walked her to an array of mirrors.

Abigail gasped. "It doesn't even look like me," she muttered at the princess before her.

"Come now, we can only bring out what's already there." The hair stylist chuckled, joining them. "Dylan said he wanted you to look like royalty, how'd we do?"

"A-amazing." Swallowing, she fought the urge to cry. "I feel … spoiled."

"Dylan doesn't do this for girls normally." The mutter made her blink. "Let's hope he approves or I'm out of the job."

"It's perfect, Gretel." Dylan's voice had them twisting in his direction as one. "And that smile on your face says you approve."

"It's amazing. They're amazing." She rushed him, hugging him.

"Careful, or you'll get makeup on my jacket. It's too soon for that." He spun, hiding his face from her as he hooked her arm. "But we're late. Mr. Morozov is at the table already and blowing up my phone."

"Oh no." Abigail held onto him tightly, afraid of tripping in the heels she had picked out. "I'm so sorry, this is my fault."

"The hell it is. I already told you I planned on you being the centerpiece in this gala." Dylan had pulled her through the casino and across to the convention center area. "This is all me."

Anxiety crept up as the butlers at the door waved them through. The ballroom was enormous. A grand chandelier hung from the center as columns of white and gold decorated the walls. She scanned the room of extravagantly dressed guests. Dylan nodded and waved as he passed them, stating names as he went and never losing pace. *He knows all these people.*

"Ah, Mr. Morozov!" They at last came to a stop and her feet ached from the trip they took across the hotel. "Sorry, for the delay. You know how it is, waiting on a lady."

Abigail gave him a death glare. Then the large mountain of an old man burst into laughter.

"From the look in her eyes, it's your fault she ran so late," he said in a heavy Russian accent, standing to his full monstrous height. "Pleasure to meet you." He took her hand and gave it a kiss. "And you are?"

"A-abigail." His eyes were so pale blue, the irises seemed almost white. "Nice to meet you?"

"Well, sit!" He gestured and Dylan nodded. "Come, they should be serving any moment."

"Where's Yvette and Satch?" Dylan's glare grew dark at the empty chairs.

"Hell, if I know. Neither will take my call or reply to a text." A thin man sat beside Mr. Morozov, though similar eyes, his accent was American. "He better show or have a damn good excuse for being late."

"So!" Dylan's voice boomed, rattling everyone at the table. "How's that leg of yours, Ghetti?"

The thin man abandoned his cell phone on the table and leaned back in the chair. "I'm out of the cast, so I can't complain."

"Wow, it's only been thirty days or so, right?" Dylan seemed intrigued by this news as servers brought salads to their table. "I didn't realize you heal fast."

Mr. Morozov laughed in a big rumble. "You forget, we come from a wilder past than your own. We still retain a lot of the ancestral traits. We didn't derive from a curse, speaking of which my dear business partner..." he pointed to Abigail's necklace "...isn't that a Devil's Stone?"

From under the table, Dylan's hand found hers and squeezed it tight. "You amaze me sometimes. I never pick up on magic like you do."

"He cheats," grumbled Ghetti, staring begrudgingly at the two empty spots. "It's our sense of smell that does most of the work."

Chuckling, Mr. Morozov took a bite of salad. Abigail squeezed Dylan's hand again and brought it across her lap. The man's eyes picked her apart, and the words from before: *I'm a shifter,* sent goose-bumps over her. *These aren't humans. They're shifters like Dylan... no. This man is something more menacing, older even. What have I gotten myself into?*

Dylan leaned into her, whispering, "Don't get scared, he can smell that too. I'm here. No harm will befall you, my Angel."

"Abigail." She jerked, hearing her name from Mr. Morozov's lips. "Where on earth did you find this amazing trinket? Pawn shop? Thrift store? No. Maybe an antique shop?"

She forced a smile, glancing at Dylan to reaffirm if she should let that information out of the bag. "My ancestor. It's an old family heirloom."

His fork clanked loudly on the plate. He glared at the amulet, then at Dylan, eyes wide.

What in the hell just happened? Did I say something wrong? Is Dylan in some sort of trouble bringing me here? Will I even live to see Philly again with a fiery stare like that?

12

ANGEL OF SMALL DEATH

"Abby." Dylan shook her hand from his and squeezed her thigh. "Looks like we have business to discuss. Forgive me, but can you excuse us for a moment."

Dammit, he knows about that legend too. This won't go well. He's gonna talk me out of keeping her ... but I don't even know if she'll really stay with me.

"S-sure." He stood, pressing a soft kiss on her lips. "Did I do something wrong?"

"No, dear." Mr. Morozov stood, giving her a sincere smile. "You've done nothing wrong. This is about ... business."

Dylan turned, marching shoulder to shoulder with the mountain of a Yeti shifter. He hated being around him, the man was smart and had lived over two centuries from what he could pinpoint. Morozov didn't slow down once. Before long they were in the elevator headed to the offices upstairs. Dylan couldn't keep his heart still. *Something isn't right.*

"Where'd you find her." It wasn't a question; this was a demand.

"She came to the casino on the rebound last night." He swallowed. "I didn't notice the necklace until this morning ... after ... well."

"I see." The doors opened, halting Satch and Yvette's laughing.

"D-Daddy." Yvette paled and she grabbed Satch's hand. "We were on our way down."

Mr. Morozov inhaled deeply. "You better put on more perfume and cologne. If Ghetti smells what you two were doing up here on your desk," he shot a wild look to Satch who averted his eyes, "I assure you the gala will come to a halt."

"Yes sir." Satch pushed past them, dragging Yvette as he muttered to Dylan, "Good luck."

The doors shut and Mr. Morozov turned, cupping Dylan's shoulders with heavy hands. "You do know I've hated how you handled this curse."

"Yea, I know." Dylan smirked, it was the reason he'd been shunned and told to stay away from other Devil shifters. "Ex-communicated for tempting the Devil's Luck."

And no one knows where the rest went ... the whole ten or so that remained after what I did as a child.

"I can't lie. Placing a bet on the fact you would be able to beat the full turn by betting your luck against it. Tell me, did you lose at the roulette table yet?"

"Yea, the night she walked in here." Dylan brushed the monstrous hands off and marched toward his office. "But I've been struggling for a few days to keep the horns down."

"I didn't think any of them existed." Mr. Morozov gave chase, spinning Dylan back to look him in the eyes.

He shrugged at the old man. "I knew that old mine closed, but to think not every stone had been returned. The girl's lucky to even have a Devil's Stone and I think..."

"Not the fucking stone, Dylan." He gave him a bewildered look and started laughing. "You didn't notice?"

"Notice what?" *What the hell has this senile Yeti noticed about her I didn't? Shit, I fucked her, have seen her naked, tasted her ... what the hell is he going on about?*

"Holy shit." He held his forehead, pacing the floor. "I don't know if I should tell you. Does she know?"

"That ... I'm a devil shifter?" Frustration seeped forward. "Of course, she knows, I told her."

"Oh hell." He froze, staring into space collecting his thoughts. "She doesn't know, does she?"

"Know what? She knows the story about the stone, she knows I'm a shifter..."

"That she's half a fucking Angel." Mr. Morozov scoffed, shaking his head in disbelief.

Angel ... is an Angel. It was a pet name. He's lost it.

"A what?" Dylan closed the gap. "What are you talking about?"

Laughter rolled out of Mr. Morozov, his gut shaking. "Holy fuck. The Devil fucked an angel half breed and didn't even notice?"

Dylan squinted, his mind stumbling and fighting over itself. "Angels don't exist."

He's crazy. They laughed at me at Brightwater over this question about an Angel shifter.

"Yea, they do. They're like an urban legend, but dammit, I've met one before during the crusades." He whistled, the laughter continuing. "Oh, boy. So she probably doesn't know. Their kind don't mix blood often, boy is someone upstairs in trouble for that one. Dammit, Dylan, that's a lucky streak worthy of legendary status."

Fuck being legendary! If I sent this poor girl's life down this path, shit! Half Angel? What does that even mean? How could she even go all this time not knowing?

"Are you implying I put this into motion?" Covering his face, he paced a few times in panic. "I made that bet, what, when I was a kid. And I stuck by it because once a devil makes a bet, even as a kid, it sticks."

"Did you ask for her birthday?" he offered.

"No, we started last night being a one-night stand and then..."

"Tasted like a peach, didn't it?"

Dylan's face sobered of all emotion. "How would you know?"

Why would he know about that?

"They say when you find a good match, it's like the sweetest fruit. It's called forbidden fruit for a reason, they don't have to be a shifter for it to happen and there can be more than one girl that does it for you, but it's hard when you made a bet on a devil's luck." Another wave of laughter, the rumbling like a distant storm, menacing and frightening. "Wait until I share this with..."

"Don't you dare!" In an instant Dylan changed. Horns black as night pushing ten inches tall, a pointed red tail snaking behind him, and large black feathered wings flaring out. "Don't you tell anyone!"

"Oh, we're serious about her, are we?" There was a sparkle in his eye. "Ok, ok... I won't tell anyone. Wanted to see if you plan on letting her go so easily."

You dick. You needed to know if this was the real deal.

Snorting steam from his nostrils, Dylan shook off the shift and threw off the ripped overcoat. "Dammit. How could she not know?"

"Because a devil hasn't given her, her wings." He followed Dylan into his office where he grabbed a spare coat. "Or so the legend goes. Look, the Devil Stones made humans devils. But an angel—or someone the blood of angels—would be immune, but it brings them bad luck, or in this case, brings them into the luckiest devil in the whole world. I didn't just go into business because you were good at what you do. You couldn't lose no matter how hard you tried."

He shoved on the coat, still fuming. "Look, I need to go down there and discuss this with her. She needs to know. I've got to get her to give up that damn necklace, but... to never know."

What kind of life is that?

"Go get her. She's lucky enough to have found you." He snorted. "Maybe the stone was responsible for that much. Maybe it's never been unlucky."

"It's fate that we met." Dylan gave Mr. Morozov one last look and ran for the elevator. "Thanks!"

The elevator never felt so damn slow. He exploded into the stretch between stores, weaving with practiced skill through the casino floor and came to a halt as he bumped into someone. They dropped their phone, and he realized the pandemonium unfolding behind him. The gala was filled with screeches. The Morozov siblings were wrecking the event in record time and he paled.

"Dylan!" Satch picked his phone up and flashed a picture. "Did this guy just throw a bikini in the fire? He did, didn't he?"

He smacked the phone from Satch's hand. "I don't give a shit, where the fuck is Abby?"

"Oh?" He turned Dylan around and they disappeared into the casino floor crowd. "So her ex-fiancé the preacher marched in and took her?"

"FUCK!" He broke from Satch, charging for the lobby.

Satch shouted after him. "I'm leaving early to pick up Bif and his girl from the forest! Good luck boss!" A trail of black feathers floated to the ground in Dylan's wake. "Oh hell, I'm not staying to see how this ends. The Devil's about to explode."

Please don't take her! I need her! She needs me!

We ... need each other.

13

DEVIL'S BACKBONE

"**G**et your hands off me." At last, Abigail broke from Pastor Bradley's hand at the edge of the lobby. "I'm not going back to Philly. Especially not with you!"

"Come on. You're making a show of this." Sweat trickled down his temple, still dressed in his clerical clothing.

He left right after the last sermon today, didn't he?

"Everyone in the congregation wanted to know where you went." His anger added friction in her core.

"Of course, they did." She shuffled backward, disbelief gripping her. *Why wouldn't they ask?* "Did you tell them why?"

His face reddened, a wild look in his eyes. "I told them you were at home sick."

He blames me for this.

"Until DeeDee spoke up."

"DeeDee?" Abigail's eyes widened. "But she never goes to church on Sunday!"

This man's looking at me as if he caught me on that baptism table.
"I know, and when she said you were stuck here at the casino... Abigail, I was embarrassed. How could you humiliate me like that before the entire congregation! People are starting to ask *me* what *I* did!" He marched toward her, and she kept the gap between them, the vein pulsing on his forehead. "You have to come home with me. Tammy's waiting in the car. This is ridiculous for a Pastor's fiancée..."

"EX-Fiancée." Abigail's rage had finally crested. "I didn't fuck the organ player, asshole. Go to hell!"

She spun around and ran full steam into the sea of casino patrons. Tears threatened, and she could hear his steps heavy behind her. *This is crazy! He cares more about his reputation than what the hell happened!* She kicked off the heels abandoning them in her wake, hiking the dress up to allow her legs to take wider strides in order to properly run. Her feet struck the casino carpet with heavy thuds matching her heartbeat. Pivoting to the right then left, she looked like she was running bases in a baseball game.

Thank you for little league, you finally came through for me! Squeezing her eyes tight, she refused to slow down. *Dylan! I need you! Don't let him take me from you! Damn my luck!*

Another pivot to miss the Blackjack table, and she smashed into someone, their arms wrapping around her tight.

"Let me go!" She shrieked, panic filling her. *I need to find...*

"Abigail." Dylan's voice snapped her eyes open, his eyes glowing red. "You didn't leave."

"Don't let him take me." A tear slid down her cheek, body shaking, the thought frightening. "I can't. He's not the one I love. Dylan, I love..."

"ABIGAIL!" A voice roared in the crowd, chills snaking up her spine.

She gripped onto Dylan's coat, pressing into him. *I'll never let you go!* He tightened his hold and twisted, as if looking for an escape. He froze and pulled her from him, locking eyes. That devilish smirk on his face, the horns starting to peak out of his forehead. *A shifter, a devil. And he loves me, and I love him.*

"Do you trust me?" He pulled her through another crowd and under the caution tape, through the tarps that had barricaded guests from a section of the casino. "He's going to look here too, but..."

Her stomach knotted. *I can't hide.* She stumbled past him to lean on a roulette table in defeat. "I don't ever want to go back to Philly. Let me stay here with you, Dylan. I know it's a crazy request but..."

"Yes." His answer fell hard in the air between them as he tossed his coat on the table. "You *should* stay here with me. Now, about our current situation. I have a devilish solution for you, my Angel."

She twisted to face him, his tie already slipping from his neck as he started to undress.

"I'll do anything to stay with you... what are you doing?"

"Promising the Devil like that is a dangerous thing." He unbuttoned his shirt and it fell to the floor revealing the rips in the backside. "What if I demand more than what you can give me, Abby?"

Her eyes lingered on the shirt with black feathers tangled in the threads. Swallowing, a wave of desire and excitement hit her. *The horns, he said they were real... but he said...* A heat stirred in her, anger and anxiety drowning under love and lust.

"What happened to your shirt?" She marveled, exhilaration bursting through her veins. "Dylan, what are you planning to do to me?"

"Fuck you." He declared, sucking the side of his cheek before closing the gap between them. "Will you fuck the Devil right here, right now?"

Abigail eyed the tarps behind him, the only thing shielding them from the rest of the casino and the crowds of people whose shadows made it ruffle as they passed. *He did say Bradley would find us.* His hand started tugging the dress further up, his knee pressing between her thighs. Her breath caught, heart beating fast and hard. *He's serious. He wants to do this, but...* Her mind and body struggled with one another. *If he found us, like I found them.* A heat of arousal rolled over her as she backed up and found herself pinned between him and a roulette table. *Is it wrong, wanting him to catch us?*

"What if I can't keep quiet?" She eyed his lips as they came closer to her own, all her want hitting her at once. *I was hoping to finish what we started in the fitting room. Why not here and now?* "What if someone hears us?"

"Not even worried about that." The stone at her neck began glowing. "You're the one who likes doing this sort of thing in public places, Ms. I-used-live-the-wild-clubbing-life. Screwing guys in the bathrooms, back alleys, fitting rooms, and now you can add casino to your naughty list."

Dylan kissed her, deeply and passionately. She leaned her weight onto the table, wrapping her arms around his neck. Their tongues wrestling with one another, rubbing hot and wet as they moaned into each other. The way he made her feel, her body alive with lust like never before. *How could I ever say no to this?* She ground against his thigh, flashes of how he felt inside her making her want him. He pulled away and before she could fuss, his hands raced up her legs to pull the black thong off once more.

"Again?" He lifted an eyebrow, the devilish grin with the red eyes and black horns making her shudder with anticipation. "If I didn't know better, you lied when you said I had bad taste."

"Never said that. Just told you how embarrassing it is to see you riffle through a bucket of lacy thongs." She laughed, *even in a moment as wild and crazy as this he manages to get me to laugh. Every fear gone; every desire pulled out to the open just for him to enjoy.* "You paid for them; you can take them back any time you want."

"Just so you know, I'm partial to black, especially lace." He began unbuckling his pants, pulling out his erection and her heart skipped a beat.

"Why's that?" She glanced at the tarp as it moved under the air vent, the excitement adding to the throb of her provocative want. "Ex-girlfriend?"

"No." His eyes glowed in the dim lighting, for the first time everything about him screamed *devil*. "Because they remind me of these."

Like magic, Dylan's black wings exploded behind him. Abigail covered her mouth, eyes widened, marveling at the extraordinary sight. They blocked her view of the tarps, so black she could've mistaken them for the night sky. He gave them one flap, the wind from them slamming into her to confirm they were indeed the real deal. She reached to touch one over his shoulder but recoiled. *How could I be so careless.*

He gripped her wrist, angling her hand until her fingertips touched his feathers. "Please don't ever pull away from me, from them."

Her heart fluttered. "They're soft and ... warm."

Nuzzling her, his voice deep as he whispered, "You're the first to touch them."

How far have you let me into your life to be so reckless? To take all the risk on betting I would stay with you, would keep quiet, and ... accept this of all things?

Before she could say anything, his lips were back on hers. They travelled down her neck, and she grew wet. The heat of his hand plunged between her thighs making her moan. Fingers dove into her folds, dripping with anticipation of what he promised and what she knew he could do to her. Slick fingertips found their way back to her swollen jewel. She inhaled swiftly, muffling the urge to scream. Reaching behind him, she groped at the muscled wings but jerked her hands back.

Where the hell do I place my hands! I'll pluck him bare at this rate trying to stay quiet!

14

FIRE UP THE NIGHT

ylan chuckled, his tongue licking the tender salty skin leading to her ear. "My wings are your wings, Angel. One day you'll have your own. Trust me on that one."

I was wild about her before, but the idea she's my opposite even on grounds as a shifter has stripped me of all my doubts. We were made for each other.

"Are we really doing..." She panted. "Doing this?"

Already breathless, are we? So we do like the risk of being caught, don't we Abby?

A huff escaped him. His hands grabbing her hips to bring her to the edge of the roulette table and allowed her to lay back. *Forgive me, I refuse to be gentle this time.* With a confident tug on the front of the halter top, the laces on the back of the dress popped and a breast came free from even the bra. His grin, toothy as he leaned in to suckle at the nipple. Pushing his hip between her parted legs, he slid his hardened length into her wet heat. *We don't have time to take this slow, it's only a matter of time before he sees us. Sees what he could have had. Sees the devil fucking what once was his angel.*

She stifled a moan, tightening on his cock. The sensation sent an enthralling wave through him, and he fought the urge to come. This made his wings flare, only adding to her tightness, adding to her sensation of pleasure. *Shit, she saw that. I better keep her at bay.* Rocking against her, he pulled the full length of his cock in and out, each push making her whimper. The tightening no longer a willing participant to its master. It took everything she had to stifle the yelps and moans, from holding her breath, inhaling deep and swift, to even biting her lip. She tightened and he moaned, another ruffling of his feathers. He pressed hard and deep inside her, lingering there hoping to wait out the teetering edge of his own full orgasm.

Releasing her nipple, Dylan gave her a wide smirk. "If you keep tightening up like that, then we'll have to worry about my loud moaning."

"I'm so afraid..."

"Afraid?" Dylan leaned back, a flash of concern on his face as his wings folded. *Because of me? Because of my shifting?*

"I'm so afraid to touch them." She tightened and the wings flared for her, a laugh escaping her. "And it's kind of fun to see that."

He snorted. "You're hopeless. Here." Pulling her arms off him, he pulled out leaving her whimpering in his wake. "If it bugs you so much," he flipped her with stunning ease. "It's easier to avoid them this way." He tugged her dress up over her ass and to the side, positioning her in doggie-style fashion as his hands roamed her body. "I don't think we've tried this position. Plus, it's cheating if you know when you have me teetering on the edge. I can't have you finishing me off first."

"Dylan, I can't." Her shaken voice came out rushed. "I'll scream."

"Oh? Is this a favorite of yours?" He slid his throbbing cock inside her warmth once more. "You better grab my coat there and muffle yourself. Wouldn't want to have a crowd forming to see you come."

"Dylan I'll squirt..." The rocking of his body connecting with her own sent her scrambling for the jacket to release a squeal into it, muffled and desperate.

I want her to scream.

He maintained his pace, slow and calculated, gauging her body. "Don't you dare hold back. Relax, Angel Abby."

Fingers dug into her hips, rivulets of the rising tide of her orgasm ran hot down her legs. She squeezed her thighs tight, but they were slick as her body arched like a stretching cat. This only made his dick dive deeper inside her pussy. One hand reached out, too short to grip the far edge of the roulette table. He reached out, entwining their fingers and pushed against her harder, grinding and throbbing on the edge of his own orgasm. She began screaming, visceral and alarming as her other arm hugged his coat tighter into her face.

Good girl, give it all to me...

There was a flash of light as she tightened her pussy on his cock, her body shuddering under his. Over his shoulder he locked eyes with the man holding his cell phone. Abigail in the throes of her orgasm hadn't noticed, and with a devilish grin he winked at the pastor still in Sunday attire. With that, he fled through the tarps and Dylan wasted no time turning his attention back to Abigail's peaking. His cock throbbed, his blood rushing, knowing full well who had seen them, who had taken an opportunistic picture and fled without a word.

Ex-fiancé, Pastor Bradley. And my, what a shot he took!

A gush of hot liquid rushed between them, his cock at its peak in Abigail's tight pussy. Unable to resist, he pulled out in a rush, cursing under his breath. Licking his lips, he watched the peach scented liquid dribble down to her ankles. His wings shuddered as he kept a tight hold on his dick, the agonizing tightness of needing to release making his skin crawl. At last, she stopped screaming, a moan all that remained of her orgasm. Reaching over, he stole his coat from her and at last allowed himself to fully come, panting. She rolled to her back, covering her face, legs clamped tight.

"I can't believe we just did that," she whined.

Another laugh escaped him. "I regret nothing. Well, except forgetting a condom. I know better."

"My legs are soaked."

"At least the dress will hide that. My pants look like I pissed myself, but I'm not complaining." He bit his bottom lip, soaking in her body as she lay across the roulette table. "And what makes you think I'm done."

"W-wait!" She tightened her legs.

His hand slipped between, the slickness proving disadvantage as he still found her swollen clit. Frantic, Abigail pulled a swath of her skirt to her mouth and squealed. Humming at each stroke of his finger, slow and steady, coaxing her to open her legs for him. At last, her knees parted wide enough he could kneel between them. His other hand joined, diving inside her and she tightened. Her back arched, knees lifting. All of it allowed his fingers to stroke deeper, rubbing the hot flesh within. Even now, she still dripped and squirted as he pulled her orgasm into a second coming.

Abigail reached down, unsure whether to push him away or pull him into her. Her legs shook, and Dylan licked his lips with anticipation. Shoving her hand to the side, his lips wrapped around her clit. She arched and gave a muffled wail as she pressed the skirt firmly against her mouth. Hungry with want he devoured her, suckling and licking. At last, he gripped her thighs, pushing her open. His tongue dove into the crevasse of her pussy.

Dammit, of all the times not to have a condom in my back pocket!

Juicy and hot, he felt himself growing hard again. Stamina and endurance were trivial when he shifted like this, even on a sexual level he could come again and again without need for reprieve. He ran his tongue up, circling her clit, until she reached down. Moaning, his skin crawled with the thrill of her fingers tangling with his hair and horns. He moaned into her silken heat and her legs jittered, making her join him with her moan.

"D-Dylan…" At first, he refused to stop, but her next words caught his attention. "I found one."

He rocked back on his heels and let her pull herself to a sitting position. She twisted the jacket and out of the pocket, a colorful square wrapper appeared. They grinned at one another, and he wasted no time ripping it open. Rolling it on, she partially hid her face, a mischief and bashful expression. The sparkle in her eyes was worth every bit of the risk of being caught in the act.

Pressing inside her once more, she tightened, and his wings flared. "Dammit."

"That's the worst tell in all gambling history." She repeated the motion, and he puffed out his cheeks unable to stop the ruffling feathers.

"Shut up and fuck me." He wrapped his arms around her, deepening their kiss, lips parting to stroke their tongues.

Grinding hard and fast into her, she synced with his rhythm. Her arms hot against his ribs as they abandoned his jacket. Hands clawed across his back and between the feathered appendages. She moaned into his mouth, another hot gush unfolding as he only continued the rocking of his own hips, peaking. One arm reached to the roulette table, and he realized her amulet had broken and the stone spun off. When they broke the kiss, he paid it more heed and laughed. The glowing stone sat on red nineteen.

"I won."

"You won?" Looking over, she realized what he referred to. "What was the bet against?"

He picked up the stone, now free of the metal backing, and he rolled it over, then laughed. "When we get upstairs, I'll tell you a funny story about your stone."

"Oh!" She plucked it from him and read the words scratched into the back. "Lucius? It's a name!"

"Yea, my name." He kissed her once more, then broke away. "When I was a boy, I tried to give away my devil's luck by putting it into a Devil's Stone. My dad took it, pawned it or chucked it in the trash, who knows. All I know, is that I never saw it again … until now."

"Wait, then that makes you over two hundred—" Pressing fingers against her lips, he winked as the wings and horns disappeared.

"Dylan's my middle name." He snorted, helping her from the roulette table. "Lucius means *light*. It's the name my mother gave me on a stormy night in 1735. Don't believe all the rumors you hear about me."

To think that bet would lead me to be here with her at this point in time. She was worth the wait.

15
EPILOGUE

Pastor Bradley slipped into the passenger side of a golden Mirage. Pulling out his cell phone, he glared at the photo he'd taken before leaving the casino.

In the driver's seat, the old redhead stared out each car window, confusion written on her face. "Where's Abigail? I thought you found her." Tammy stared at him, but he ignored her. "Pastor Bradley!"

"Shut up!" He snapped, never breaking his glare from his phone.

He brought it closer, picking apart each detail, deciphering which part was his imagination, and the rest, real. Losing sight of Abigail had sent him into a panic attack, spinning in circles from the dizzy casino neon signs. That's when he'd heard voices. He recognized Abigail's.

When the muffled scream unfolded, he pushed through some tarps and froze. There before him, the Devil had been fucking his once beloved fiancée. At first, he locked eyes with the halo above her head. Another moan from her made him realize they were in the throes of passion. He will never erase the image of her, bent over a roulette table, screeching as she reached out. The devil held her down, its wings spread wide, its pointed tail swinging wildly.

He did the only thing he could do; he snapped a photo, using his phone.

The flash went off. Red eyes and a fanged grin looked his way, and he stumbled out. All hope had been lost. The cheating pastor was powerless against a real-life devil. *They never said we'd come face to face with one!* He'd rather save his own soul than throw himself between her and whatever he saw.

"Bradley, where's Abigail?"

"Drive! She's lost to the devil!" Panic filling him, he deleted the picture as she leaned to peek. *If anyone found out I gave an angel to...*

"Did you catch her with someone?"

He tossed the phone to the floorboard, disgusted. "Something."

Tammy drove out of the hotel roundabout. "Well, I suppose that's karma."

"You don't understand, Tammy. What I've done, what we did..." He covered his face. "I'm leaving the church. I can't be a pastor. I'm not cut out for this."

This isn't what I signed up for ... hell, not even what they trained me to go against. I was to counsel people on normal life problems. Not face demons and devils! Maybe I just imagined it, but that picture...

"What?" Tammy's face flushed. "What about me?"

"Who the fuck cares about you?" He balled his hands on his thighs, his eyes still on the phone. "Far as I know, you were in on the deal."

That's right. She was temptation and I fell for it. I failed the test. I'm not fit to lead a congregation.

"What on earth are you talking about?" she shrieked. "If I recall right, you're the one who put your hand up my skirt!"

"I lied."

"Lied about what?" She marveled, struggling to keep driving in her lane as they reached the busy highway.

"She wanted ... *more* but she's so damn pure... Well, she used to be." He paled, remembering the winged creature. "I settled for you because I was a coward. And because of you, I committed a sin. It's my fault she led herself to the devil!"

For a moment, Tammy grew quiet. The only sound was the rain pattering on the windshield.

"I caught her fucking the Devil, Tammy. Right there in the casino!"

Tammy laughed. "Holy shit, I'm jealous. She upgraded to a billionaire! They say you're lucky if you get the chance to sleep with The Devil at the Saint's Hotel and Casino. Wow, Abigail will have to tell me how she pulled that one off. Now, where do you want to eat?"

Bradley puked on the floorboard.

The End

HONEY CUMMINGS

A passionate, award-winning author of Fantasy, Honey has turned her aim toward erotica. Blending everyday scenarios, and crafting them into steamy, blood-boiling moments for every shade of audience. Whether you want something short and hot, like a student-teacher hook up to the more paranormal flair, where Sleep with Sasquatch has unexpected bonus, look forward to erotic short stories, novellas, and hopefully a Trilogy in the future. Honey's debut erotic short landed at No. 3 in Urban Erotica and continues to satisfy readers time and time again. Be sure to leave her a review and let her know what you think!

amazon.com/Honey-Cummings/e/B07WFX5FDX
AuthorHoneyCummings.com
instagram.com/authorhoneycummings
twitter.com/HoneyCummings2
facebook.com/Author-Honey-Cummings-101408818012749

More Honey Cummings Books

Sleeping with Sasquatch
Cuddling with Chupacabra
Naked with New Jersey Devil
The Erotic Cryptid Collection

Laying with the Lady in Blue
Wanton Woman in White
Beating it with Bloody Mary
The Erotic Ghosts Collection

Beau and Professor Bestialora
The Goat's Gruff
Goldie and Her Three Beards
Pied Piper's Pipe
Princess Pea's Bed
Pinocchio and the Blow Up Doll
Jack's Beanstalk
Pulling Rapunzel's Hair
The Urban Erotica Fairy Tale
Collection

Curses & Crushes: KU short story

Queen's Incubus: YONDER webnovel

Writing as Valerie Willis

Cedric: The Demonic Knight
Romasanta: Father of Werewolves
The Oracle: Keeper of the Gaea's Gate
Artemis: Eye of Gaea
King Incubus: A New Reign
Queen Succubus: Holder of the Crown

Val's House of Musings: A Mixed Genre Short Story Collection

Writer's Bane: Research 101
Writer's Bane: Formatting

Writing MM Romance as VC Willis

The Prince's Priest
The Priest's Assassin
The Assassin's Saint

The Champion's Lord: YONDER webnovel
Champion's Love: KU short story

More books from 4 Horsemen Publications

Erotica

Ali Whippe
Office Hours
Tutoring Center
Athletics
Extra Credit
Financial Aid
Bound for Release
Fetish Circuit
Now You See Me
Sexual Playground
Swingers
Discovered
XTC College Series Collection

Aria Skylar
Twisted Eros
Seducing Dionysus

Chastity Veldt
Molly in Milwaukee
Irene in Indianapolis
Lydia in Louisville
Natasha in Nashville
Alyssa in Atlanta
Betty in Birmingham
Carrie on Campus
Jackie in Jacksonville
A Humorous Erotica Collection

Dalia Lance
My Home on Whore Island
Slumming It on Slut Street
Training of the Tramp
The Imperfect Perfection
Spring Break
72% Match
It Was Meant To Be... Or Whatever

Nick Savage
The Fairlane Incidents
The Fortunate Finn Fairlane
The Fragile Finn Fairlane
The Complete Package

LGBT Erotica

Dominic N. Ashen
Steel & Thunder
Storms & Sacrifice
Secrets & Spires
Arenas & Monsters
My Three Orc Dads: a Novella
Before the Storm: a Novella

Eskay Kabba
Hidden Love
Not So Hidden
Signs of Affection
Deeply Devoted to Him
Honest Love
A Plane and Simple Connection

Grayson Ace
How I Got Here
First Year Out of the Closet
You're Only a Top?
You're Only a Bottom?
I Think I'm a Serial Swiper
Lookin in All the Wrong Places
What Makes Me a Whore?
A Breach in Confidentiality
Back Door Pass
My European Adventure
An Unexpected Affair
Finding True Love
The Dr. Cage Chronicles

Leo Sparx
Before Alexander
Claiming Alexander
Taming Alexander
Saving Alexander
The Fall of the House of Otter
The Case of Armando

Robert Lewis
Someone to Love
Someone to Come Home To
Someone to Kiss

Discover more at
4HorsemenPublications.com

www.ingramcontent.com/pod-product-compliance
Lightning Source LLC
Chambersburg PA
CBHW050022120726
47903CB00006B/1875

* 9 7 8 1 6 4 4 5 0 7 0 9 4 *